Denver's Calling
Calling

Cooper's Ridge Series Book 1

Cover design by JC Clarke at The Graphics Shed
Edited by Petra Howard at Dragonsfly Edits
Formatted by JC Clarke

For everyone brave enough to follow their heart, and take a risk

Prologue

"You're kidding me? You have to be fucking kidding me? Married? You're getting married? Who the fuck to?" I've been home for twenty minutes tops, after a week away at a conference, where I was keynote speaker. I've been feeling so good after the lectures were well received. I went away, annoyed Alec didn't want to come but it all makes sense now. I look at the man in front of me and realize I don't know him anymore. Scanning around our living room, I notice some of the book cases are empty and photographs and artwork is missing. *He's already moved out.*

"Den, calm down. Please, let me explain." Alec stands in front of me, in our home—*our* damn home—and wants me to calm down. Dressed casually, his hands bury deep in his front pockets. *How can he be so calm? Is this easy for him?*

"Who the hell? Shit! How long has this been going on?" My hands are on my head, pulling on my already messy hair; it's this or punch the bastard. "Who else knows? Am I the last, damn idiot to know?" *Fuck! I'm such a fool.*

"His name is Michael, he's a pediatric doctor over at Mercy General. I never expected this, Den, I thought you were it. I thought we were happy, until I met him and then I realized we weren't happy. We were complacent." Alec takes in a deep breath, in what sounds like a well-rehearsed speech. "We've grown apart: you're never home, I need something more than work and that's all you are interested in. I stopped being happy with you a long time ago."

I must interrupt him. "I'm happy. At least, I was until ten minutes ago. Complacent? No way! Damn, we are still having sex, for god's sake! Have you been using condoms? Please, tell me you have?"

"Of course, I would never do that to you. And, think about it, Den, when was the last time we had sex? When was the last time you were home and awake enough to actually *want* to fuck me?" Alec's voice fades as he realizes what he's done is so much worse than a fuck without a rubber.

"Oh, for God's sake! D'you hear yourself? You would never *not* use condoms! But you're happy to cheat and lie. As for fucking, I think it has been me that has tried with you the last countless times. At least, I now know why!" I hear the flatness in my voice, I don't want to hear any more of this. I'm done. "I think it's best you go now; I don't want to see you here again." I watch his mouth open as he tries to contradict me. "You lost the right to be here when you decided to fuck someone else, Alec. Go to Michael's, I'm sure he's waiting to hear just how badly I acted, so he can soothe you and tell you it's all my fault."

Alec finally shows some remorse and seems lost, I don't know what sort of reaction he wants from me, but I'm sure as hell not breaking down. Not while he's here. After staring at me, looking for more from me for a few moments too long, I make a move and step past him, stalking to the front door and opening it. I hear two sets of steps behind me, Alec looks at me hopefully for a brief second.

"Not a fucking chance, Alec; she stays with me." I observe our dog, looking confused at us, then turn back to Alec. He nods and walks out.

Chapter
One

DENVER

The further I travel, the more miles I put between me and the only life I've known for the last twelve years, the lighter I feel. The easier I breathe. Being a doctor—a healer, a surgeon—has been all I've ever wanted, and all I ever planned to be. Until a month ago. A month ago, my life was structured and organized. It had focus and it had a bright, shiny future, one I expected to spend with Alec. I thought we had the whole nine yards: the house, the dog, excellent jobs, and plans to marry.

Then he changed, the man I thought I knew and loved met someone else: he went from supposedly being in love with me to planning a wedding with someone else. How the fuck am I supposed to rebuild my life now? I heard the hospital gossips going to town on my life, all 'oh, poor you, you must be devastated' to 'what a fool, how could he not have known?' It seems Alec has been seeing this other guy for months. Again, I ask myself how I could have been so stupid. *How did I miss all the signs?*

Alec had been my everything for over five years. We met as we became surgical residents. It was fun, the whole flirting and getting to know each other while we worked and competed against each other. We clicked immediately, we got each other's jokes, were the same type of goofy. It only took a month for us to find a house, together with some other friends, and the next, simple move was sharing a bed. We were accepted as a couple by our peers and by each other's families.

At least, Alec did the decent—ha! Decent, my ass—he moved out as soon as he broke the news. He'd already packed all his belongings while I'd been out of town at the conference, waiting for me on my return to tell me without apologizing once. He simply said he'd met someone else and they were getting married. There was no 'where', and sure as hell no 'why.' It was so matter of fact. He left after that and the only thing he looked sad about leaving was our dog. *There was no way he was going to take her!*

For now, I've left everything behind: my house, my job, and my friends, and I'm on my way to my old home town. My folks are overjoyed, my mom is already planning to feed me constantly and my dad is looking forward to having some help around the ranch. I don't have any plans, and certainly no job to rush to, for twelve to fourteen hours a day. I haven't spent much time here since I left for college, I have no doubt it will still be the same, small town I left. There's not much need for fast food joints and shopping malls in a town of only a few thousand occupants and it's exactly what I need. A hassle-free zone: somewhere for me to recoup, mend my broken heart, and decide what to do next. The drive has been a long one and poor Missy did not want to get back into the truck I bought, trading in my sporty number for something more practical for living on a ranch.

We are only a few miles out, so I lower the window on the passenger side and let the dog stick her head out, taking in the sights and smells of the countryside. There won't be dog parks to walk her here, all clean and tidy and regimented. It will be forests and hiking for her, at least she's used to the heat. The next couple of miles pass and I drive up to the town, there are new amenity buildings, a good-sized school takes up a large part of town before you get to the high street and I'm wrong about the mall; it is on the outskirts, opposite the school on the main road, boasting a Cineplex with bowling and ice rinks attached to it. The high street seems more like I remember it, a few new restaurants and bars that look like the sort of places I would like, which means they don't scream cowboy at me. Not that I have a problem with them but they have never been open to gay men or the whole LGBTQ life. Maybe things have changed in the twelve or more years I've been away. I chuckle at the thought, but then a fleeting memory of a secret kiss and forbidden fumbling with a boy I went to school with pops up. Hell, I can't even remember his name—let alone his face—but at the time I didn't feel so lonely and isolated, trapped in a gay teenager's nightmare coming to terms with a sexuality I never expected.

Luckily, I have the best parents in the world: they totally accepted me and smothered me with hugs and love. They totally understood and supported my decision to live away from here; I was happy with who I was by the time I left for college and knew I would never be happy here. I needed to be where I could be myself and that was never going to happen in Cooper's Ridge.

A few people look at me as I drive through, but I may simply be overthinking things; for the past month, I've felt all eyes were on me. *Ha*, I chuckle to myself. They *were* all on me, I felt like I was in a cheap soap opera as they waited for me to fall apart and start a fight with Alec. Even though my bosses tried to talk me out of it, I handed in my notice the same day I found out, knowing I was done there. Not with medicine, but with that hospital. There will be other jobs, but the sale of the house has left me with a tidy sum of money and I can take a step back for a while. I know I'll go back to it, but when I'm ready and right now I'm *so not* ready.

I'm soon out of the town again and back in the spectacular countryside. After so many years in a city, I forgot how beautiful these wide-open spaces are. I take in the lush, green grass that will yellow in the scorching summer sun in a couple of weeks, the mountains that will be snowcapped through the winter months but, for now, the craggy rocks absorb the warmth. I take a left turn onto another asphalt road that will turn to dirt in a mile or so as I get closer to my folk's place, but I'm surprised when I make it all the way to the gateway and then on to the house without once going over a pothole or leaving a cloud of dust behind me. *What made them do that?*

Driving up to the front of the house, taking in the large stone-and-timber ranch house: the shutters are painted a blue that matches the sky and hanging baskets of bright flowers are suspended on wrought iron hangers around the outside of the porch. It really is a spectacular place. I can imagine the visitors' first impression as they admire the house and the large, red barns that house the horses they have come to ride and trek through the forests and fields on.

The door opens and my mom stands, a huge smile brightening her face and her eyes sparkling with love, raising her hand in a wave. Switching off the engine, I climb down from the large cab and let the dog jump down from my side. She sits patiently by my leg, awaiting her next command.

"Oh, Denver, it's good to see you. And look at the monster truck you've turned up in." The smirk on her face has me laughing.

"Oh, you know me; I always want to fit in with the locals." I reply sarcastically.

"Yeah? Maybe you should have bought a ten-year-old beat-up version then, this one screams city boy." Her laugh makes me join in.

Striding up to her, I pick her small frame up and swing her around. "It's good to see you, Mom." I put her back down on her feet.

We walk back up the few steps to the porch and in through the front door, my mom's arm wrapped around my waist. I look around the warm and welcoming room, the photographs of me and my brother growing up still covering the surfaces and walls. There are plenty of my brother's family as they grow, but I realize my absence has led to a lack of pictures of me as an adult and guilt washes over me. They gave me so much and I haven't returned the favor by being around them as an adult. *Do I know them properly anymore? Are they sure they know me? Am I sure I know who I am anymore?*

"Coffee, Denver?" My mom breaks my reverie, making me turn

and smile, but she's my mom and she knows me and, as she sees my smile falter, soothes. "Oh, sweetheart, you're home now."

And, for the first time, I give in and cry.

Chapter Two

EAST

"You're killing me here! Seriously? A glory hole, in the restroom?" I'm laughing so hard, I nearly tip over the chair I'm leaning back on.

"It's not fucking funny, you asshole. I just want to know if you can come over and fix it." Kester tries not to laugh, I can hear it, but I love winding him up.

"For you, baby, anything; I'll get another divide and come on over." I drop the legs of the chair back down on the floor.

"Thank you, I'd like it done before opening tonight." Kes sounds more relaxed.

"Only because I love you, but there's one condition: we have to try it first." Damn, the thought of that has my dick throbbing.

"Hmm, maybe. It depends how quickly you can get here." He

chuckles.

"I'm on my way." I end the call and pick up my keys. I'm still smiling when I hit the builders' merchants. I have no problem choosing the correct piece since it was me who fitted out the bar when Kes bought it and needed to refurbish the whole place.

I shake my head as I remember seeing Kes for the first time in years. I knew him, of course, but he's older and we were never friends at school and I would never have been brave enough to approach him anyway. Kester Dereham was the coolest kid in school, smart, baseball captain and so damn hot in his tight white pants, I spent hours dreaming of him. And jerking off. Hell yeah, plenty of hours whacking one off with his face in my head. He'd gone off to college, only coming back for the summer and the holidays, and we never socialized in the same circle.

I was surprised when I heard he'd moved back for good—and saddened for the reason why, I was more than ready to do the refit for him. I wasn't prepared for him to remember me, let alone come on to me. I had no idea he was gay, but hell, I was never gonna turn him down. That was two years ago. Now we have a house together and have been accepted by our normally closed-minded community as a couple.

I pull up outside the bar and grab my tool bag from the back of the truck, leaving the partition where it is for now. Sauntering up to the door, I tap on the glass and wait for him to reach me, giving me time to take all of him in, standing taller than me at six foot to my five foot ten, with dirty blond hair that is long enough to tie back at the nape of his neck. Under the tight, black T-shirt with the bar's name emblazoned across the front, I see the outline of his firm, muscular body, the one I know intimately, having traced every plane of it with my tongue. His hazel eyes spark and his smile widens as he reaches me.

"Hey, baby, you have moved quickly. Always so eager to please." Kes' voice lowers as he leans in to kiss me. His mouth hovers over mine briefly, but long enough to make me sigh in need, then presses firmly onto mine.

"Hey! You sounded desperate; I'm the superhero here, rushing to the aid of the needy bartender. So, come on then, show me your hole." I snigger and run my hand down his cheek to cup his jaw.

"I might just do that." He winks before wandering towards the restrooms at the rear of the bar. I follow, staring at his tight ass in his black pants, planning what to do with him when he finishes here tonight.

When I walk into the restroom, I can't stop from laughing: Kes stands with his hands on his hips, looking every inch a prude. I don't think now is the time to remind him of the dirty shit we get up to, so I hold back my smile and bite my tongue.

"Just look at it! I mean, who the fuck comes into a bar with something that can cut through a Formica partition and line the fucking hole with tape? It's not something you have on you on a normal night out!" I watch as Kes runs his hand through his hair for probably the hundredth time today. He pulls the tie loose, only to drag his hair back and tie it up again, a sure sign of his annoyance.

"Kes!" I call out but he's still ranting, "Kes! I've got another panel. So, shush. Now, do you want to stick your dick through that hole or are you gonna suck mine?" I wink.

I observe as my lover stops, his hand still in his hair, and look at me. I have finally reached through his ranting and focused him back on me. I watch as his eyes sweep down my body, lingering on my dick as it twitches in its confines.

"I think I want your dick through that hole, sugar. Then I'm gonna fuck you hard with your hands on the mirror." Kes leans into me and bites on my bottom lip, tugging it between his teeth.

"Fuck, yeah!" I'm inside the toilet cubicle with my dick out before Kes can blink. "Get on your knees, Kes, and get ready to suck me hard. Make me come, baby." My dick is hard and through the hole in seconds, eager for Kes' hot, wet mouth.

My smile is massive as we walk out of the bathroom ten minutes later, after the dirtiest blow job and fuck I've ever had. I run my hand down Kes' back and cup his ass as I lean into him and whisper, "I'm taking that fucking partition home; that was the sexiest fucking thing ever."

A shudder runs through Kes' body and he gives me a heated look that makes me gasp. "You'd better do that, sugar: it's my turn next." He peers around the bar, checking everything is ready. "The girls will be here soon, I'd better get ready to open. Will you be back here, later?"

"I'll come back and help you out behind the bar, but you'll need to feed me? I've been asked to go over to the Sinclair ranch; they've got some work for me. It should be good, they are expanding their holiday home business and I'm hoping to get the contract to construct the cabins." I smile, this would be a monumental job for me and exactly what I need to get noticed around here.

"That's great news, East. You'll get it for sure. I used to know the older brother but he hasn't been around here for years now. They are a good family and know a good job when they see it; you'll be just what they need." He drops a kiss on my lips and pats my butt. "Now, get going."

"I need to grab my tools and the board, and I'm gone. Love you, hon." I smile and saunter back to get my kit.

I drive out to the ranch with my head full of the ideas and plans I can suggest to the Sinclairs. I haven't been out this way for a long time. I went to school with Cal, the youngest son, but he got married and has a couple of kids, so I don't see him about much, even if he's our town veterinarian. We were good friends all through high school; maybe I should reach out to him again.

When I arrive at the ranch, I notice a brand-new Ford truck parked next to the barn, I hope it's not another constructor; I don't want to have to compete, especially not with someone who drives a top of the range vehicle. Nerves build up inside me as butterflies swirl frantically in my stomach. *Don't be stupid, East; they asked you here,* I tell myself. The door opens and Mr. Sinclair steps out and waves.

Switching off the engine, I climb out of my truck and walk over to meet him.

"East, it's good of you to come out. I haven't seen you for a long while. How's life treating you?" He offers his hand and I shake it firmly, his friendliness boosting my confidence.

"I'm good, Sir. Thank you for asking me here. What can I do for you?"

"I think I've got lots of things for you to do, let's take a walk and I'll talk you through my plans."

We set off, strolling comfortably together, as he explains the trekking holidays they already offer but plan to expand to skiing holidays for the winter and fishing breaks, too.

"No hunting offers?" I question, thinking this is prime hunting land and am surprised when he shakes his head.

"No, I'm not keen on hunting: the wildlife here is too beautiful to kill for sport. I'll stick to what we've got." He smiles.

We reach the first of the cabins already in place, situated in the woods but not too secluded, the tracks to drive up well established. The view of the lake from any of the six existing cabins is spectacular and I see the space available for maybe another six, depending what they want.

As we get closer to the first cabin, I see someone sitting quietly on the decking. With his back to us, it seems like he's sketching something, a small table next to him holds an empty mug and empty plate.

"My son, Denver, is staying in this one. I think, after a month of his mother fussing around him, he has decided to retreat to the quiet out here." Mr. Sinclair chuckles.

We carry on past him without any more being said, surveying the land he wants to develop to the level of luxury he wants to offer. These are no ordinary range holiday cabins, not by a long way. I offer suggestions, which seem to be accepted. I really want this and can see my mark over his visions.

I continue the visit, concentrating on Mr. Sinclair's vision. We complete our circle and end up back at the ranch.

"So, East, what do you think?"

"I think you've got a great thing going on here, I would love to be a part of it." I smile, genuinely excited about doing this job.

"Then, let's talk some figures and I think we have a deal."

The next hour is spent running through the logistics and costings and I think we are both satisfied. I glance at my watch and realize I've been here for nearly three hours.

"I think I'd best be going. I think all my suppliers will have finished for the day, so I will call them first thing and get my orders in and then I can get my machinery up here to get the ground work done. I think we will have this ready for your first round of summer visitors."

My drive back home is quick as my head is full of ideas I can't wait to share with Kes. This will give us the injection of cash we desperately need after the expensive renovation of the bar; we scraped every bit of cash we could to get his dream up and running and, so far, it is not letting us down. In fact, if I don't hurry, Kes will be rushed off his feet, keeping his serving staff replenished.

A quick shower later, dressed in black pants and the bar T-shirt, I'm ready to go again.

Chapter Three

KES

I look around as the bar starts to fill and come alive. I have dreamed of this for so long and still have to pinch myself to believe it's real. I glance at the clock hanging above the mirrored wall and glass shelves housing all the best liquors, and see East should be here soon. I hate he has to come and help out in the evenings; I'd much rather watch him sitting on the other side of the bar, keeping me company.

I know, if he gets the job for the Sinclairs, he will have to stop. The hours will be long enough for him there, without the five or even six hours he puts in here three or four times a week. I need a new bartender; I'll get an ad sorted. Who'd've thought an openly gay man running a bar in a straight-laced town like this would go and be a success? Without being a gay bar, I have managed to keep it a gay friendly place. The locals have got used to it as word got about and people come over from the surrounding towns, too. The motels get the trade, as some stay over at the weekend rather than risk a DUI.

Cal Sinclair walks in with another guy; I can't quite see his face under the baseball cap he's pulled down over his eyes. I make eye contact with Cal and he tips his chin in response, then the other guy takes his hat off and looks around. *Fuck!* My heart stutters when I recognize Denver Sinclair, the man I haven't seen since high school, the first man I ever kissed. His strong, chiseled jaw is covered with a couple of days growth but the dark blond scruff suits him. His longish, floppy blond hair has been flattened by the cap but his long, slender fingers run through it, returning it to a haphazard tumble of curls. It's his eyes that capture attention next, the electric blue orbs are hidden by a shadow, there's no sparkle or shine, they merely look tired and sad. I give him a smile of recognition and raise my hand in a half wave. He returns my greeting with a small smile that seems as sad as his eyes.

I cast my eye over his shoulder and see East strolling in behind the brothers. He smiles openly at me and my heart splutters again. Here he is: my man. I match his smile as he walks up to the bar, we lean over at the same time and kiss hello.

"Sorry I'm late, babe, the meeting with Sinclair took up all afternoon. I've managed to have a quick shower but I'm here now and you're gonna have to feed me, I didn't have time for anything."

"Did you recognize who you walked in behind?" I ask as he steps back, ready to stroll around to my side of the bar.

"No, who was it?" East lets his eyes roam over the room before looking back at me.

"Cal Sinclair and he brought his brother, Denver." I let my eyes travel to the booth in the corner where they sit. "I haven't seen him in over twelve years."

"His old man told me he was back today; he's in one of the cabins. I ought to go say hi to Cal."

"Leave it till he comes over, I don't think Denver wants to be recognized. He looked like a deer in the headlights when he walked in. Cal will be over soon enough. More importantly, how did you get on?"

I watch as East runs his hand over his short, dark hair then grins slyly at me, his sea-green eyes flashing with pride. "Yeah, I got it. I start tomorrow. I'll call the boys to start clearing the land. It's big, Kes. I mean, we could get out of debt with this."

"Oh, babe, I knew you could do it. I'm so proud of you." I drape my arms over his shoulders and step into his embrace for a kiss. "Let's talk about it later. C'mon, get to work."

When I scan over the room, I see Denver watching us. He seems, shit, I don't know. No, I know: he looks wistful. I give him a smile and my heart swells when he returns it. I glance over at East and he smiles as he watches our interaction.

We work long and hard tonight; the crowd doesn't seem to thin out until after eleven. The kitchen shut at ten, so all the tables have been cleared and it's just the drinkers. I survey the room and happiness blooms inside me, I'm so lucky to have the place I only ever dreamed about. Add East in as well and I can't believe I have such good fortune; he loves me as much as I love him. When I look over, he's laughing with Cal Sinclair at the bar—I'd forgotten they were good friends all through high school. College took Cal away but he came back and brought his girlfriend with him, he married her not long after and he's the town vet.

Denver sits alone, so I take my chance and saunter over to reintroduce myself. I wonder if he remembers me.

"Hey, Denver, it's good to see you again after all this time, how are you keeping?" I hold my hand out to shake his but I'm in no way prepared for the sparks shooting up my arm as he grips it. I watch his eyes widen with surprise; he felt it, too.

"Yeah, I remember. It's Kester, isn't it?" His warm smile brightens his face and his eyes flash for a moment. He runs his hand through his hair again, is it a nervous habit?

"It is, but I tend to go by Kes now. Kester reminds me too much of my mom hollering at me." I chuckle.

"It's good to see you again, Kes. You've got a great place here. Is it always this busy?" Denver peruses the room and the good thirty plus people still here, this late on.

"It's getting that way. It took a while for us to be accepted, but now it's doing great. Problem is, now East has the job at your folk's place, I'm gonna lose him as my bartender. I think I'm going to need to employ someone else." I look over at East and he nods, letting me know he's okay there.

"Why weren't you accepted? I would have thought this is exactly the sort of place this town needs." He looks genuinely quizzical.

"Oh, the bar wasn't the problem, the problem was me being gay and in a relationship with East. I've never hidden who I am but a few of the busy-bodies and bible thumpers caused a fuss."

With a dry laugh, Denver looks at me, "I guess I've been living in a city for too long, your sexuality would never have been an issue there."

"Is this just a visit then? You've not been back for a while." I hope it doesn't sound like I'm fishing, but I am interested in what has brought this man back here and for it to make him look as broken as he does.

"I'm not sure how long I'll be here; I'm taking some time out. I need to clear my head for a while." His answer is cryptic, but this is a bar, not a therapy room, so I leave well alone.

"Well, for what it's worth, it's good to see you again. You know where to find me if you get bored out on the ranch." I look over my shoulder again and see I'm needed back at the bar. "I'd best get back to work, it's really good to see you again, Denver. Don't be a stranger." I clap my hand on his shoulder and turn away. Denver's smile falters as he nods. The sadness in his eyes makes me want to reach out to him.

East clears away the last of the tables as the final drinkers leave, while I lock up behind them and start the cleanup. We've got into a pattern and its only minutes before we have squared away and cashed up.

"C'mon, baby, let's go home." My arms wrap around East's broad, muscular shoulders, tugging him against my body and leaning in to capture his mouth with my own for a soft kiss.

"What did Cal have to say about Denver?" We walk out to East's truck, having locked up. My interest in him is perplexing.

"Not a lot, he just said he has had a bad break up and needed to get away." East presses the button on his key fob, unlocking the doors and switching the headlights on. "Why?"

"There's just something about him that intrigues me, I can't put my finger on what it is though." I have always been honest with East and he knows I enjoy a ménage à trois and we have played a few times when we've been out of town.

"He is still as gorgeous as I remember; his time away has only made him better looking. I had such a crush on you and him." East chuckles as he opens his car door and climbs in.

"You and me both," I laugh, "he didn't look too good tonight though. Yeah, he's still a handsome fucker, but he's not happy."

The drive home is quiet, even if we continue to talk. "I'm going to advertise for another bartender; you are going to be so busy, I can't ask you to work evenings with me. Plus, there's Ellie to think of. She doesn't see enough of you as it is."

"Ellie is fine; she's happy, and well adjusted. She knows how hard life can be, she found out the hard way." I watch as my handsome lover's face tightens, the tick in his jaw prominent as he bites his tongue.

"I know she is, but she does need her father, especially as she's getting so grown up now. Plus, you miss out on time with her, too."

"Okay, as long as you think we can afford to pay someone, but only if you can arrange to get a night off, too. I'll never see you otherwise and what would be the point in that?"

"I agree, I'll put a notice in the window first but if that doesn't get me anywhere, I'll put an ad in the paper." I reach across and squeeze his thigh, smiling when he turns his head and winks.

When we get home, I'm beat and ready for my bed. East goes to the bathroom and is stripped off and under the water by the time I get in the bathroom. I tut as I pick up his clothes and throw them in the laundry hamper; something I have to do every night.

"Hey, save some hot water for me." I laugh and nudge him out of the way, but he simply pulls me under the spray with him. The water deluges over us as our mouths come together.

"Hmm, you taste good." East murmurs as his mouth travels down my neck, kissing and nipping my heated flesh. My hands tangle in his hair as he lowers himself to his knees and takes me deep in his mouth. The heat from his mouth has me moaning as he takes control and soon has me whimpering and begging for relief.

"Please, baby. I'm so close." I pant as my head clunks back against the shower wall, water pounding down my chest. Picking up speed, East quickly has me crying out his name and pouring my release down his throat.

Standing back up, East smiles and leans in to kiss me, I taste myself on his lips and tongue and moan again. "Your turn, I think."

Chapter
Four

DENVER

For the first time since I got here, I feel better; I think being dragged out by Cal last night did me some good. Seeing Kester Dereham again made me smile, and seeing him openly affectionate with East Brookman was a huge surprise. It's time to get back up on my feet and sort myself out. Alec has had too many hours of my time over the last month; I need to focus on the future. I'm not sure where it will take me but I can follow my feet for a while longer and see where they lead me.

I look at myself in the mirror after brushing my teeth and see a different person then the one I left behind, the dark shadows under my eyes have gone, my face is tanned from the afternoons sitting on the deck and my blond hair is even lighter. But it's my eyes that I notice have changed the most, the blue is brighter than I remember, the tiredness has dissipated at last.

"C'mon, hound! Let's get running." Whistling to Missy, I finish lacing up my running shoes and wait for her to come racing through the woodland. I love running and the joy of being free. I used it as tension and stress relief after long, tough shifts at the hospital. Alec would scoff, laughing that a few beers and a blow job would do the job quicker and a lot less painfully.

Running here, in the countryside, is so different: the air is clearer and the roads a lot quieter. I feel safer here. Missy doesn't have her leash and runs freely beside me. As I jog past my folk's place, I call out to mom who waves me on my way. It's good to be here, the pain and confusion of Alec's betrayal eases away, but my anger is still with me. I think that will be here for a while yet, but I'm not going to feed it anymore.

After a couple of miles, a truck passes me, the driver waves and I raise my hand, not sure who was driving, but hey, I can be friendly. After he's gone, I recognize him as East Brookman, the other half of Kester Dereham, the bar owner. This sets me thinking again about how easily they kissed each other last night. I know it was brief, but it was also sweet and loving, but mainly it was how accepted it was by the patrons. Something I never thought would happen here. I enjoyed talking to Kes last night and would like to be friends with him. Then my mind switches on and I remember my first kiss and the image of the other man comes to me, *shit! It was Kes, how could I have forgotten that?*

I keep on running, my feet pounding the road as my mind runs away with me. As I realize exactly how far I've come when I enter the main street, I slow down to a jog before I stop and bend over, my hands on my knees as I take in deep breaths. I look to my side and Missy has lain down, puffing out some hard breaths, too. Standing upright again, I take in my surroundings and find myself standing outside the bar. Glancing up, I wonder if it's open and push on the door to find it opens; I need to ask for a bowl of water for the dog and a refill of my bottle.

"Hi!" I call out and wait to see if anyone is around. Kes pops his head around a door at the side of the bar, he smiles in recognition and the ease of it sets butterflies off in my stomach.

"Hey, Denver, it's great to see you again." Kes' easy smile turns into a laugh when he sees precisely how hot and sweaty I am. "It looks like you could do with a cold drink and a towel."

"Um, yeah. That's what a came in for, do you have a bowl I can put some water in for my dog?" I look over my shoulder and Missy is sitting still, looking at me through the glass.

"Sure, bring her in, she probably would benefit from being out of the heat, too." Kes looks at her, then strolls behind the bar and picks up a tall glass and lifts it towards me. "Water?" He questions before grabbing a clean towel from a shelf by the tills and passing it to me.

"Please." I wait while he pours a bottle of water into the glass, leaving it on the side while he collects a plastic bucket from the floor and filling it with tap water for the dog.

"Here you go." He hands both over.

I head back to the dog and open the door, calling Missy inside. She comes immediately and sticks to my side, waiting for my next command.

"She's a beauty and very well trained." Kes comments and leans down to offer her his hand to sniff.

"Yeah, she has to be. Pitbulls have such a bad reputation but they are softies, really. Missy, here, is a rescue dog, she was seized by the local animal society in a raid on a dog ring. Luckily, she hadn't been used for fighting; she was just a puppy machine to the bastards that had her locked in a filthy shed. She was so grateful to be free, she threw herself into training and we have been together for two years now."

"What a great story, I hate the thought of animal cruelty. It's good she found such a loving forever home." Kes smiles at me again; he really is a good-looking man. Shame he's in a relationship, I wouldn't mind spending some time with him.

"I was passed by East on my way here; he's doing the building work for my dad, isn't he?"

"He is and he's very excited about it: he's so good at his job but he has had some setbacks that have stopped him working as much as he should. I'm just trying to sort out an advert for another bartender. East is going to be so busy, I don't want him having to come here to work, too." Kes runs his hands through his hair, raking the long strands through his fingers, then pulls a band from his wrist and ties it back. *Christ, he's a sexy man.*

"What sort of hours are you looking for?" I don't know why I've asked; maybe I think it would be good to work here a few hours a week.

"You interested?" His eyebrow rises, not sure if I'm serious.

"Yeah, I think I might be." I surprise myself but it suddenly sounds very appealing, so different from my real job back in the real world.

"Why don't you call back later, we can grab something to eat and have a beer and talk it over. East will be calling in too, he can help us work out a schedule. He'll have a better idea of what's going on at your dad's place."

"That's a great idea. I think I need a shower and a change of clothes before we sit down together." I wipe the towel over my face and neck and when I look at Kes again his eyes are dark and I watch him swallow hard. *Is he attracted to me? What about East?*

"Shall I give you a lift back? I'm not sure your dog is ready for the long run home." Kes looks at my dog, lying flat out on the cool, wooden floor and we chuckle.

"If it's not a problem? I would appreciate that. She's not the only one that would struggle." I smile, grateful not to have to run home again.

"It will be my pleasure." Kes looks at me and the tip of his tongue slides slowly across his bottom lip, making it my turn to swallow hard. "I get to see East again, too."

"Of course, yeah." I try to shake the image of me and Kes kissing from my mind. It's another ten minutes before Kes is ready to leave but I'm in no rush. I'm hoping I don't stink, I don't even think I can blame it on the dog if I do.

"You ready?" Kes asks, breaking me from my reverie and the images of me and him, and then of him and East.

"Yep, I'm good to go. Are you sure you're okay with the dog?"

"Dude, when you see my truck, you'll understand why I'm laughing." Kes opens the door for me and locks up behind us. His hand briefly skims across my back then it's gone and he leads me down to a beat-up truck.

"Okay, I get it." I laugh. Letting him drop the tailgate to let my dog jump in, I climb in the passenger side and look over at Kes. He's shoved a baseball cap on his head and he gives me a quick wink before he starts up the engine. *Damn, he's hot!*

"What have you done for the last however many years it's been since we last saw each other?" Kes flicks his eyes to mine as he turns his head to reverse out of the parking spot. His eyes darken again, I wonder if he remembers our kiss.

"I'm a doctor. A trauma surgeon, to be specific." I don't really want to get into this, I know it will lead to questions about why I'm here and I'm not sure of that answer myself. I'm questioning if it looks like I ran away, which I did but not for the reasons my colleagues will choose to think.

"Wow! That's awesome, Denver; congratulations on achieving your dream." He smiles broadly at me as he reaches across and squeezes my shoulder. The bolt of lightning coursing through my body surprises me, making me gasp.

"Do you remember that? I'm surprised." And it's true, we didn't spend much time together in high school but we were friends.

"Oh, Denver, baby, I remember a lot about you." His wink throws me off, *is he flirting with me?*

I flush, not knowing how to reply to that, so I don't, I look out of the window watching the countryside flash past.

"You can tell that I never got away, not very far anyway. I went to college but hated it and felt it was a waste of my folk's money, so I left. I lived over in Denton for a few years; my folks had trouble accepting me for who I was, so it was easier to stay out of their way. Then my brother was killed in Iraq and we needed each other, my parents are totally behind me now and we have a good relationship."

"I'm sorry to hear about your brother; that must be extremely hard to recover from." I knew a few good men back home who had lost limbs out in the desert.

"Thanks, it got me back here and to East; I don't regret my time away from here but I'm happy to be back." His smile is still there but not quite as easygoing as it had been.

"Have you two been together long?" I'm interested in how he can flirt with me and be with East.

"Over three years now, he's a wonderful man. He's had his own difficulties in life but we are great together. We live over on Laurel Drive, in a house he renovated himself. You should come over for dinner one night soon."

We've reached the ranch before I have time to answer but when I glance across I see he's waiting for an answer.

"I'd like that, thank you." I accept his offer. I look over to the barns and see East standing, smiling as he sees us. "There's your man."

"So he is." Kes smiles, but he keeps his eyes on me.

EAST

As soon as the merchants are open, I'm on the phone to place the orders; the accounts for Sinclair are already set up, making my life so much simpler. The excavator will be at the property by ten o'clock, and Doug and Eddie will meet me there. Dean is sorting out the plant machinery and will join us out there, too. This is going to be a good day. Kes wakes up and wanders through to the small room we've set up as an office, his smile makes my heart pound a tiny bit faster, even after all these years.

"How's it going, baby?" Kes leans down to kiss me.

Swiveling my chair around, I spread my legs, allowing him to step between them. I reach out for his hips and draw him closer to me. Planting a kiss on his bare stomach, right above the thin line of dark blond hair travelling down and disappearing under the band of his slip shorts, I nip the skin as he pulls away from me. He makes me chuckle and I kiss the tender skin.

"It's good; I'm heading out in a few. I have a good feeling about this." I look up at him, then stand up. "C'mon, lover, I've got a few minutes to spare." Tagging hold of Kes' hand, I lead him back to the bedroom.

The sun is heating up and I know we are in for a scorcher of a day. Driving out to the Sinclairs ranch, I see a man running, his dog alongside him. As I get closer, I recognize him—Denver, damn he's fit! His long legs are muscled and tanned, sweat causes his running vest to cling to his body, outlining some very defined pecs and abs. Maybe Kes is right, there's something about him. I lift my hand and wave smiling, as he returns the gesture. I hope he's not out in this heat for too long, it's easy to dehydrate if you're not used to it.

When I pull up at the ranch, my two team members are here already and lean against Eddie's truck. I pull up next to them and call out.

"Hey, guys, you ready to work hard today?" I laugh: these are two of the best guys I could have on my team, quiet but hardworking, ready to get on with any job given to them.

Climbing down from my cab, I grab the prints and plans of the cabins we will be building, Mr. Sinclair knew exactly what he wanted and had the architect draw the plans. We head down to the site and mark out the initial site, ready to excavate and flatten the ground; the hard core will be here tomorrow, so I want the beds ready for that. It takes us longer than I'd planned, as we decided to get all six foundations ready in one go rather than have to bring the heavy machinery back again. The ground is going to take enough of a hit, getting all the timber purely for the basic structures, let alone the interiors, through here. Luckily, we had budgeted for a landscaper to come in afterwards to spruce up the area before the first holidaymakers come along.

I hear a shout and see the flatbed truck bringing the excavator. Dean apologizes for being late, I hadn't realized how much time had passed but within fifteen minutes we're in business. I leave the guys and head back up to the ranch house; I want to talk over the arrangements again with Mr. Sinclair, keeping him up to date with the change of plans.

Standing by the main barn, I spot Kes driving down the wide asphalt, I grin even harder when I see who's sat next to him. Denver Sinclair in the ever-loving flesh.

"Hey, guys, whatcha doing?" I stroll over to them then wait while Kes lets the dog I'd seen running earlier down from the truck bed.

"It seems like I ran further than I should have and I didn't want to put Missy through the run back again, your very helpful boyfriend offered us refreshments and a ride home." Denver smiles broadly, he seems much happier today then last night.

"And it seems I may have found a new bartender, too, if we can work out a shift timetable, and, of course, if he survives the trial night." Kes laughs and nudges Denver with his shoulder, making him blush.

"Oh! You never said anything about a trial; maybe I'm not interested now." Denver jokes back, I'm pleased to see how well they are getting on. *Hang on! Shouldn't I be worried or jealous of the way they are acting?* I should, but I'm not, unless wishing I was standing with them counts as jealous.

"Anyway," Kes carries on, ignoring Denver's comment, "I've suggested we all get together later and work something out. What do you reckon, babe?"

I've reached the two of them and reach out to touch Kes' hand then quickly drop a chaste kiss on his lips. I turn and smile at Denver and offer my hand. "We didn't get to speak last night, Denver. It's good to see you again; your brother seems excited to have you back."

As he grips my hand, a zing of electricity sparks between us and we both look wide-eyed in surprise. Kes observes us, his eyes flicking between us, then a small, smug smile flickers briefly across his lips. I know my man: he saw what happened and is intrigued. His brain works visibly as he assesses the situation, wondering if there is something more here. It sure feels like it.

"I'm enjoying it here; I need to acclimate to the weather. It's a very different type of heat that I'm used to, I feel like someone has just opened the oven door and not told me to take care." He sniggers.

"What time will you be here till today, East?" Kes enquires.

"I think I'll be away by six from here, but I need to call in at mom's; I promised Ellie I'd call in tonight." I run my hand through my hair, suddenly embarrassed I'd mentioned my daughter in front of Denver. That's a story for another day, or not, depending on whether Denver becomes a friend. Kes looks at me in surprise; I guess he didn't expect me to mention her either. But I feel very comfortable around Denver, he feels familiar to me.

"Okay, maybe we should leave it for tonight. It sounds like you've got a packed evening already." Denver looks disappointed and gives us a small shrug as if it's no big deal. But, I think, for him it is. I watch his body tense, accepting the rejection.

"I'll be fine, let's make it eight o'clock; I'll be all done by then. It will be good to catch up with you, Denver."

He smiles again, relaxing. "Okay, shall I come back to the bar for eight then?" I watch him look between me and Kes, waiting for an answer.

I flash a silent question at Kes; I know he has the night off. Maybe we should get him to come to our home. Kes understands and gives me a slight nod.

"Come to our place, it's my night off. We can talk without being distracted by work." Kes smiles and touches Denver's arm with his fingertips, it looks like a casual touch but I see the static run through Denver as the short, pale blond hairs on his forearm stand on end.

"Yeah, sure. You said Laurel Drive, right? What number?"

Kes gives him the address and we swap phone numbers. "I need to get back to work, guys. I can't be seen slacking by your old man, Denver." I laugh then lean in to kiss Kes, Denver averts his eyes from our personal moment but not before I see a flash of heat in his eyes.

Kes smiles and gets back in his truck. "I'll see you both later then." He starts up the engine and gives us a smile.

"Thanks for the ride, Kes." Denver calls out as Kes turns the truck around, his arm waves out of the open window as he drives away.

We stand together silently, before Denver gives a little cough and mutters he'd better get back to his cabin and get showered.

"I'll walk back down with you, if I may." I ask and he nods. We saunter down to the waterfront and the cabins. "It's beautiful here, a good place to clear your head, I guess."

"It certainly is and, so far, it's doing its job." Denver seems suddenly somber, reflective even.

"I hope we don't disturb you too much with all of our noise and mess." We have reached his cabin and I turn to face him; he really is a very good-looking man. I watch as his eyes flicker down to my mouth as I lick my dry lips. They darken for a moment then, with a blink, Denver steps back and the moment is gone.

"I'm sure I'll cope." He smiles. "I'll see you later, East."

Chapter Five

KES

My head is in a spin, I can't get Denver out of it. His scent, as he sat next to me, was intoxicating: the pure man essence made my mouth water. But the reaction from him with every touch, not just from me but from East, too, has had my dick hard all afternoon. I'm prepping some food for tonight, keeping it simple with some homemade pizza and a few beers that are already in the fridge.

East will be home soon, Ellie won't keep him there too long. She simply likes to spend an hour or so, a couple of times during the week, then spend time together at the weekend; I've got used to it now but it was a shock at first. I was surprised when East mentioned her this afternoon but Denver didn't pick up on it, or at least he didn't question it. Maybe he knows, his parents and brother will have filled him in on all the town news when he got back here. And Cal definitely knows.

The door opens and I turn to see East walk through, he looks tired but his smile brightens up his face as he sees me.

"Everything okay?" I ask as I wipe my hands on a towel and walk towards him. I lean in and capture his lips with mine.

"Yeah, Ellie is good. She's got a school dance this Friday and wanted to show me her outfit. She's growing up way too fast." East chuckles. "I'm gonna grab a shower then I'll come and help."

"It's all done; take your time, baby. Do you want me to come and scrub your back?" I waggle my eyebrows.

"I don't think there's time for that." East smirks, and heads down the hallway to our bedroom. It's a large home, all on one level but there's plenty of space; East did an awesome job on renovating and restoring the old building. I follow him and sit on the window seat as he strips off his clothes. He looks over at me. "What do you think of Denver then?"

"Now there's a loaded question, baby." I lean forward and rest my arms on my knees.

"You know what I mean. Shit, Kes, the reactions we get from him are hot as hell! He's sexy as fuck and he seems to be interested." East wanders to our bathroom, making me get up and follow him.

"I get that feeling, too, but he does seem confused and I'm not surprised: he must be getting some very mixed signals from the two of us. On one hand, we are affectionate to each other and then we are casually flirting with him. But fuck, East, the smell of him this afternoon as I drove him back home had me fucking hard."

I watch as East starts to soap himself, his hand runs down his tight body and onto his dick. As soon as he touches it, it starts to swell. "Yeah, I noticed; both your dick and his scent." He winks. "So, the question is, what do we want to do about it? Are you looking for just a bit of fun? Because if that's all we want, giving him a job probably isn't the best idea."

"I think this could all be hypothetical, he may not be interested.

We could have this all wrong, but you are right: this can't just be a casual fuck. The thought of watching you and him together has been running through my mind all afternoon. The thought of having both of you has been driving me crazy." I watch as East carries on rubbing himself. "You're gonna have to stop doing that, baby, or I'm getting in there with you." I growl.

East shuts of the shower and steps out, grabbing a towel and rubbing the water from his body. "I want you to fuck me while you tell me what we'd be doing to him." His voice is thick with desire.

I drag him to the edge of our huge bed and bend him over, spreading his legs wide. Running my hand down the damp, heated skin of his back, I stroke every muscle as it ripples under my touch. Kneeling behind him, I spread his cheeks wide.

"I'd have you on your hands and knees and he's eating your ass out." I swipe my tongue over his tight pucker, "His tongue is spearing you as his hand tugs on your balls, stopping you from coming. My cock is in your mouth, plunging in and out of your throat as you groan."

My finger slides into East's tight ass as I carry on talking, my breath hot over his hole. "When you can't take his mouth anymore, Denver's dick lines up to your begging hole and pushes deep, filling you in one stroke. My dick is still hard in your mouth as you suck me harder with every thrust from him. Denver reaches around your body and grasps your weeping, desperate cock and wraps his fingers around you."

I copy my own words and thrust hard into East, his channel clenches tight around me, his heat burning me. I start to fuck him hard, bent over his back with my mouth to his ear. "As you get closer to coming, I pull out of your mouth and shoot my load over your face. Denver pounds hard inside you, gripping your hips now. As he pulls you up against his chest, I lick your face clean of my cum then take your cock in my mouth. Denver cries out, filling your ass with his cum, pounding your soft spot, making you come. You fill my mouth with your molten release, crying out our names as you shudder through your ecstasy."

Feeling my orgasm flashing through my body, I pull out of him and flip him onto his back before plunging back inside him. I wrap my hand around his dick and bring us both to climax. As East comes, he cries out my name and shoots his load into my fist as I fill his ass. Collapsing on him, I bring my fist up to my mouth and suck his cum into my mouth then, stretching up, I kiss him, letting him suck on my tongue to taste himself.

Pulling away and out of East, I smile at his totally blissed out face. "God, I love you, East. I love you so fucking much."

His eyes slowly open and come into focus, "I love you, too, Kes." His voice is floaty and ethereal as he comes back to me. The doorbell rings and we jump.

"Shit! You get dressed and I'll go let him in." *Fuck*, I look down at myself and grab East's towel to wipe my cock clean before I tuck myself in. I'm smoothing my hair down as much as I can before stalking out of our bedroom.

"You totally look like you've been fucking!" East calls out to me.

"So do you!" I shout back, but his comment works and I'm laughing when I open the door. Denver stands nervously on our front porch with a six-pack of beer. "Hey, Denver, c'mon in. Sorry to have kept you."

Denver blushes bright red; "Um, did I come at the wrong time?" He peers down at his watch and frowns.

"No, no, of course not. East is here, he's just got out of the shower. Let's go through, he'll be with us in a moment." I lead him through the house, down the corridor, into the kitchen.

"This is a great place." Denver looks around the large, open kitchen, I see he is genuine as his smile spreads. I watch as he walks over to the wall covered in photographs; his eyes are wide and his smile grows as he looks at the happy memories we have framed all over the large wall.

I open the fridge, "You up for a beer?" I ask, pulling his eyes away from the catalogue of our lives.

"Huh? Oh, yes, please. Here, I brought some, too." Denver hands over the carton of drinks I think he'd forgotten about.

East walks in behind Denver and smiles at me. His eyes still sparkling, he reaches over and snags the beer from my hand before dropping a kiss on my mouth. Turning to Denver, he runs his hand over the nape of his neck and down his back. Denver's eyes widen in surprise but he doesn't step away.

"Hi, Denver, it's good to see you again." East smiles easily at our guest but I know my man, and he's eager to know how Denver feels about us. I should feel bad for planting the images of the three of us together in his head, but I want this, too. "You found us okay? The town has grown bigger since you were last here, I guess."

"Yeah, it sure has changed but I haven't forgotten *that* much of the layout." I watch him twist the cap off the beer bottle then look around for somewhere to put it.

"Here, let me take that." I hold out my hand, letting my fingertips slip slowly over his wrist and down the palm of his hand. His eyes widen but then he coughs an embarrassed huff and looks anywhere but at the two of us. Okay, I get the message: it's time to tone it down before he runs for the hills. I look over Denver's shoulder, catching East as he stares at our guest's ass. I give an infinitesimal shake of my head and East nods.

"I did pizza, I hope you like that?" I smile easily and watch as he shakes his head clear of any confusion.

"Yeah, pizza's great, thanks." Then, when I pull the made-up meal from the fridge, Denver lets out another cough. "Jeez, I thought you meant you'd called one through for delivery."

"The guy who cooks for me at the bar makes them better than me, but it will be good, I promise." I laugh and let my hand touch Denver's fleetingly, but enough to make goosebumps appear on his tanned skin.

I wait for a second, maintaining eye contact, then turn away to place the pizza in the oven. East pulls some chips from one of the cupboards and tips them into a bowl. "Shall we eat outside?" He asks and I nod.

"Is that okay with you, Denver? It's nice and cool here now, don'tcha think?"

"Yeah, outside is good." He takes a long swallow from his beer and then follows East as he walks to the large, open glass doors. "Whoa!" I hear him say and I smile.

We have a great back yard; it's larger than most of the others in our street, the land was a disaster when East bought it but we have cultivated and planted a gorgeous garden. The swimming pool is mainly for Ellie but we have fun there, too. The wide, decked area has plenty of comfortable chairs and loungers along with a larger grill, all under a large, canvas canopy. I'm very proud of our garden. I amble out, after setting the timer on the oven, and stand next to our guest.

"You like it out here?" I enquire and rest my hand on his shoulder.

▢ ▢ ▢

DENVER

What I like is his hand touching me, I liked the way East ran his hand down my back. I try and clear my head and speak, *shit! His touch courses through my body like lava, fuck. Denver, get your act together.* I try to put together a coherent sentence and clear my mind of the thoughts rushing through my mind. Thoughts of these two men naked, with me sandwiched between them. *Fuck! I'm screwed!*

"Yeah, wow! It's really something out here. You two have done an outstanding job, so many individual sections but they meld together so well. It's exceptional, Kester." I gaze over the green lawn surrounded by lush, green shrubs and trees. The borders have an abundance of bright flowers accentuating the space and tranquility of the whole garden. The pool surprises me, but it's fenced off and has large tubs of flowers in its corners and vines climbing through the low fence make it less obtrusive.

"It took a long time but we enjoyed doing it together; East had already done most of the house by the time I moved in, and we wanted to do a joint project." Kes stands close to me but takes his hand away and I miss his touch immediately.

I don't know what the hell is up with me. After Alec cheating on me, how can I even be thinking these thoughts? But it's not only Kester's touch I like; when East touched me, I had the same thoughts. Even when he simply smiled I felt the flutter of excitement in my gut. I look up at East and he gives me a lazy, appraising smile, his bright green eyes sparkle with mischief.

"Are you ready to work with Kes, Denver? He's a fusspot and likes everything done his way." East jokes and tips his beer at his lover in a salute.

"Ignore him, Denver. He just doesn't like to be told what to do." Kes sticks his tongue out at East, a gesture so childish it has us all laughing. A ringing sound from the kitchen draws him away. "I'd better go and fetch our pizza."

I watch him walk, his tight, round butt cheeks firm in his shorts. Hearing East snicker, I flush when I realize I've been caught.

"Don't worry about it, Denver. He's got a great ass, well worth ogling." He laughs and my face gets hotter as my embarrassment heightens. "You should feel it, it's one hell of an ass."

Kester came out with the pizza on a large, circular chopping board. "I thought we could just muck in with our hands, if you don't mind? Saves us having dishes to do later." He looks at my face and turns to East. "What have you said to him?"

I cough and splutter as East laughs. He catches my eye and winks. "Nothing, we were just chatting."

The pizza gets placed in the center of the table and my stomach gives out an embarrassing rumble.

"That looks like a good pizza; if this is what you serve in the bar, I think I may end up working full time with you." I reach across and take a slice, picking up a paper napkin as I do.

Kes smiles and reaches across to grab a slice then sits back down next to me. There are six chairs around this large, round table but I find myself sandwiched between the two men. Their chairs are close and when one of them moves, they brush against me, either my arm or the side of my legs. We sit quietly as we eat the first slice then Kes pulls a folded sheet of paper from his back pocket and hands it to me.

"Those are the hours I'm gonna need some help; I'm not asking you to be there without me, so it's not going to be too full-on for you. I have Monday and Tuesday nights off and I am happy with the cover those nights, one of the girls, Shelley, is interested in picking up another shift, so that cancels out Thursday nights for you too. So, really, it's Friday, Saturday and Sunday shifts I need filling. None of the others wanted anymore weekend hours, so these are yours, if you want them."

I look at the sheet and see the hourly rate at the bottom and raise my eyes: he pays well. "You don't need to pay me that much, Kes. This is more about helping you two out. East is going to be busy at my place. I feel bad making you pay someone for work East would normally do for free."

"That's the going rate, Denver. I have to offer that, or my tax man will be breathing down my neck." He looks at me and smiles, "and not even in a nice way." It's his turn to wink at me.

They are definitely flirting with me, *is this a game, a challenge, to them?* I'm not into playing games; I'm not going to be someone to mess with. Have I got all the flirting all wrong? A feeling of anger builds inside me as I think of how much Alec and his new lover must have laughed at me for being so blind to what was going on under my nose. My hands have clenched into fists and I take a deep breath in and blow out slowly to calm down.

When I open my eyes, I see both men watching me with a look worry of on their faces. I exhale once more and relax my fingers, stretching them out over my thighs.

"Denver, what's wrong? Have I said something to upset you?" Kes asks as his hand reaches out and covers mine. I tense up again.

I look at him and his expression is troubled. His eyes flick over to East, making me look that way also. Looking equally concerned, East rests his warm, calloused hand on my arm, the heat sending a tremor through my body. Confusion floods my head and I push myself up. Turning to them, I still can't decipher their reactions.

"Why are you doing this?" I ask, questioning their motives.

"Doing what, Denver? We are only talking work hours." Kes stands up and he's close to me, encroaching on my personal space.

"It doesn't seem like that to me. I don't know if this is some sort of joke to you, if this is a way for you two to get your fun. I'm not interested. I'm not here to play games." I try to walk past Kes but East stands up too. They stand in front of me, not so much incasing me, but not allowing me an easy route out of their home, either.

What I don't expect is East to lean forward, his face mere millimeters from mine. "This isn't a game, Denver. I promise you that." His warm breath washes over my skin and my eyelids flutter at the sensation.

Kes moves half a step closer, his body heat registering as his chest comes in line with my own. "You are no plaything, Denver."

As he leans in, his mouth slides so softly over mine, I could almost have imagined it if it hadn't been for East's sigh. My eyes are fixed on Kes as he pulls back then turns to East and does the same to him; this time it's me who makes a sound. I gasp at what I'm seeing and what I'm feeling because, as Kes steps away from East, his eyes fix back on mine while East steps closer and touches his lips to the soft, sensitive spot below my ear. This time, there is more pressure and my hands reach out to him. My fists clench in his T-shirt. I don't know why this is happening but it feels good.

Kes steps up, his hands resting lightly on my hips; East hasn't moved away, instead, his nose skims up and down my neck, inhaling and emitting a low moan as he exhales. My eyes are tight shut when Kes' mouth touches me and I try to embrace what is happening and why it feels so good. And, as his lips press harder against mine, I find I'm returning the pressure, feeling the vibration in his lips as he hums.

I feel bereft, alone, when they move back, their eyes dark and heavy with desire and I'm sure mine match theirs. My chest heaves as I draw in a large, deep breath and shakily release East's T-shirt from my fists.

"No games, Denver. Nothing more than what you want, if you want anything at all." East's rough, lust-laden voice breaks through my own thoughts and confusion.

"Okay." I manage to whisper. Kes moves away until he is in front of his chair. East follows him and then they sit in front of me. Glancing down, I see the stiff outlines of their dicks pressed tightly against the fabric of their shorts.

Kes lets out a gruff bark of embarrassment and rearranges his junk, breaking the tension surrounding us as we laugh.

"Fuck! Do you interview all your prospective bar staff this way?" I laugh shakily and lean against the table, my hands curling around the edge.

Kes blanches and East curses quietly.

"Denver, what just happened has nothing to do with work. It has everything to do with you, this is your call. We like you, *we like you a lot.* You can take the job regardless; it's yours. I'm happy to be your friend again. Twelve years is a long time away, and I'm guessing you could use a couple of friends around you right now."

I look over to East and he smiles; there's no guilt or embarrassment and neither of them looks contrite nor ashamed, only open and friendly and so damn, freaking hot. *Fuck! I have never thought of anything like this before, but two men? Really? Could I possibly be thinking about this?*

"Okay, how about we start with friends, and a new job for me, and see how it goes. I may be so bad at bartending, you have me out of the door after the first hour." I smile at the two men and see them relax; I hadn't even noticed they were tense until I answered.

"I can't imagine that, but that sounds good." Kes smiles and reaches his hand out to mine, his fingertip strokes over my knuckles. "How about another beer to celebrate your new job?"

☐ ☐ ☐

"Denver, are you okay?" East's voice breaks through my daydream.

"Huh? Yeah, sorry; I was miles away then. What's up?" Coming out of my daze, I look at East. He's working on the construction of the timber cabins for my father. I'm keeping him and his crew hydrated as they work, bringing them bottles of water, I got caught up at the sight of East's tight ass in his well-fitting jeans. They must be an old pair because the denim has gone soft and worn and clings to his ass like a second skin. My mind was full of images of him lowering them for me, teasing me as he strips off his clothes. His scent fogs my mind as the smell of clean sweat, soap and the musk of his own, natural odor floods my nose.

I glance down and see the bottles are still in my hands. "Sorry, here you go." I hand them to him then turn to leave.

"Hey, Denver, hold on." East calls, "I want to talk to you." As he reaches me, he strokes my back; I know he feels the shiver that runs through my body because he presses a bit firmer, his finger digging into my skin.

"Do you want to come inside for a minute?" I'm back at my cabin and push open the door, welcoming the cool air from the air conditioning. East has come up to the cabin before but we stayed outside; having him inside my space feels strange. Not that this is really my home, but it's the closest thing I've got to my own place. I've added my own touches, hanging some of my photographs and artwork on the walls, my vinyl records are stacked on a bookcase and the player sits in the corner next to my guitar. For now, I'm happy here. I don't know what the future holds and I'm comfortable with that.

When I turn back to close the door, East is looking around, a small smile hints its presence on his lips. *God, I want my mouth on them!* I watch as he sucks on the plump, full bottom lip, making me want to tug it between my teeth.

It's been three weeks since that night at their home and Kes and East have kept their word, letting me adjust to my new job and my friendship with them. That doesn't mean there haven't been some heated looks and a few more than casual touches; they are a very tactile couple. I can't help but watch as they interact with each other, they never pass each other without making some sort of contact. It may be a soft touch from their hands, or a quick kiss, or even a jokey bump of a hip. All of it makes me aware of what I didn't have with Alec, not for a long time anyway. What I thought was comfortable and content, I now realize was boring and lackluster. We lived alongside each other, communication was humdrum and quick, and I hadn't realized how long it had been since we laughed and messed about like these two do.

"Denver, Kes and I are going to the Oasis club in Denton tonight; do you want to come with us?" I watch as East scrubs his hands through his hair and then down his face. "What I mean is: Kes and I would like you to come, too."

"Oh!" I'm surprised: *is this a date or another friend thing? Will I be the third wheel?* "I don't want to get in the way of your date night, but thank you for thinking of me."

"Denver, it's not a date night, it's a night out, relaxing, having a couple of beers and a dance if the mood takes us. C'mon, Denver, it will be fun." East looks at me, his cute puppy dog eyes make me smile. A night out does sound fun.

"Okay, thank you. What time shall I meet you?" I'm wondering if I need to drive over to Denton or if we'll go together.

"Come to us for nine, is that okay?" His smile is a mile wide and his eyes are sparkling; he looks so adorable.

Before I know what I'm doing, I reach out and run my knuckles down his cheek. His eyes widen and his tongue darts out and dampens his lip. Quickly pulling my hand back, I step away.

"I'm sorry." I manage to splutter but East grabs my hand and I find myself wedged up against his solid chest.

"I'm not. Don't worry, Denver, it's all good." Licking his lips again, he presses them firmly against mine. A few, short seconds later, he moves back a step. My tongue slides across my bottom lip as I capture his flavor while he mimics my action, a soft sigh escaping me as I continue to gaze at his beautiful mouth, then back up to his eyes.

"It's all good, Denver, I promise. I'd better get back to work. We'll see you at our place at nine." With a wink, he's gone.

I spend the rest of the day in nervous turmoil but I prep myself for every eventuality and dress in dark jeans and a tight fitting, grey T-shirt. As I splash some cologne on, I can't help my mind from wandering to new places: the thought of two men surrounding me. Of their hands on my body, stroking, caressing my body, taking me to heights of passion I never imagined.

Chapter
Six

EAST

The thought of Denver coming with us has me thrumming in anticipation; I've been trying to get Kes into bed since I got home, but he's not joining in.

"Just suck my dick then, Kes. I've been hard all afternoon." I'm whining, I hear it but I don't care. "If you don't, I'm only gonna jerk off in the shower."

"For fuck's sake, East! Just hold on to it, imagine how good you'll feel if he joins us tonight. And, if he doesn't, I promise to let you fuck me raw." Kes smirks and pops a kiss on my cheek as he walks past.

"You're on!" I call out to him as he strolls out into the garden. I start the shower and as much as I want to rub one off, I heed Kes' words and keep my hands off. I do make sure I'm all prepped and ready, in case Denver does make a move on us.

We've kept our word and have not mentioned our interest—fuck, it's gotten so much stronger than interest; it's our desire to be with him. I know he's not immune to us. Because, although we haven't spoken, I know both of us have found it hard to keep our hands to ourselves. Not grabby, hands-on, over the top groping but I can't keep my hands away from him and the slightest of touches only heightens my need for him. As I step out of the shower and back into our bedroom, Kes sits on the edge of our huge bed, definitely big enough for three of us.

"What's up?" I take in his worried mien and begin to panic. "Has he called to cancel?"

"No, I'm just wondering if we've made a huge mistake, that he's not interested. Have we set ourselves up for disappointment? Fuck, East, what we have together is amazing; it's everything I've ever wanted. I've dreamed of a home and a man—a really fucking hot man—to come home to, and I've found that with you." Kes looks up to me as I step into the space between his parted legs. "I never want to be without you, I just feel that we could be what he didn't know he was looking for, what he needed. But, and you need to understand this, if he turns us down then I am still the happiest man alive, because I have you. I fucking love you, East Brookman."

"Oh, Kes, baby. I feel the same way: you have accepted me, all of me. All the baggage that came with me—and I'm not ashamed or embarrassed by my daughter; she is a wonderful part of my sad, past life. But you never batted an eyelid, you just accepted her as part of me, as part of the package, and I'm not prepared to lose what *we* have on the chance of something different."

I lean down and cover his mouth with mine, pouring the love I feel for him into this kiss. "We are good, baby. With or without Denver sexy-as-fuck Sinclair, we are the real damn deal."

Kes reaches his arms around my body and clutches me against him, his cheek resting on my stomach. My dick reacts—well, shit, of course it does—and starts to swell. Kes chuckles and starts to move away. My hands clasp his head lightly.

"C'mon, baby, you're halfway there already." I know I don't stand a hope in hell of him sucking me, but damn. Kes pulls the towel from around my waist and his hot breath skims over the tip of my, now swollen, head. The heat from his mouth as he engulfs my length deep into his mouth has my fingers digging into his scalp. The sensation of his hot, wet mouth has me quickly begging for relief. Kes knows exactly how I like my cock sucked and, *damn*, he's doing his best to kill me right now.

"Fuck! Yeah, baby. Take me deeper, swallow me down." My mouth always turns dirty when he does this to me. Hell, when he does anything to me, I mouth off like a horny sailor. I feel the tingle start in my toes then race like wild-fire through my body. My butt clenches in his tight grip as my climax fires from me. Kes swallows my thick load and licks me clean as I soften in his mouth. "Oh, baby, you are going to get so lucky later."

Kes stands up and wipes the back of his hand over his swollen mouth and grins. "I'm fucking counting on it." He swats my ass as he steps past me. "Now, get dressed; he'll be here soon."

"Do you think we should have gone out for dinner?" I glance over my shoulder at Kes as I zip up my jeans.

"I thought you told him it wasn't a date: dinner implies date. This is just a night out for some fun." Kes steps up to me, wrapping his arms around my waist. "Just chill, babe. It will be a good night, whatever happens."

"It's just that he's a doctor, hell, he's a surgeon. What would he see in us? I know we're damn good at what we do, but we're not exactly his caliber. We're just two guys who never got very far from home." The panic running riot in my head surprises me as much as Kes.

"East, we are good people; we work hard and are successful. We don't have to be doctors or lawyers, we simply need to be us, plain and simple but good." He looks me in the eye and doesn't break contact until I nod. "Good. Now, come on, no more critical analysis." Popping a kiss on my mouth, he smiles again.

Wandering out into the back garden, each with a beer, we wait silently. It's not long until we hear the deep rumble of Denver's truck. Kes looks at me and winks.

"Ready?" He questions.

"As I'll ever be, I guess." I listen to the sound of the engine being switched off and then... nothing. We wait, not wanting to rush to the door, but after a minute of no car door being opened and no knock on the door, I look at Kes and he shrugs.

"C'mon, let's go see." I stride through the house and pull open the front door. Denver looks up through his windshield and gives a weak smile. Walking down the three steps of our wooden porch, I head to his car. As I put my hand on the door handle, it starts to open; I look over my shoulder and see Kes on the porch, his hand resting on the wooden upright.

"Hey, Denver. Whatcha doing sitting here?" I make light of it as he pushes the door open properly.

"I was just finishing a call. I'm sorry, my phone rang just as I got here." He smiles and climbs from cab.

"You had us worried. C'mon, let's go inside while we get all locked and ready." Kes smiles and steps back, giving Denver room to walk past. I'm not sure he's telling us the truth but if he needed a minute to get his head together, then that's fine by me. He's not running away of whatever he thinks is going on.

"You look good, Denver." Kes lets his eye roam over Denver, he really does look good. Almost black denim clings to his ass and thighs and I see the stretch of his dark grey shirt over his muscular shoulders down to his tapered waist. He is so unaware of how damn hot he is, whoever shot him down should be beaten.

"Thank you; I wasn't sure what to wear. It's been a long time since I've been to a club." He looks over Kes and his smile is more genuine as he acknowledges we are similarly dressed. "Looks like I did okay, though."

"We just need to grab our keys and lock up, then we're on our way." Kes winks and laughs.

□ □ □

The first couple of beers went down well and I watched as Denver relaxed, his eyes roaming around the darkened room. Tuesdays are a good night here: the music is loud and dirty, it never seems to bother anyone it's a week day, the dancefloor is full, and the men are getting good and sweaty as they grind against each other. It's a good club, I'm not saying there aren't men fucking in the bathroom, but it's not a meat market.

"You having a good time, Denver?" I'm standing close, my mouth barely brushing his ear. As he turns quickly, our lips almost touch but he moves back minutely so they miss by a hair's breadth.

"I am; it's been far too long since I've had a good night out. It's good here, a nice crowd, by the look of things." He turns to scan the room again.

"Anyone here catch your eye?" I nudge—*please, let him get the hint.*

"Er, well, no. Not really. It's more of a look-and-learn night for me. I need to get back into the swing of things, I've moped about for long enough now. Now thanks to you and Kes, you've restored my faith in mankind." His smile is genuine as his eyes roam my face, focusing finally on my lips.

I watch as he tips his bottle up to his mouth and drains the last of the beer. My eyes follow the trail as he swallows. Finding it hard to concentrate, I decide it's time to dance.

"C'mon, let's get our groove on." I shout as the music suddenly gets louder. Kes smiles and nods before grabbing my hand.

"You too, Denver." Kes reaches out his other hand but Denver shakes his head.

"No, you two go, I'll be fine here. I haven't danced for a long,

long time." Denver smiles but it doesn't reach his eyes. "Go, go." He shoos away, smiling.

Kes nods and pulls me into the crowd on the dancefloor. "Leave him, East; let him make up his own mind. Baby steps, remember?"

I let the music take hold and soon I sway to the beat, my arms over my head and Kes' hands on my hips, keeping me close to him. Kes keeps his mouth against my neck as he leaves long, wet kisses on my already heated skin, his hips rock, keeping me close to him as we grind sweetly together.

□ □ □

DENVER

I'm such a damn coward. I berate myself as I watch the only two men who have my interest tonight. *Just grow a pair, Sinclair, and go dance with them.* I watch as they move together, they could be the only two men in the room for all I know: they have my total attention as the room fades, leaving only them in my sight.

The song changes and a harder, dirtier beat comes through the speakers. I don't recognize it, but it's good. I watch as Kes turns East around so his back is pressed against Kes' front. East's hips sway, rubbing his ass over the front of Kes' jeans. It's so fucking sexy.

Whether it's the couple of beers I've had or the noise of the music or the heat coming from the bodies around me, but something has me intoxicated. The urge permeates through me, directing my thoughts to the two young men I walked in with not ninety minutes ago. My feet move of their own volition as I weave between the writhing, sweaty bodies. Kes has his mouth on East's neck, sucking on the soft skin. The bright, multi-colored lights bounce off their skin serves to highlight the sensuality of the kiss on his damp flesh.

A moan creeps out of me as I reach them and—again—with no forethought, my hands are on East's hips as I press my lips up to his. East parts his lips fractionally and the hot tip of his tongue slides over the seam of my mouth. Opening to him, I let my tongue slip tentatively over his. *Fuck!* The taste of him sends me reeling, my head spinning as I lose myself in him. I can't get enough.

The kiss intensifies as I pin my body harder against his. In unison, we roll with the beat. Kes' hands are on my hips as East grips my head, holding me in place. Our tongues dance a lazy dance as we learn each other's mouths. My eyes open when I feel the hard length of East's dick pressing into me; he nudges me with his hips, eliciting another soft moan from me.

"My turn, I think." I hear Kes' gruff voice and feel East pull away and twist around.

Suddenly, I'm the one in the middle, East's front against my back, and I look at Kes. His eyes are dark and heavy, his desire apparent as he draws me closer.

"Oh, baby, I've been waiting to do this again for so long." Letting the tip of his tongue slip over his bottom lip, leaving a sheen in the roving lights, Kes whispers as his mouth skims over my already kiss-swollen lips. His tongue slides over my bottom lip before he pulls it between his teeth and gently tugs. Then it's on! His tongue invades my mouth, dueling with my own, his dominance obvious but so sexy. He sucks on my tongue and I groan hard, my hands wrapping around his shoulders and into his hair.

East's hands are around my waist; his fingertips ease up under my T-shirt and caress my highly sensitive skin, leaving what feels like scorch marks in their wake. I need more, I don't know what it is I need—but this isn't enough. East pushes his groin into my ass cheeks and I gasp at the feeling, the hotness of his hands, along with his erection, send all sorts of signals to my befuddled, kiss-drunk brain.

Kes slows his kiss and ends with delicious nips and nibbles over my lip. "I think we need to get out of here: we've become a show."

I open my eyes and notice the men around us staring, not with disapproval but with desire and envy. I feel East's warm chuckle against my neck as he plants his mouth on my skin.

"Ready to go, Denver?" He asks huskily.

I have to swallow a couple of times before I find my voice and the depth and roughness of it surprises me. "Yeah, I'm ready."

I feel drunk as Kes takes my hand and East rests his on the small of my back, the heat of his touch still scolding my skin. Those two kisses have left my brain reeling and turned my legs to jelly, my bones weightless in my limbs. I appreciate the support and strength of the two beautiful men.

Kes presses his key fob and the lights of his truck flash as the door locks release and pulls behind the wheel. I wait for East to open the passenger door to sit next to his lover, but he opens the rear door and waits for me to clamber inside before settling in next to me, slamming the door shut.

Kes looks at us through his rearview mirror and smiles, "Ready, boys?" His eyes flash with heat as he gazes at us.

"Yep, let's get home." East replies easily.

I don't think the power of speech has fully returned to me yet, so I keep quiet. Resting my head against the headrest, I relax, knowing we have at least thirty minutes of driving before I have to make any more decisions.

East sits close, his hand casually on my thigh, his fingers splayed, pale in contrast to my dark jeans. I revel in his touch and move my head to lean on his shoulder. His hand flexes as I inhale his scent, so clean yet masculine. The sweat from the dancing only heightens my desire, fueling the fire already burning brightly inside my chest, making my heart beat faster. The need for these men to own me courses through me like red-hot, all-consuming lava.

His head drops and I feel his lips in my hair as he kisses me, my eyes flick up to his face and he smiles. It's a heart-wrenchingly beautiful smile, full of promises. I return it then shift so I can reach his neck, my mouth presses against the skin at the juncture of his neck and shoulder, I had no plans to take it further but I moan when my tongue slips between my lips and I taste the salt from his overheated body. Pressing my lips more firmly, I let my tongue slide over the pulse spot beneath his ear.

When I pull my mouth away, his flavor captured on my tongue, East lifts my chin with two fingers and kisses me. Not a soft, full of promise, kiss but a head-spinning, heart-bursting, dick-throbbing kiss that has me squirming into his body. My fingers clutch at his shirt again, keeping him pressed against me. His hands tangle in my hair and tug, a groan vibrates through my chest and is swallowed by his constant kiss.

A loud chuckle from Kes breaks us apart; we are breathless as we gaze into Kes' dark eyes through the mirror.

"We're nearly home so pack it in now, at least until I can join in." He laughs but his voice is low and full of promise, sending yet another lick of flames through my bloodstream.

I look out the window and recognize the street we drive down as the one they live on, I should feel nervous—or, at least hesitant—but I'm not. I'm horny and want more from these amazing men, I want to see what they expect or plan, most of all I want to be pressed between them again.

When the car pulls onto the drive, Kes turns off the engine and, without hesitation he is out of the door. He yanks my door wide open and then I'm pulled out. Kes crushes his body up to mine and captures my head in his hands. His kiss rockets through me, I can taste the need and desperation on his tongue as he strokes mine.

His forehead touches mine as he drags his lips away. "Fuck! I needed to do that. Watching the two of you kiss for so long was killing me. I don't know how I kept my eyes on the road long enough to be safe."

"I hadn't realized we'd kissed for long." I stutter, but I know why the journey seemed to go so quickly.

"Denver, baby, you owned that kiss." East murmurs behind me.

"C'mon, let's get inside before the neighbors' curtains start twitching. The things I want to do to you do not need an audience; the three of us is enough."

It's Kes' turn to groan and he grabs my hand before dragging me the few, short steps to their porch and front door. His key slides into the lock and he looks back over his shoulder and winks. My stomach turns, awakening a thousand, coiling, roiling snakes, writhing, but in a good way, an excited, 'hell yeah!' sort of way. I nudge his foot with mine, encouraging him to twist the key and push open the door.

East presses against my back as we tumble through the doorframe. My hands claw at Kes' clothes as we stumble down to, what I hope is, their bedroom.

As soon as we are inside, the door closes firmly behind us and we stand panting in the soft glow of the side lights. Kes crushes his mouth over mine as East latches on to my neck, the sensations sending me higher and higher and I don't want it to stop.

When he breaks away, I watch Kes' chest heave as he reins himself in. The blown pupils shine jet black as his desire pulses from them.

"Denver, do you want this? Are you sure you want to go further? Because I can't back away from you, unless you tell me." The raw huskiness of his voice beats into my chest. I check his hands furl and unfurl as he keeps them to himself. "East, are you sure you want to do this, there's no going back. We need to all agree on taking this further."

East steps away from my back and walks around to stand in front of Kes, "I want this, too, baby. I want you and I want him." He leans in and kisses his lover passionately, then turns to kiss me just as much.

"Shit, Kes, you were the first man I ever kissed and working with you has brought all those feelings back. East, the sight of you at my place these last few weeks has been driving me wild. I want this, I want you both." I step closer to them, reaching out to touch them both. "I have never done anything like this before and I have only been with one man for the last five years, and only a couple more before him: you need to lead the way here." I'm surprised I have been so open with them, but this is no time for untruths.

"Oh, baby, that's not going to be a problem." East smirks then pulls his shirt over his head before tossing it to the floor. I stare as the body I have been sneaking peeks at for the last three weeks is suddenly unwrapped; his broad chest is even better than I imagined, the fine hairs covering his chest have me itching to run my fingers through them and swirl my tongue over.

Kes reaches the hem of my shirt and slides it slowly up my body, his fingertips trailing my ribcage as the fabric slips up. I moan and lean into him. Pulling the T-shirt over my head, he discards it along with his own, then his mouth is on my shoulder, leaving hot wet kisses over my inflamed skin. When East runs his hands over my chest, my lungs fill and I push my chest into his hands. As his fingers stroke and pluck at my nipples, Kes reaches around me and has pulled my belt undone, I hear the pop of the top button as East's mouth covers my nipple and sucks.

"Ahhh! Fuck!" My head drops back and my eyes close tight at the sensation of four hands over my body. My dick painfully presses against the remaining buttons on my jeans, dampness spreading on the tight fabric of my briefs.

"What do you want, baby?" Kes' voice breaks through my lust-crazed thoughts as his mouth heats up the shell of my ear, his tongue tracing the edge before he bites on the lobe to send bolts of lightning through my body.

"More, I want so much more. You, East: I want you, both of you." My words sound alien to me; I have never heard my voice so needy, so desperate. I have never been this desperate, this aroused. What have I been missing out on? Why has this taken so long? Has my life been so devoid of passion? The sad answer is yes.

East's mouth travels down my body, his teeth and tongue caressing my torso, I feel him humming against my skin as he tastes me. Then I'm turned around and facing Kes, he sweeps his tongue briefly over my lips then he's on his knees—*oh god, he's on his knees.* I have never wanted a man's mouth on me as much as I do now.

His mouth hovers over the edge of my briefs as his fingers pluck the last of the buttons on my jeans, his hot breath washing over the damp patch on my briefs.

"Fuck! I used to dream of doing this to you. Christ, Denver, I wanted you so much in high school." Kes whispers over my skin.

East holds my hips steady as Kes pulls the rough denim down my legs; kicking my shoes off, I let him shuck off my jeans. Standing in only my briefs, I should feel self-conscious but I simply feel wanted. East's fingers find their way under the band of my briefs and I hold my breath as he slides them down, dropping to his knees as he lowers them. *Christ, are they both going to blow me?* I won't last a minute, I know I won't.

"Look at us Denver; watch what we do to you." Kes moans then flicks his tongue over the swollen head of my dick. "Fuck! You taste even better than I imagined."

East licks from the base all the way to the crown, I watch as the gorgeous men lick at my slit, their tongues tangling together. My precum drips copiously and they take every drop. Then Kes covers the head and slides down the length. I've never thought much about the size of my dick but watching Kes stretch his mouth round the girth and slide up and down, I see I look big. Then his eyes reach mine and he winks. My hips jut forward of their own accord, pushing deeper inside him; his moan tells me he likes it.

East's mouth surrounds my sac, the scorching, wet heat has my balls screaming for release but his suction and the swirl of his tongue has me crying out loud. My legs shake but their hands hold me still.

"It's too much, I can't last." I beg for release but East stops sucking me and pulls down on my sac, halting any release. Kes pops of the head of my cock and grins.

"Let's get on the bed; I'm not sure your legs are going to hold you up for much longer." Kes stands and quickly strips out of his jeans, his boxers following rapidly. I gaze on his impressive cock, standing long and proud. It's about the same length as mine, but not quite as thick; the weeping head makes my mouth water. I want to wrap my mouth around it, then I turn my head and gaze at East. Keeping his gaze locked on mine, he pushes his jeans down.

When he takes a step closer, I reach out and grasp his thick length, pumping hard once. His eyes roll back in his head and his mouth drops open at my touch. I feel so empowered; Alec never reacted to me like this. Never made me feel so wanted or so sexy.

Kes kneels on the bed and holds onto my other hand. "C'mon, baby."

I let go of East and his whimper at the loss of my touch makes my chest swell with desire and pride. We climb up next to Kes and lean in to kiss him. The touch of two mouths, two tongues, has my mind reeling. I clutch at them, desperate for more. As Kes slides his tongue into my mouth, East licks my lips.

"Touch me—please, god—I need your hands on me." I entreat for more.

"What do you want, Denver? Do you want me to blow you till you come, do you want my cock in your ass while you plow yours into East, do you want to suck East with my cock buried deep inside you? Maybe East can blow you as I fuck you hard. Can you imagine the feeling of me deep inside you, pounding you from behind?"

"Yes, yes, yes! I want it all. Fuck me, Kester, fuck me hard." I lean over and take East's dick in my mouth. Working my mouth up and down his thick length, my hands cling onto his ass as he kneels in front of me.

"That's it, baby. Suck me, suck me hard!" East's hands run through my hair, knotting and tugging as I swallow him deep. I groan loudly and pull back, only to take him again.

Kes is behind me, his hands on my ass, his fingers running up and down my crease. He pulls back and I hear a drawer opening but, wrapped up in sucking East, I don't pay it any mind. Then a cold trickle of lube runs between my parted cheeks and over my hole. My pucker twitches and Kes' finger circles softly, round and round.

"Fuck, Kes, I'm not gonna last, his mouth is so fucking awesome." East's cry breaks through my fog and I pull back, ease off sucking, and start licking him, up and down his length, down and over his balls, torturing them the way he did mine. I love giving head, Alec never wanted to waste time doing it, I get the feeling East would let me do this for hours, the idea fills me with hope.

Kes pushes a finger slowly inside me, pulling back to repeat, pressing deeper each time. I push onto his finger as he withdraws only to add another.

"Your ass is fantastic, Denver; if only you could see my fingers sliding in and out." I feel him stretch and twist his fingers, opening me further. "Are you ready?"

I nod furiously, my mouth back around East's dick. I hear the tear of a condom and a mewl escapes me as his fingers slip from inside me, then it's more cold lube and the press of his cock against my hole. The sting of the first push gives way to pleasure as he slides slowly inside me. Kes stills as he breaches the tight ring of muscles, I feel him shudder and hear him pant before he continues to push steadily deeper inside me, my body quakes as the ripples from Kes surge through me. East moves to lie down so I'm bent over him, sucking him deep again.

Kes bottoms out; I feel his balls against my taint as he fills me. *Fuck! This is perfect, this is heaven.* These two men give me everything. I'm not going to be able to last long once Kes starts to fuck me but I don't care, I merely want to feel this good forever.

As Kes pulls back, the room fills with the sound of his groan, so passionate, so wild—I love it. Then he starts to fuck. This is what my life has been missing, the feeling of being wanted. The sounds from East as he encourages me, telling me how good it feels and how close he is to coming, mixed with Kes' grunts and groans has me soaring.

The feel of their hands, in my hair and on my hips, keeps me centered, then it builds up. My orgasm starts to climb, growing in power and size, like a wave on the ocean. Then, like a tsunami, it crashes over me and I come. I fire cum over the sheets as East roars and pours his hot release into my mouth and down my throat. His hands grip tightly onto my hair but I don't mind how painful it is, it's only heightens the explosion pouring from my cock. I gulp and swallow, eager to take every drop, as his hips punch into my mouth. Then Kes falters, his rhythm stumbles and his hands squeeze me so hard I'm sure my hips will have his finger prints as bruises. He cries as he comes, the heat of his orgasm filling the condom and still managing to burn my channel as I pulse and clench around him.

口 口 口

KES

How the fuck did I manage to get us all home? My eyes kept drifting to the mirror as Denver claimed East, his mouth fixed tight as they kiss. Then, as he tugged East's lip with his teeth before sucking on it, I had to hold back my moans. But now we are home and my dick is so hard, it feels like it's going to burst out of my pants if we don't get it on soon.

I observe him as I offer him an out, my body hard and desperate for him to say yes, to agree to this. I wanted him in high school and we shared a kiss that has been fixed in my mind since then, always searching for a kiss that will match it. I found it in East. Our first kiss set my heart alight; I knew I had to have him. And now, with Denver standing here—his chest heaving, his eyes wild and needy—I have the taste of him still on my tongue and I know it's not enough.

As soon as he walked into the bar that morning after his run, sweat making his vest stick to every contour and outline of his defined chest and stomach muscles, I knew I wasn't over him. I have what I want with East but having Denver Sinclair will complete me.

I have talked this over with East. It isn't a matter of him not being enough, because if I had never set eyes on Denver, I would have had everything I want and wish for. Now, I just want it with both of them. Is he going to want to do this?

When East confirms our desires, and demonstrates his wish so exquisitely, I wait. But then it's on, and—*oh, fuck*—this is going to be good. I need him naked and in my mouth. East pulls off his T-shirt, leaving me to remove Denver's. I slowly lift the fabric, my fingers skimming gently over his skin, thrilled at the trembles coursing over him, then I get to see his skin. His tanned chest ripples with muscles in anticipation of being touched. The defined, broad shoulders undulate with tense muscles, the deep tanned skin suits him. I run my mouth over his shoulders, tasting the rich, unique flavor of his skin, and fill my lungs with his scent.

Then East kisses his chest, sucking on one of his nipples. Fuck, my dick is going to burst at the sight of these two men—my men. The thought resounds in my head; yes, these are my men.

I kiss him quickly when East turns him to me, but it's not his mouth I want. Dropping to my knees, I undo the last of Denver's buttons and get to his dick. I pull his jeans down and wait for East to remove his briefs, precum from his aching dick has left a damp patch and it urges me to take him.

Then, with a flick of my tongue, I finally get a taste of him and *damn*, there's not much that tastes better than this. Together, we work him over until I know he can't take much more and I need to be out of my clothes; my dick is about to blow in my pants.

Our first three-way kiss is better than I could have hoped for: we fit together, there's no fumbling or teeth clashing, it just works. As I start to tell him all the choices he has, I feel the need building up in him, the shudders as I get coarser and dirtier wrack through his body, then I get the words I've been waiting to hear.

"Yes, yes, yes! I want it all. Fuck me, Kester, fuck me hard." Denver begs as he bends down to take East into his mouth. Fuck, I could watch this all damn night. East loves this, his hands grip the soft strands of Denver's hair as he gets taken to higher levels of bliss.

But with Denver's tight, high ass in front of me, I need to get inside him. My finger trembles as much as his pucker as I stroke the lube over and around his hole, yet nothing prepares me for the heat and tightness of his ass as I slide my finger inside him. My other hand strokes slowly down the ridges, dips and peaks of his spine. It takes mere moments to have him rocking back on my fingers, his ass begs for me. The second finger glides as smoothly—this ass, this man, was made for me.

I watch as East gets closer and closer to coming. Jeez, Denver knows what he's doing with that amazing mouth of his. As East implores, Denver eases off; he's loving this as much as we are. I can't hold off any longer; I need to be inside him. Ripping open the condom wrapper, I sheath my cock and lube it up. Here I go.

The first nudge of my needy cock against his pucker has Denver pushing back into me, and I slip smoothly into the tightest and hottest ass I have ever been in. The muscles let me in and then grip around me. I feel the ripples from his muscles as I slide against them, my dick swells as I push further in, as if I need to feel every part of him.

Thank god East lay down; I can get a proper grip on Denver's hips. My balls slap against him as I pick up speed, my body taking over from my mind as I watch. Fascinated at the levels of pleasure East reaches. I don't have long; I know I can't keep this up, I only want to come. Soon, it's too much for them and Denver comes, spurting thick ribbons of cum over the sheets. All this without anyone touching his dick—*fuck, he's responsive.* East follows, his hips piston into Denver's mouth; the sight of the man I love, and the man I'm falling for, coming apart has my climax tearing through my body and it's a mere second before the white-hot heat burns through my body and I come, pouring my heavy load into the condom. *God, what it would feel like to go bare?* The thought sets me off again and I pulse into his ass, his muscles clamping around me, milking me for every drop.

Denver collapses onto East's stomach, East's hands stroke

soothingly through his hair as he whispers quietly to his latest lover. I relax my hands then see the bruises already forming on Denver's hip—one for each finger—I hope he's okay with that. I fucking love it.

Easing back, I pull out of his body. Grasping the top of the condom, I watch as his asshole tightens shut again—*fuck, that's hot*. I knot the condom and chuck it in the waste basket before flopping down next to Denver, with my head close to East's. Tipping my head up, I seek out his mouth and slide my tongue between his lips, pouring all my emotions into this kiss.

Denver lifts his head and opens his heavy eyes; his smile lights up his whole face and the totally blissed-out look on his face says it all. I reach out and stroke my fingers down his chiseled face, the roughness of a slight stubble sensitizes the pads of my fingertips. I trace over the full bottom lip, swollen from sucking on East, and sigh as he kisses my middle finger and draws it in to his mouth.

"Hey there, baby." I smile and continue to run my hand down his neck.

"Hey." He whispers back. His eyes blink heavily, sleep desperately trying to take him over.

"You okay?" I bite my bottom lip as I start to worry. Even though Denver smiles, is this merely post-coital bliss? Has what we have done registered with him yet? He spoke of only having a few partners in the past. *Oh, fuck! What have we just done? Shit!*

"Kester, look at me, honey. Please, Kes, look at me!" The determination in Denver's voice makes me pry my eyes open again. "This has been the most amazing experience I have ever had. If this is a one night only thing, then I can cope. I'm a grown man with my own mind. Do not doubt what you have done. You and East have given me so much; I just hope I have made you feel as good as I do now."

I watch as East props himself up on his elbows and looks down at Denver. I know East, and I know his lack of diplomacy. "Are you fucking kidding me?"

Denver's eyes fly to him, wide-eyed and confused. "I just want you to know that I understand that you are a couple and that you love each other. I'm the third for tonight, and I'm grateful. Fuck me, I'm grateful! This has been the best night of my life."

East's eyes fly to mine, I read his mind as he silently screams at me to stop this; Denver is ours now, as much as we are his. I raise my eyebrows, soundlessly asking him what he wants from me and I see his plead. East feels as much as I do, and as much as Denver does.

"Denver, you are not a third. You are with us. For as long as you want us; we are yours." I look at him and see nothing but surprise.

"I... I don't know want to say." Denver looks at the two of us, his eyes flashing rapidly between us.

"Baby..."

"Kester, I'm realistic. Can we just see how we all feel in the morning? East, thank you: for you, for giving yourself to me." Denver drops his head down onto East's stomach.

"You're going to stay?" I hear the enthusiasm in my voice, and so can East by the sound of his chuckle.

"Kester, you've just fucked me into another realm. There's no damned way I'm leaving this comfortable bed tonight."

With that, Denver clambers up and over our two bodies, heading for the bathroom. I look at East and he sighs heavily.

"What the fuck just went on?" East exclaims as he sits up. "Does he think this is a one night only gig, because if he does then fuck that! I love you Kes, you know that, but fuck me, his mouth around my dick was like something fucking else. Don't you dare fuck this up by overcomplicating things!"

Denver stops before he reaches our en-suite bathroom and looks back at us, his eyes flashing with lust but only momentarily. "You may want to sleep on it, East; it could look and feel very different in the morning."

□ □ □

EAST

"Denver, I promise you: this is not a high-on-euphoria emotion. What we just did was—well, fuck me," I chuckle when I realize what I've said, "maybe later. No, this was amazing, this... this was so much more. I'm not great at putting what I feel into words, but I think what we shared was the start of something. I don't want you to think we won't want more, because dammit, you are like a drug to me. I can't wait to have more of you, over and over again."

Denver walks back to the bed and stands looking at us. "I don't want to push my luck; I don't want to believe that something this good can last. I'm trying to get over the betrayal of someone I thought was supposed to love me. I don't have the confidence to trust this right now." He shakes his head sadly then glances around the room. "It's late, I'd better head for home."

Picking his clothes from the floor, Denver looks so lost I can't stop myself from jumping off the bed and reaching for him.

"No way. There's no way you're leaving here tonight, Denver. C'mon, let's get back into bed, I need to hold you, I need to feel you with us." I look to Kes who swings his legs out of the bed and joins us.

"He's right, Denver; you need to stay with us. We want you here. If you leave, you will talk yourself out of ever being with us again." Kes kisses Denver gently, "Please, don't leave us."

Denver leans into our embrace and I feel him trembling as he ducks his head and rests it on our shoulders.

"Will you stay?" I ask softly and feel his nod rather than hear his answer. "C'mon, let's get back into bed."

Denver lies between us, Kes has his back and I face him, my hand on his hip. As I lean in to kiss him, he whispers, "Thank you."

"What for, baby?" I ask.

"For wanting me." I hear the tremor in his voice, his eyes closed as if afraid to look at me.

"Denver, I've wanted you for fucking years." I chuckle. "You sure as fuck were worth the wait."

"Come on, we need to get some sleep." Kes murmurs from behind Denver. His hand reaches around Denver, clasping my hand briefly, "Love you."

I hear Denver sigh at Kes' words. Does he wish they were for him? Because, I think they were for both of us. "Love you, too." *Or is it two?* I wonder, then the heaviness of sleep takes over.

□ □ □

My alarm startles me awake, my mind still a sleep-fogged jumble, then I feel a hard cock against my butt cheek and I remember last night. I hope this is Denver's dick, but he may have left. *I fucking hope not!* Twisting around, I see Denver—*thank fuck!*, I take the chance to look at his strong, handsome face while he sleeps unaware. I itch to touch his dark blond stubble-covered chin, and his full lips are slightly parted as he sleeps peacefully. I watch his eyelids flicker and flutter as he dreams. Kes still has his hand resting on his hip. The mark of possession should bother me, I should feel jealous that Denver has his touch instead of me, but I don't. Kes' fingers twitch and Denver stirs. I watch as his eyes flicker and open. Slowly, they come into focus and remind his brain where he is.

"Good morning, baby." I whisper quietly to him. I see his shy smile and his tongue peeps out to dampen his lips.

"Morning, East. So, not a dream then?" He questions.

"No, not a dream." I lean in and let my lips brush over his.

"Thank fuck for that."

"No regrets?" I smile then kiss him again.

"I can't regret the best night of my life. I never knew I could feel that good." Denver sighs quietly as he reaches up and cups my face, a touch so tender I swallow hard at the emotion building in me.

"Mine too. You know we don't want this to stop, don't you?" I kiss him again, not giving him the chance to answer. Quickly deepening the kiss, I have time before I have to get up and I want more of this man before I go. As I kiss him, my hand trails down his chest and abs until my fingernails scrape through the scruff of his pubic hair.

Denver's tongue slides languorously over mine, making me sigh; I wrap my fingers around his thick length. I stroke him equally as lazily as his tongue caresses me.

"Fuck!" He moans into my mouth as his hips push into my hand.

"I need to taste you." I groan, sliding my mouth down his neck as I shuffle down the bed. I smell his hot musk as my mouth hovers over the head of his cock. A hand rests on my head and I know it's not Denver's: Kes has woken up. When I raise my head, Kes leans over Denver and kisses him heatedly. The sight spurs me on and I engulf his crown with my mouth, sucking hard as I slide my tongue around the ridge, letting my tongue trawl, glide over the satin-smooth skin—fuck, he tastes good. Pumping his length with my hand, I take him deeper, my tongue gliding over the thick vein on the underside and tasting a spurt of his precum as I pull back up. I know he's getting close when his sac draws up tight and I increase my sucking; I want my mouth full of his release. I want to spend the day thinking of this, having his flavor in my mouth.

A deep groan registers and I look up again to find Kes playing with Denver's nipples, plucking them, pulling them tight in his fingertips. As I work him harder, Denver punches his hips before stilling as his orgasm burst from him, filling my mouth with its thick cream. I mewl at his intense flavor, swallowing every drop before licking him clean. When I slide back up his body, Denver has collapsed back to the pillow, but Kes grabs the back of my neck and plunges his tongue into my mouth. Sucking mine into his, he captures Denver's tang.

"Fuck, Denver, you taste good." I chuckle and bend over to kiss him.

"You are going to kill me; I don't think I'll be able to cope, you are such trouble." His eyes open as he tries to glare but the smile breaking through the false scowl makes us all laugh.

"I need to get up and shower. Some of us have to work all day." I swing my legs out of bed. Getting to my feet, I stretch my arms over my head as I let the kinks out of my back. I hear them laugh. "What?"

"What are you going to do about that?" Kes grins at my stiff dick.

"Have a cold shower, I guess." I shrug. "You can sort it out for me tonight. I'll offer up my ass to you," I look at the two of them, "you can flip a coin to see who gets it."

"I need to get up, too; my folks have got the dog, so I need to go fetch her." Denver follows me and grabs his clothes. "I'll shower when I get home."

Kes lies back in the bed, his arms behind his head. "I can't believe you are both leaving me." He grumbles.

"What time do you want me in tonight, boss-man?" Denver looks to Kes as he pulls his jeans up—I notice he doesn't bother with his briefs.

"Whenever you want, sugar; I'll be there from about three. Why don't you bring Missy with you, then you don't have to go home tonight?" Kes smiles as he casually invites Denver back here tonight.

"You sure you don't mind?" Denver queries.

"Nope, she's a good dog and I want you back in our bed again."

Kes sighs.

"Okay then, I will see you later, Kes. East, I'll see you back at the ranch?" He questions.

"Hell yeah, who else is going to keep us hydrated in this heat?" I smile, then lean forward to kiss him. "I'll see you later." I wink and head off to the bathroom.

I hear Kes saying goodbye and then the bedroom door shuts. Moments later, the rumble of Denver's truck starts up before fading down the street. Turning on the shower, I look at myself in the mirror, there's a sparkle in my eyes that makes me smile. I turn and see Kes striding towards me.

"You want me to take care of that for you?" He smiles and looks down at my now semi-hard dick.

"Nah, I'm good. I'd rather wait for all of us being together again." I smile and kiss him.

"Yeah, it feels weird now, just being us two. I guess we need to work a few things out if he does decide to carry on: some rules, like." Kes scrubs the back of his head as he works out the thought of us going from a couple to a trio.

"I don't think we should put that sort of pressure on him too early. I need to tell him about Ellie, too. That could be a deal breaker. He doesn't strike me as a man that would be put off easily, but an eleven-year-old kid is a lot to take on."

"It never put me off. Ellie is part of you, part of us. We need to think if this could impact on her, though. Maybe you should tell him about her today, give him time to think it over before he decides. Although, I'm pretty sure he has made up his mind."

I step past him and get under the hot water. "Yeah, me too. He would've left last night if he hadn't wanted this. I'll think it over and maybe catch up with him on my break."

Kes wanders back out again, leaving me to get ready for work.

Chapter
Seven

DENVER

Why am I not freaking out? I've spent the night with two men. Christ, I blew one while being fucked hard by the other. But, instead of panicking, I grin and feel the twitch of my dick as it agrees with me. *Damn, that was the best sex ever! Fucking hell, Alec never made me come that hard or feel that good. Not even when we first started dating.* I still feel Kes inside me. *Hell, he knows how to fuck!* The taste of East isn't going to fade away anytime soon, and I don't want it to.

But I need to be careful: these two men could hurt me and I'm never going to let someone hurt me the way Alec did. A shadow clouds my mind when I realize they could hurt me more than he did; I already feel more connected to them than I ever did to him. They are a couple, a couple that loves each other very much. How do I fit into that love?

My head is full of them and I almost miss the turning to the ranch. Swinging quickly onto the road, I pick up speed and soon pull up outside. I know it's still early but my mom will be up, getting breakfast ready for the guys working for my dad; she always has fed them after they have done the horses and checked on the cattle. There's been so much going here, with all the building work, I forget this is still a working ranch, providing good quality beef to major high-grade grocery stores and butchers.

Missy sits on the porch but she jumps up when she sees my truck and starts wagging her tail frantically before letting out a couple of excited barks. My mom opens the porch door at the commotion and waves when she spots me. I don't want to be here too long but I know I need to say hi, and at least thank her for keeping my dog.

"Hey, Mom." I climb out of the truck. I don't want to get too close; I'm sure I stink of sex and I don't think she would appreciate that. A chuckle builds up but I quash it quickly, turning it into a smile.

Hi, Den, you have a good night out? Of course, you did, you're only just coming home." She smiles cheekily.

"Yeah, but I think it was one beer too many to drive back. I crashed at Kes and East's place." I smile and bend down to greet my dog.

"You look better, Denver; I think it did you good. Missy was fine here." She smiles and gives me a little wink.

"Yeah, it's was fun; we did a lot of catching up. I'll be off now, I'm working an extra shift tonight, and I want a lazy day."

I drop the truck's tailgate and Missy jumps up, she loves traveling like this. I wave once more to my mom before driving down to my cabin.

Missy races down to the water's edge and barks at the birds to make them take flight, so she can chase them; the move never fails to make me laugh. I let her run before calling her back, she returns on my command, looking like she's smiling as her tongue lolls out of the side of her mouth.

"Come on, you: I need a shower and some breakfast." Walking to my cabin and unlocking the door, I feel so different this morning then I did when I left last night. I feel so much lighter, happier. And that's a feeling I don't think I've had for a while. Maybe long before Alec dropped his bombshell since I've felt this good. Have I simply been going through the motions for a long time?

Grabbing a towel, I head to my bathroom. As much as I love the smell of East and Kes all over my body, with the sweat from the club and then the amazing sex, I need to clean up. Stripping out of my clothes, I dump everything in the clothes hamper then turn to look in the mirror. Do I look any different? I feel it, but is it showing on my face? Apart from the stupid grin that doesn't seem to want to go away, I think I look the same but then I look down my body and stop, my gaze glued to my hips.

There, in Technicolored beauty, are four bruises on each side, with a larger one below my kidneys when I twist around. *Fuck!* That's from Kes' hands gripping me as he fucked me; I remember how tight he had held me but it was never too much. If anything, I wanted more. My smile gets even bigger and turns to a full laugh. Talk about marking your territory. *Am I his now? Do they both want me? Do I want to be in a relationship again?* And this sure as hell won't be an easy one. The town accepts them, but would they accept a threesome? I can't let anything ruin the reputations they have worked so hard for, I won't be the reason their businesses suffer.

Fuck! I'm talking myself out of it, much like Kes said I would. I shake my head and get into the shower. Letting the hot water wash away my negative thoughts, I drift back to the feeling of East's mouth around my dick this morning. Growing hard as blood pumps back into my dick, my hand slides down my soapy body but, as I go to grab it, I remember East saying he was going to wait until tonight. *Fuck*, I want to be in his ass tonight. I spend the rest of my shower thinking of all the things I want to do and have done to me, it's not until the water starts to cool that I stop my imagination from running wild.

After drying and dressing, I grab some cereal and a coffee and take my breakfast out to the decked area in front of the cabin. This used to be my quiet time, my sit-with-my-kindle time but, ever since East turned up to work, it's become a gaze-at-the-hottest-construction-guy-ever time. I chuckle to myself and eat my breakfast; I'm on my second cup of coffee when I hear the sound of the workers coming down the road behind my cabin. I wonder how long it will be until I see my man.

I see East a few times throughout the morning and hear him calling out to his team but, apart from a few glances and small smiles, he works hard and stays away.

When I walk out of my cabin with six bottles of water, I stop in my track when I see him hand out bottles of water from a cooler he's brought. Why would he do that, when he knows I always bring them over? An icy chill runs down my spine as I realize he's avoiding me. I retrace my steps, hoping he doesn't see me, but he turns his head and gazes at me as I reach my door. A frown appears on his face; my face must give away everything I'm feeling.

I close the door behind me and crouch down, my eyes closed tight as I try to deal with the rejection. I knew it was too good to be true. They must have talked things over after I left and realized I wasn't worth it. No surprise, really. I'm not very sexually experienced; I spent my adult life either studying hard or working harder. I've never done the gay scene. I'm not ashamed, I never have been and I never will be. It's never been a secret but I've never felt the need to flaunt it. But, last night, I got a taste of what my life could look like, and it was a bright, colorful life. One I could learn and discover more about, living life as a gay man rather than simply being gay. I don't want to be humping nameless men in dark clubs, but I would have liked to have had more time with Kes and East in social environments. *Oh, fuck! What the hell have I done?*

Standing upright again, I decide to go for a run. I'm not hitting the road in this heat; I'll stick to the woodland trails we have here. I ran them for years when I lived here, so I can't imagine them changing that much. Quickly changing into my running gear—before I change my mind and go and hide—I'm out of the door. I don't see East as I leave and I take the route in the opposite direction from the work site, picking up the trail easily and I start clearing my mind. I concentrate on putting one foot in front of the other on this uneven terrain as Missy darts ahead of me, proving that four legs are far superior to two. I smile as she flushes out some small animals, knowing she'll not harm them.

I run until I'm breathless and desperate for a drink. Stopping and bending over, my hands resting on my knees as I draw deep breaths, before standing up again, I gulp mouthfuls of water from the now warmish water in my water bottle but it goes down well. I wander down to the water's edge and find a fallen tree to rest on as I throw a short branch into the lake for Missy to dive in after. Still trying to keep my mind occupied, I think about looking for a job at a hospital. I doubt I'll walk into a job as high up as mine was at Cedar Greens, being chief trauma surgeon for not only there but for the other hospitals too is not something that comes up anywhere else very often. But I love surgery and the bustle of hospitals. Besides, playing bartender is not something I'm going to be able to do now. My heart stutters and it tightens at the loss of Kes and East. But hell, I'm a big boy; I can take it. I'll go in tonight and talk to Kes, tell him I won't be carrying on there; I'll stay until he replaces me. That's if he wants me to, he may be equally as keen to avoid me as East seems to be.

After about ten minutes, I'm ready to head back. Checking my watch, I notice I must have run for over an hour, so I head back at a steadier pace, so as not to overwork my muscles. As I run out of the trees near the cabin, I slow to a walk but stop when I see East sitting on my steps. I lift my head and walk slowly towards him, my eyes trained on him and I watch as he seems uncomfortable under my scrutiny.

"East, what can I do for you?" I keep my voice neutral and watch him flinch at my tone.

"I guess I deserve your reservation, Denver. I'm sorry." His voice breaks at the end and I want to reach for him but hold back. "Have you got a few minutes to spare me? I need to explain to you."

"You don't need to say anything, East; I got it this morning." I look everywhere but at him to prevent myself from breaking down and beg him to reconsider. *So much for clearing my mind.* "I need a shower, so it's not really a good time."

"Denver, please, it's not what you think. I have something I need to explain to you and then you can make up your mind." East pleads. I nod and walk past him to push my door open.

Missy bustles past me and heads for her bowl. I pick it up and replenish it with fresh water as East hesitates in the living area and I relent. "Take a seat, East; you don't mind waiting while I take a shower?" I watch his eyes flare and his pupils dilate but he nods and goes back to looking at the floor.

I stalk off to the bathroom and take a shower. I ponder what he could possibly need to say that isn't a simple 'thanks but no thanks' conversation. Scrubbing my body, I take my frustration out on myself. Rinsing off before switching off the water, I stamp my way through to my bedroom, wrapping a towel around my waist, but I stop when I see East sitting on the edge of my bed. His eyes rake down my body and he fixes on the couple of finger bruises peeking over my towel. I rest my hands on my hips, essentially covering the marks made by his lover.

"I didn't expect you to be in here, East; why are you?" My eyes narrow as he cringes.

"I really need to talk to you, Denver. Do you want me to leave this room?" He looks so lost, almost broken.

Dropping my towel, I reach to my drawers and pull out a pair of briefs then, from another drawer, I grab a pair of shorts. Stepping into my underwear, I look up and see him gazing at me, but I also see him readjust himself.

"You are giving off so many mixed signals today, East, I don't know if it's Christmas or Easter." I drag my shorts up my legs and snap the button closed before dragging the zipper up. "For god's sake, East. Please, tell me what the fuck you are doing here."

"I have a daughter."

My mouth drops. I have no words.

☐ ☐ ☐

EAST

My mind goes back through the years as I drop my head in my hands. I feel the bed depress as Denver sits next to me but I'm not ready to look at him yet.

"I need to tell you what happened. It was over ten years ago, and I felt lost and alone, my sexuality was hard to deal with. I thought my parents would never understand, so I tried to conform. I met Stacey, she was a year older than me and I hooked up with her once. She has been the biggest mistake of my life, but Ellie isn't: Ellie is proof that something good can come out of the darkest times of your life. Please, will you let me explain?"

Taking a deep breath, I recall the evening that changed my life.

"Walking through the door, I hear Ellie crying. No, scrap that: Ellie is screaming. Rushing to her room, I see her standing in her cot, still in the sleepsuit I put her in last night, a soiled and soaked diaper hanging low between her legs. Her bright red face is covered in snot and tears but, as she sees me, her body starts to shake and her tears stop, morphing into heart-wrenching hiccups and sobs.

"Up, Dadda. Up." Her little arms reach up for me as I haul her from the crib that seems to have become her cage.

"Where's momma, Ellie-babe? Where's your momma?" I hold her close to me, even though the pee-and-poop-soaked suit seeps through my shirt. I don't expect her to answer as I rock and soothe her trembling body but I freeze when I hear her answer.

"Momma gone." Ellie's body shudders as the tears start again.

Striding to the bathroom, I run a bath for her; there's no way I can get her clean enough any other way.

"C'mon, baby; let me get you cleaned up." I try to set her down on the floor so I can strip her out of her clothes but her arms cling to my neck, not wanting to let me go. *"Come on, Ellie; we need to get you washed and then we can find some supper. You hungry?"*

Ellie nods her head against the crook of my neck and then loosens her grip on my neck. As her feet hit the floor, she stands steady, her chubby baby legs barely strong enough to support her. I pop the popper down the front of her sleepsuit, the diaper falling down her legs at the weight of the pee it carries. My anger rises again and I wonder where the hell Stacey is. What the fuck has she done?

Seconds later, I place Ellie's stinky body in the bathtub and grab a cloth to clean her off. The clothes she had on are only good for the trash. Ellie's resilient nature soon has her clapping her hands as she plays with the bubbles and toys I've dumped in with her.

I look down at my T-shirt and see the stains over it; I pull it over my head and drop it with the other filthy garments.

After washing her, I lift my daughter from the bath and wrap her in a towel before carrying her back through to her room. I take in more this time and see two empty bottles in her cot, so she has had something to drink today but there is no other sign that she has been left alone. Grabbing some clothes and a fresh diaper, we go into my bedroom and here the story unfolds. All the dresser drawers are open and empty, along with the closet—well, Stacey's side at least. Our bathroom looks the same: all the doors are open on the vanity unit and the medicine cupboard and the contents are either gone or strewn over the counter.

I manage a wry chuckle when I see her 'Fuck you, asshole' message written in lipstick on the mirror. So, she finally followed through. But my back stiffens with a fury that burns through me as she has made good on her threats to leave her daughter, with a dirty diaper and only two bottles of formula to keep her going. I clutch Ellie closer to me, dropping a kiss on her sweet-smelling, damp, blonde hair.

"C'mon, baby girl; let's get some supper."

I carry her through to the kitchen and search through the cupboards for something we can both eat and realize exactly how badly Stacey fucked us over. Confusion of my sexuality and a split condom on a drunken night out ended with

Ellie: a mistake I can never regret, but the makeshift life I made with Stacey was a mistake from the first time I set my eyes on her. The only woman I'd ever had sex with, and only the one time. She was only interested in a good time and ignored all the signs of pregnancy until it was too late to do anything else but have a baby. She never wanted it; she never changed her lifestyle, even when she was due. She would still be out with her girlfriends, never listening to my pleas for her to stay home. We were only eighteen and nineteen, way too young to cope. I had to try, but she didn't want to.

Her moving in was the only way I would be able to keep my eye on her and I got to be with her when she went into labor. I was there for Ellie's birth and have been here every damn day since. Stacey never wanted me; I merely put a roof over her head when her own folks threw her out. I was a meal ticket, that's all.

Still searching for something to eat, I realize there's nothing and pull out my cell phone and make the call my mom has been waiting for.

"Mom, she's gone," I mutter, "she left Ellie alone all day in her crib. There's no food here for us." I feel defeated, she has finally broken me.

"I'm on my way, East, honey. I'll bring dinner. Is Ellie okay?" My mother's voice softens when she speaks her granddaughter's name.

"She is now. She left her, mom; how can someone do that? She's been crying all fucking day, and that bitch just walked out of the door."

I wait with my baby in my arms, rocking her gently, terrified of what I am going to do and how I am going to manage. I'm frightened, not noticing the tears running down my face until my mom wraps me in her arms, telling me it will be okay.

"Please, Denver, don't saying anything. I need to get this out: I need to explain this so you can make a decision. A decision about us, about you with me and with Kester."

"Why do you need to tell me this? I mean, why do you think this would be a deal breaker? Shit, East, so you have a child, why do you think that would affect the way I feel about you?" I scrub my hands through my still damp hair, in frustration as well as annoyance. "Is this what all the shit this morning has been about? Why you have shunned me, made me doubt everything we went through—not just last night, but this morning, too?"

His outcry shocks me: he's angry with me, and I can understand why, but it's not for the reason I expected. He doesn't mind, he doesn't even seem to be concerned by it. He is angry with me for my silence, for what seemed like my rejection of him.

"I don't know what else to say." I mutter.

"Well, I fucking do! How fucking dare you? You made me doubt everything we experienced last night! Shit! East, I had my resignation from the bar planned, so I didn't have to embarrass or shame you, either of you. Why didn't you just come to me this morning?" Denver stands and paces the floor of his bedroom. The tension in here is beyond my capabilities, I don't know what to do or say.

"Denver, I'm sorry. I don't know what else to say. I know I've let you down. Please, don't give up on me, or on us." I stand up, desperate to pull him into my arms. I want to plunge my hand into his messy hair and kiss the ever-loving breath out of him, but I can't. At this moment, he is not mine, and I'm sure as hell not his; he could kick me out right now, everything over before we've even had chance to start.

"Oh, for fucks sake." Denver strides up to me, making me take a step back, nervous, hesitant. But the fire in his eyes makes me gasp. His hands grasp the side of my head and his lips land on mine. As his tongue plunders my mouth, I feel his anger and frustration as well as his need and want.

I grab his hips and pull him closer, crushing my body to his, feeling the nudge from his dick as it swells against my own. Pouring my apologies and emotions into my kiss, it doesn't last long and Denver pulls away. I know I look confused but his smirk eases my fears.

"East, you promised up your ass to us tonight; there's no way you're getting any more from me." Denver kisses me again then moves away. "You need to get back to work."

"Denver? Please, are you really okay with this?"

"Honey, I can't wait to meet her. When you think the time is right—I'm not pressurizing you, I just want you to know I'm okay with this, with you and your daughter. But, don't introduce us before you know where we are going, that what we have is worth sharing with her. Because, from the sounds of it, she has had enough people leave her already."

"Fuck! Denver, I think…fuck! I don't know. Thank you, baby. Thank you." I pepper his mouth and face with kisses until he laughs and moves away again. "Can I tell you a bit more about her?"

"East, honey, you can tell me anything you want." The sparkle is back in Denver's eyes, *thank fuck!*

"She's amazing. Ellie is eleven now and knows it all, as you can guess. She lives with my mom but I see her nearly every day, when she's not too busy with school stuff. It worked out easier that way when I was only nineteen and struggling, the place I lived in with her and her mom was damp and not very nice. I moved back home with her and it just made sense for her to stay there as we grew up. Ellie would have been there all the time instead of daycare or afterschool care anyway. My mom adores her but is still as strict as she was with me, but Ellie loves her just as much." I smile at Denver.

"It must have been hard to build your business up and look after a child, so I can see why you went home. Have you ever heard from Ellie's mom again?"

"Just one time. I needed her to hand over any claim she had on Ellie in the future; I needed to know that she would never be able to hurt her again. She moved over to the west coast and hasn't been near us since." I sigh as I remember precisely how hateful Stacey really was. I look at my watch and realize how long I've been here. "Shit! I need to get back to work. Thank you, Denver, thank you for listening and for being so understanding. You really are amazing."

I move over to him as he sits on the edge of his bed and smile at how readily he parts his knees for me to slide in between. Running my knuckles down his face, I watch his eyes dilate as he leans into my touch. He reaches up and pulls my face down to his.

"You'd better kiss me goodbye then." He whispers, his lips a mere breath away from my own.

"I think you're right." My lips press against his gently. His tongue coasts over the seam of my lips, parting them.

Denver stands up, our lips still together. I let him take control, allowing him to be in charge after the strain I put him under and the hurt I caused. As his hand slides through my hair, his other reaches behind my back and tugs me into his lean body. Moaning into his mouth as his tongue dances gracefully with mine, he pulls back and nips my bottom lip sharply before immediately kissing the sting away. My hands reach around to grab his firm ass, our dicks rubbing against each other through the layers of our clothes, getting harder and harder.

Denver skims his hand down the back of my jeans and I feel his finger slide down my crease, *fuck!*

"I'm taking this ass tonight, honey." Denver murmurs against my lips, my cheeks clenching as his finger slips up and out of my jeans. "You keep thinking about that this afternoon."

We break apart and I watch as Denver's dark eyes return to normal. He sucks his bottom lip into his mouth and bites down. I can't stop the moan that falls from my mouth as I watch him.

"I think I'd like that, baby." I whisper, unable to find my voice. Stepping away, I laugh as I try to rearrange my junk in my jeans; I don't need my crew seeing this.

"You doing okay with that?" Denver jokes.

"It's okay for you; you don't have to go back out there." I shake my head but keep smiling. "I'll see you tonight."

Chapter Eight

DENVER

The bar is busy when I walk in, the tables full with the late lunch crowd. The patrons are mainly women, a lot of them dressed up prettily and laughing with their friends over large glasses of wine and the odd cocktail. Kester is at the bar but he hasn't noticed me yet. Walking past the bar, I head to the office where we can hang our jackets; the girls leave their purses safely in here.

Missy walks closely to me but, when the ladies having lunch see her, she starts to wag her tail, desperate for some fuss. I let her wander over to the objects of her attention and laugh with them as they greet and pat her; Missy loves any attention. After a couple of minutes, I walk on—Missy back under my command. When I look over at the bar, Kes is staring at me, his body language as stiff and guarded as East's this morning; they obviously discussed whether or not to share East's daughter with me. I don't want to leave him second-guessing my feelings: I smile and give him a wink then watch him relax, relief visibly spreading over his face and through his body.

"C'mon, girl, you're in here for the afternoon." I stride down the short hallway to the office and let Missy settle with a bowl of water and a dog chew. Leaving my bag by the door, I walk out again and closing it softly behind me.

Entering the hallway, I find Kes leaning against the wall, his arms folded across his chest and his feet crossed at the ankle. He's still on edge; as a doctor, I'm trained to notice any signs of distress, agitation and pain that the patient attempts to hide from me. Kes is still worried: his brow is creased and he's chewing his lip.

"Kes, it's all okay." I approach him, getting close but not close enough for anyone to think anything inappropriate.

"My office, please, Denver." His voice is low and desperate. Glancing past him, I see Shelley looking casually at us.

"Sure, everything okay?" I let him pass me then follow a couple of paces behind. The door shuts with a thump and I hear the click of the lock as Kes reaches behind me.

"East called me. Fuck, Denver, I've been a right mess." Kes runs his hands through his hair, pulling the band out before retying it. I love the length of his hair, right above his shoulders but enough to need to be tied back. I want to spend time simply running my fingers through it, the caramel blond that makes him look so fucking hot, with his twinkling hazel eyes that sparkle with mischief.

"Yeah, well, I wasn't fucking happy. I know we don't know each other very well and we haven't talked about why I came home…"

"I was inside your fucking body, Denver. I think we know each very well." Kes interrupts.

"That's not what I mean, and you know it. I have had my whole life thrown back in my face, all I thought I had and how my future was going to be… ripped up and thrown away. So, my self-confidence is at rock bottom. I had begun to believe in myself again since I've been back, and the last three weeks working here have made me so much happier." I take a deep breath, "And then, last night. Last night was something else, it was everything. I thought, when I left this morning, it was the start of something good."

"It was, baby; it still is."

"But it didn't feel like it an hour or two later, when East ignored me. I was reluctant to listen to him but he wasn't going to go away. Planting himself in my bedroom while I was in the shower was probably the best way to get my attention. I can understand why he was unsure whether to tell me and I am totally okay with him having a daughter; I'm just pissed at the way he handled it. He should have come to me first thing, that way we all could have had a better day." I let out a heavy sigh and look up at the ceiling, collecting my thoughts and getting my emotions under control before I get to work for the next six hours.

"Come here, Denver." There's a roughness to Kes' voice.

I step up to him and let him put his hands on my hips, reminding me of the bruises he made. I rest my hands on his arms and lean into him.

"I'm sorry, baby. I told him to wait until we were all together, but I'm so fucking relieved you're here. I can't wait 'til we get home." Kes leans in and captures my mouth with his, this is a rough, hard and so fucking hot kiss that I pull away panting. "So, you're having East's ass tonight, I hear?"

"Too damn fucking right I am; he'll be lucky if he can sit down by the time I've finished with him." I smirk and kiss Kes again.

There's a knock on the door and Kes lets go of me. "C'mon, let's get this over with."

I think we both want this shift over with. Kes keeps his distance as much as he can and I'm grateful; the longer I'm here, watching him move so smoothly behind the bar, the more I want his hands on me.

"Excuse me, gorgeous. Can I get a drink?" A pretty, young girl smiles at me, breaking me away from my dirty thoughts of Kes and his hands.

"Of course, what'll it be?" I smile and see her eyes focus on my dimples. Her tongue darts out and licks across her gloss-slicked lips, it's her turn to lose her concentration.

"Huh? Oh, sorry: a cosmo and a mojito, please. And your number, too, if I can?" She smiles and I see exactly how cute she is; any straight guy would be lucky to get her number. I mix her drinks and think of a way to politely say no.

"Oh, I'm sorry; we're not allowed to give out our numbers. Rules from the boss." I smile, wanting to let her down gently. Sliding the two glasses over the polished mahogany bar, I keep my smile fixed.

"That's okay, here's mine." She grabs a napkin and writes her number down with a cute smiley face and a heart next to it. "I'm Lucy; give me a call, maybe."

With a swish of auburn hair, she sashays back to her friend at a corner, high-top table. Her friend looks over and smiles too, hell. I feel Kes' eyes on me and a small smirk plays across his lips when I turn my head to the side and peek at him, not wanting anyone else to notice our interaction.

Kes walks behind me, his hand gliding over my lower back sends goosebumps over my body. "Nicely done, baby." He murmurs as he carries on.

I turn back to my customers and serve a jug of beer to a big guy in workman's clothes. He doesn't offer any conversation; he simply wants to chill out with a couple of buddies after a long day.

"Thanks, man." Is all I get when I hand him his change.

I know the evening is coming to an end when I see East striding through the doors, he's looking so damn hot, in a tight white T-shirt tucked into his dark jeans. He smiles at me and says hi as he walks past to Kes. I watch as he comes out from behind the bar to embrace his lover. They kiss briefly, then Kes is back to work. Pain shoots through my chest as I watch how easily they greet each other when I only get a brief nod. *Fuck, that hurts! I want that too: I want East to kiss me as he walks in.* Absentmindedly, I rub my chest and catch East watching me, looking as pissed off as I feel. His sad smile only makes it worse.

Are we really going to be able to do this? Will him kissing me, as well as Kes, ever be accepted by this still straight-laced community? I guess this is something we need to talk about. There's a lot of things we have to work out if—and it's a big if—we want this to work. *Am I confident enough to be part of a trio? Can I pull it off, knowing it's what my heart wants and needs? Will my parents, my brother, accept it? Is this going to cause problems for Ellie?* Suddenly, I feel trapped as so many questions run through my head; I need a break. I look along the bar and see everything is under control.

"I'm taking five, boss." I call to Kes, who's busy serving so I know he can't follow me. I walk into the corridor but, instead of going to the office, I make my way to the back door, leading into the side alley where the dumpsters are kept. Pushing the fire door open, I step into the cool, night sky. Making sure the door doesn't completely shut, I lean against the wall. Tipping my head up to the sky, I search out the constellations to clear the confusion from my mind.

I feel the door next to me open and without looking, I know it's East. It's not only his cologne I smell: it's him, pure East.

"You okay, baby?" He asks quietly before standing in front of me.

I sigh but it comes out as a ragged gasp, bordering on a sob. "Fuck!" My hands are up in my hair when I feel East's lips on mine.

"Shh, baby. It's okay, we just need to work it out. It hurt me just as much: I wanted to kiss you, too. I promise, we will work it out. It's worth it, it may not be easy, but nothing worth having is."

My arms wrap around him and I hold on tight as everything that has happened today comes crashing down. Then I realize, the pain I feel is the pain of not being with them, not the worry of acceptance or understanding from the people around me.

"Fuck, I need you both so much. Is it too much, too soon?" I hold back the thought of falling for them both, I can't deal with that now.

"No, baby, it's not. Not for me and not for Kes. You're part of us, it's like we've been waiting for you." East murmurs sweetly in my ear.

"Oh, fuck!" I groan, "Is this really going to happen? Fuck, this has to wait until we are all together tonight."

"It is and, yes, we can talk it over later." His mouth presses hard on mine but far too briefly for my liking. "But not until you've had my ass. You need to understand just how great this really is going to be."

"I have to get back inside. Thank you, East; you seem to know just what I need." I push away from the wall and we walk back inside.

"Baby, we *are* what you need." He answers gruffly and nudges me forward.

He may have a point.

□ □ □

KES

Thank fuck! I watch as Denver walks in for his shift, the fact he has his dog with him relaxing me. But, maybe he's simply not prepared to leave her alone for a long night shift. He resettles a backpack he has over his shoulder; *is that overnight stuff or bits and pieces for Missy?*

I watch as a group of yummy mommies coo and fawn over the dog—*or are they interested in the man standing so tensely next to them?* As Denver moves away, he looks across the bar at me and, with a miniscule smile and wink, he walks past the bar to the office. *There's no fucking way he's walking out here to work before I have spoken to him.* I let him move through with the dog to get her in my office and settled before I have a quick word with Shelley, then follow him.

I hear him talking to Missy then it goes quiet. The door opens and closes and I give it a couple of seconds before he sees me.

"My office, please, Denver." I hear the roughness in my voice; I hope he doesn't take it as a rebuke. I observe his eyes widen in surprise.

He trails me and, as soon as we are in, I lock the door. I told Shelley I didn't want to be interrupted, ignoring her surprise: I run a smooth shift and rarely have to talk with one of my team but, as a newbie, I think I can get away with talking to Denver privately.

I want to drag him to me, to touch and kiss him—damn, I want him bent over my desk so I can fuck him till he screams but, by the look on his face, that isn't going to happen. When I explain that I've spoken to East, I watch his face turn from unease to angry, and I understand that. *East totally fucked up! Why didn't he do it first thing? Or carry on with his day and we could have all been together and handled it so much better.* But hearing why he is nervous of trusting us, even without saying much—I can't tell whatever happened to him—it is obvious it was bad. That's a tale for another day.

How can he think we don't know each other? Does he not feel the connection? Being inside him changed me! The thought of us never doing that again kills me.

Finally, I get the chance to taste him again, and there's no way this is going to be a sweet, loving kiss. This is a play-hard-and-fuck-harder sort of kiss and, by his labored breathing, I think he gets the point. Shelley knocks on the door and we must get to work. I wonder if I've brought him back on board with me and East.

Denver settles into his shift comfortably. He has no idea how hot it is to spy him smiling and joking with the customers. They flirt shamelessly, men and women alike, but he simply carries on serving them. I watch a girl sidle up, her finger twirling her long, red hair as she orders her drinks. She asks him something and I see him blush. Shaking his head, he manages a laugh. Oh, it gets better: she writes her number down and winks. I hold back a chuckle when he glances at me.

"Nicely done." I murmur as I walk behind him. My finger skims his back and I revel in his tremors.

By the time East walks in, I'm ready for this night to be over with. The crowds have thinned, making it easy for him to walk over to me. As our lips touch, I see Denver flinch. *Damn! I should have thought about this, how our open affection can hurt him. Fuck, fuck, fuck!*

I notice him walk out but I can't leave the bar. With a nod to East, he follows him out. *I hope he can help. Damn, we have so much we need to talk about, tonight.* But I want him with us, I want us to be seen together and it needs to be done before the crowds start turning up for the holidays. This town fills up from Easter onwards with trekkers and back-packers: the visitors need to know Denver is off limits.

Calling last orders, I start to close. Pulling tabs up before shutting one of the cash registers down, I send Shelley off to help two servers clear the tables of bottles and glasses. I don't notice my men walking back through the door but I feel Denver's presence behind the bar as I load up the washer with glasses.

"Sorry about that." Denver speaks quietly.

"It's okay, baby. We'll sort it, I promise." I answer equally as hushed as I straighten and face him. Looking around the bar, I search for East.

"He's in the office with my dog." Denver laughs; East has fallen in love with Missy.

"Let's get finished up here then." I call over to the girls, telling them they can leave. Shelley grins as she closes the door behind the last customer.

It's another thirty minutes before we are done. I lock the takings in the safe then close and lock the office door behind me. When I walk in the bar, East and Denver lean together in a darkened corner, the only lights on are the ones over the bar. I can turn them off with a switch by the front door as I leave. Sauntering up to them, I see East run his hands through Denver's hair and pull his face to him, kissing him softly; it's beautiful to watch the tenderness that has grown so quickly.

"Hey." I murmur as I wrap my arms around them. "Rough day, huh?"

Denver nods and tilts his head to mine. "Too fucking rough to deal with again. We need to talk it all through. Not what went on today: that's over. But us, whether there is even going to be an us."

East growls. "There already fucking *is* us, I'm not backing out. No fucking way." He pulls Denver closer to him. "d'you hear me?"

"Let's go home." I kiss Denver then East and pull away.

Denver reaches down and picks up his bag. "I brought a change of clothes with me, in case I stay the night. Is that okay?"

"If it was up to me, you'd never leave." I answer. I laugh, as I close the door, at the three trucks parked outside. "I think we need to organize our rides better, don't you?"

I wait while Denver gets his dog in the cab before heading to mine. He looks up and smiles, "I'll follow you."

East gives us a wave before backing out of the space and heading home. The few blocks we have to drive seem to take forever this evening, Denver on my tail as we eventually pull up on our driveway. I grin at the size of it, maybe it's meant to be so we can easily fit all three pick-ups side by side.

The lights come on inside as East goes in ahead of us. Denver climbs out and walks to me. "Why am I more nervous tonight than yesterday?"

"Maybe you've worked out what you want, but you don't know how to reach it? I know I feel the same. C'mon, we need to be inside and with East before we start talking."

East is in the kitchen when we make our way down the hallway, a bottle of beer in his hand and leaning against the tall cupboard. I see the tension in his body as we near him, his eyes on us as we walk in. There are two more bottles on the countertop; I pick them up and pass one to Denver.

"Okay, how are we going to do this?" Denver questions as he pulls out a chair and drops down on it.

"This is your call, Denver: we know what we want. My issue is simply setting a few rules to make it easier." East answers before tipping the beer bottle to his lips and swallowing deeply.

"It's not as easy as that, East, and you know it. Denver didn't come back here to stay: he is here while he sorts out the mess in his head. Are you really prepared to throw yourself headlong into a three-way relationship before Denver knows what his future is going to be?"

"Maybe you should know what brought me running back here after over twelve years." Denver offers. "And how I planned to move forward."

East pushes himself upright and walks up to the table to sit opposite Denver, a scowl already forming on his face. I join them and take the seat between them.

"I met Alec when we started our internship and had been together ever since. So, for six years, we worked at the hospital and lived together pretty much the same amount of time. First with a bunch of other doctors, then we bought our own place. I thought that was it, we would eventually get married. My time here has made me look more deeply at a relationship I thought was a good one, a solid one. I loved Alec. But I can now see where the cracks were and when they started to show. I think it started with Alec's choice of orthopedics as his specialty. He's good at it, but he didn't make the waves I did.

"I moved up the chain of command quicker than he did and with that came more responsibility, with longer hours and more commitment. I never thought he minded—he loved what he did—but we did change. Alec stopped traveling with me when I had conferences to go to, and I stopped minding being by myself. What I didn't know was, he had found someone else."

Our eyes shoot up and we stare at Denver; he gives us a small smile, but it's full of sadness. East reaches across the table and grabs his hand as I rest mine on Denver's shoulder.

"Yeah, our friends all knew, but I was so busy working I never found out. I'd been at a conference in Atlanta for five days and when I got back he told me he was getting married. He'd packed up and moved most of his stuff while I was away. He told me he got tired of waiting for me to stop working. That it was my fault, because I had neglected him. I had no idea, no fucking clue. Maybe he was right, maybe it was my fault. But, instead of talking to me about it when he first felt neglected, he chose to look elsewhere. We had seen it happen throughout the hospital—friends of ours had cheated on their partners—I just never thought it would happen to me. I handed in my notice and we sold our house, and I came back here.

"I spent a month licking my wounds and then one night I walked into your bar and well... hell, you know the rest. I had ideas that I would go back to work—not at the same hospital, I could never go there again. I'm not missing it yet, but I know I will do soon."

"What an asshole! I can't believe anyone would do that to you. How can he not have seen that you are the best he could ever get?" East looks so pissed.

"Okay, so, I guess the question I have to ask is, would you look for a hospital position around here if you stayed with us?" I'm not sure I want to know his answer but at least we would know where we stand.

"Yes, but I'm cautious. You must understand just how attracted I am to both of you, but you *are* a couple and it's hard to see how I will fit in with you. Am I going to be the one left alone when you decide that two is better than three? I'll be the one left picking up the pieces of my broken heart and have to move away again."

"I think we've already moved into a trio; I hated not showing my feelings for you tonight, Denver. I want to kiss you when I see you, just as I do Kes. I can't see past being with you both anymore. I want this!" East exclaims.

"I agree with East, Denver. I want this, I think we have both been brought back to here to be together. Please, Denver, can we try? As long as we promise to communicate all the time, I think we have something too good here to miss. But here's another question for you, both. Do you feel jealous of each other? Or of me?"

"I was jealous when you kissed him and not me. But I wasn't jealous of the kiss, just the openness of it." Denver answers honestly.

"I'm not jealous either. Watching you with Denver last night, Kes, was one of the sexiest fucking things I've ever seen. Seeing you take him, and how much he loved it, spurred me on and I had one of the best orgasms I've ever had. I want to see him take you, I want to feel him take me. I want to explore every part of Denver's body while you take me, Kes."

"Fuck!" Denver grunts. "We need to get naked, right now. East, get in that bedroom; I want your ass."

"It looks like we have come to an agreement for tonight." I stand up and pop the button on my black pants, my dick already hard and throbbing.

Chapter
Nine

DENVER

I'm not sure we have decided on anything but the images East brought up got me so damn hard. At least, I think, the jealousy issue was cleared up. East pushes the chair back and pulls off his t-shirt as he strides to the bedroom. Kes smiles and holds out his hand for me.

East is naked when we saunter into the room, I'm amazed at how in tune we are. Maybe Kes is right, and we are meant to be together.

I fix East with a stare. "You're going to watch us. I don't care how fucking turned on you are, you keep your hand off your dick. We will be giving you all your pleasure tonight." *Jeez, where did that come from? Who cares,* the gasps from East and Kes is enough to know it worked.

East clambers up the bed and sits with his back against the wooden headboard. He bends his knees and opens his legs, giving us a perfect view of what I'll be having later.

Turning to Kes, I pull his T-shirt over his head then kiss him hard, dominating him in a second. This is new to me but it feels so damn good. As I carry on plundering Kes' mouth, his hands work the zipper on his pants to let them slide down his legs. His hands grip my hips as he steadies himself to kick them off, then he does the same to my pants.

Mere seconds later, we are both naked. Grabbing our dicks in one hand I start to pump them. Kes moans as he kisses my neck, his teeth scraping over the heated skin. I look over at East: his hands are clenched into the sheets, his dick dripping precum down his length.

"Fuck, you look so good together. Suck his dick, Denver: take him deep in your throat." East implores, "I want to see you gag on his cock."

I want to admonish him but the thought of Kes in my mouth is too much. I drop to my knees and cup Kes' balls in my hand then, lowering my mouth, I suck on the smooth, bare sac. I hear both men moan. Encouraged, I suck harder, rolling my tongue over the spheres then, with a pop, I release them and lick from the base up to the head from the underside of his long, thick dick. Then, with open-mouthed kisses, I cover him with my saliva so I'll be able to glide down, taking him all the way: I love deep-throating. Alec never liked it and would rarely suck me hard. These men have both had me in their throats already.

Sucking hard on his crown, I flick my tongue into his slit and groan at the flood of precum that bursts onto my tongue. Gliding down, my mouth stretches over his rock-hard length but soon my nose is against his pubes as he slides down my throat. Kes runs his palm over my throat as I swallow, feeling how deep his dick is.

"Fuck! Denver, fuck! I'm gonna come if you keep that up." Kes grips my hair tightly in his fists as I slip him in and out of my throat. I pull up and lick over the head then, standing up, I wipe my chin before plunging my tongue in his mouth.

Turning to East, I notice his dilated eyes and his heaving chest as he tries to control himself. "You ready for us, honey?"

In tune, Kes and I crawl up the bed and pull East flat by his legs. Kes takes East in his mouth and sucks him while I straddle his chest, pinching his nipples to make him gasp. Then, leaning over him, I swipe the slick tip of my dick over his lips. His tongue darts out and licks at the precum dripping copiously from my slit. But I pull back and smile.

"Ready for me, East? Ready to take my dick deep in your ass?"

"Fuck, yeah. God, you are so fucking sexy!" East pants.

Kes lets go of East's dick and moves to get condoms and lube from a drawer.

"We are going to fuck you tonight, East. I'm going to pound you so hard, then Kes will finish you." I know I want to cover his body with my cum, to mark him as mine, but I need him tight around me first.

East grabs behind his knees and pulls his legs up to his chest. The need to taste him overpowers me and I bend over to cover his ass with my mouth. Licking and stabbing at his hole, I feel the tremors in his legs as he thrashes his head from side to side. I slide my finger inside him, slowly fucking him before adding another finger.

Kes has hold of East's legs as I slather his hole in lube and roll the condom down my length. As soon as I touch his pucker East pushes back, desperate to have me inside him. I slide balls deep in one go, moaning as he clenches around me, greedy for more.

"Move for me, baby; take me." East groans as I slowly drag out of him, only to pound back in. Slow out, fast in, slow out, fast in.

Suddenly, I can't hold back, I grab his ankles and pound inside him, Kes' fist is tight around East's balls to hold his orgasm back as East moans and groans, grinding his ass onto me.

Looking up at Kes, I signal him to get ready to take over. As soon as he lets go of East's balls, I pound against his prostate, hitting it square on until I see his balls draw up and he starts to come. His muscles clamp down on my dick as his orgasm shoots from him. As he comes down, I pull out and rip off my condom before swapping places with Kes.

I watch as Kes pushes deep inside East, still quaking from the tremors of his orgasm.

"Fuck, no! It's too much. Fuck!" East grabs at me as Kes fucks him hard, his hips driving in and out.

"Fuck, you feel good, baby; so hot and tight. You ready to come for me again?" Kes tips his hips and I know he's going for East's spot.

My hand is around my dick as I match my actions to Kes' thrusts. I lean over East, his chest and abs already covered in his own release. I frantically stroke myself, I know I'm not far off.

"Kes, I can't hold off." I cry out and, with two more thrusts, East comes again, crying out, calling our names.

"Look at us, honey; watch us worship your body." I croon. East opens his eyes as he finishes coming, his stomach striped with his release.

Kes pulls out and copies me, tearing off the condom. Leaning over between East's legs, he cries out and we come simultaneously, our cum flying over East's stomach and chest. Twisting, I hit his neck and chin: I want him to feel me all over his body.

"Fuuuuck!" I cry as East wraps his mouth over the sensitive head of my cock. He sucks hard, drawing more from me, then I fall back on my heels.

Heaving huge gulps of air into my lungs, I look back at East's prone body, crisscrossed with spunk. A chuckle builds inside me as I straighten up and look at Kes' broad smile, then I hear a laugh come from East.

"Fuck! I'm wrecked. You bastards have nearly killed me." He laughs and I lean over, slicking my tongue through the ribbons of cum, then I kiss him. East sucks on my tongue, taking our three flavors into his mouth.

Kes rests his hand on my shoulder and I turn to him. He, too, has licked across East's stomach and we share a wet, dirty, and so damn sexy kiss.

"I think we need to shower." East mumbles from beneath us.

"C'mon then, let's go get you clean." I kiss him again then get off the bed, holding my hand out to him. Kes has already moseyed over to the bathroom and I hear the shower start up as I lead East to it.

I take my time washing East; letting us have him like that, he deserves our attention. As I wash his body, Kes shampoos his hair, and we pepper kisses over his body as we clean him. I see how we have tired him out and it's got so late, he needs to sleep.

We quickly wash ourselves as East sits on the bench seat built into the shower—he really is a master builder; he thought of everything as he built this.

Kes switches off the shower and we grab soft towels to dry East off. I let Kes take him back to bed and, a towel wrapped around my waist, I go check on Missy and make sure the house is locked up. It already feels like home to me: I guess I've got my answer. I think I'm going to give it a chance with these men. *What have I got to lose, compared to what I can gain?*

When I get back in the bedroom, Kes and East are already tucked up, East rests in Kes' arms as Kes whispers to him. Surely, this is the moment I should be jealous, but I'm not, I'm happy East is still being cared for. I love that they look at me and smile, inviting me to join them.

As I clamber up and kiss East's lips before leaning over to do the same to Kes. I know I should say something, but I'm nervous. I wait as we settle down together, our feet intertwining comfortably. Our bodies mesh together, as if we were made for each other. As I hear their breathing slow down, I take my chance.

"I'm in, if you'll have me." I whisper.

"We were never going to let you go." Kes whispers back.

"You are meant to be here, Denver." East mumbles as sleep takes him over.

□ □ □

EAST

"C'mon, Denver, you know you want to!" I laugh at my man as he digs his heels in; he's a stubborn mule when he wants to be.

It's Saturday and, once a month, Kes has an open mic night. It's all good fun: some are serious musicians looking for a gig, others are tipsy girls wanting to sing Cyndi Lauper as loud, and as badly, as they can.

"You weren't supposed to find it. I don't like being in the public eye like that. Please, just forget it, East." Denver turns his back on me and walks back to his cabin.

"Baby, please. You are amazing: you'll knock blocks off everyone else. Please, please. For me?" I've caught up with him. "I'll do that thing you really like." I waggle my eyebrows suggestively.

"East, you love that as much as I do, you're going to want that anyway!" he shrugs, exasperated, but I'm not giving in.

We've spent the last four nights learning everything about each other, mainly exploring each other's bodies, but we have talked so much, too. When I saw his guitar resting on a stand in the corner of his living room, I had to hear him play. Denver doesn't do anything badly so I know he will be outstanding, not to mention as sexy as fuck.

"Why not? What happened? Is this your fuckwit ex, did he stop you playing?" I'd really like to kick his ass for the shit he put Denver through.

"No." Denver looks at me and chews his thumbnail. Knowing he's not being truthful, I lift my eyebrow and he sighs. "Well, sort of: he never wanted me to play, he just wanted to chill out and watch TV when he got home, said it annoyed him too much. After a while, I gave up playing. Now it just reminds me of feeling rejected, a nuisance."

"Oh, baby. I can't wait to hear you play. I can promise you, it will not annoy me. Kes will be so impressed. It's another part of you we get to share that your douchebag ex denied you. You have shared so much of yourself with us, don't deny us this."

"Let me think about it, East. I promise, I'll think it over."

"You know how good we are together, Denver. And we know you'll learn to trust again; I do understand what you're going through. When Stacey left me and Ellie, I swore I would never trust anyone again. But, you know what changed me or, more importantly, *who* changed me? I met Kes and everything made sense. All the hardship of learning to look after a little girl, all the lonely nights, and the most difficult part for me was accepting my sexuality. Kes made it all good; he took his time and let me grow and become the man I am today. He was so determined to never hide who he was, he was so true to himself, I knew it was time for me to be, too. So, trust us, Denver. We want you with us, and that means all the parts you want to hide. They are the pieces of you that we will embrace, and we'll encourage you to be true to yourself."

"I get it, East, I really do and I agree, but let me take my time; this is all still new to me."

"Okay, baby. I'll give you some time, but we're still taking that guitar with us, even if I do have to find a way to persuade you." I wink and watch him swallow hard.

Lightening the mood, and because I want him, I press up against Denver's back as we reach his door, nudging my hips into his ass. The door opens and I push him inside, kissing the back of his neck as we go. Wrapping my arms around his waist, I reach down to rub his dick. Popping the button and sliding down his zipper before twisting him around to face me, I drop to my knees, tugging his jeans to mid-thigh. Rubbing my face into his groin, I inhale his rich musk and groan at the heady rush it gives me. Dragging the front of his briefs down, I run my nose up his length then, when I'm pulling his dick out, I hear his head clunk against the wall and he spreads his legs as wide as he can with his pants stuck halfway done his legs.

Swallowing him down, I work him quickly, my hand and mouth pumping and sucking him over and over. Pulling off him, I spit on my finger and go back to blowing him. Then, right when his legs stiffen, my finger nudges his hole then slips inside, sliding to his prostate and gliding over the soft spot.

"Fuck!" Denver's hands are in my hair, keeping my head in place as he pours his release into my mouth and throat.

I lick and suck him through his aftershocks, then pull back and tuck his soft cock back in his briefs before standing up. I capture his face in my hands and kiss him hard.

"Fine! I'll take it with me and if, I mean *if*, there is a spot, *and* we are not rushed off our feet at the bar, I'll give it a go." Denver grumbles, making me laugh.

"Awesome! Right, I'd better go, I'm watching Ellie play soccer this afternoon." I wink and head for the door.

"You're kidding me; you only came out here to get me to agree to play tonight?" He looks incredulous.

"You got a blow job, so what's your problem?" I laugh.

"You preyed on my weakened state of mind! Maybe I won't bring my guitar after all." He gazes petulantly.

"Yeah, you will; you want to, really." I shrug, smirking.

I'm almost to my truck when Denver calls out and jogs over. "Hey, can I come? I get it if you don't want to introduce her to me, but I'm bored here and I'd like to come."

I look at him in surprise: I never thought he'd be interested in grade school soccer matches. "Really? You want to come?"

"Sure, we haven't hung out much in the day; you're normally working or I am. Is Kes going to be there too?" Denver looks excited about being out with me. "I'm not asking you to hold my hand, you don't even have to talk to me much, but I'd like to come."

"Of course, I'll talk to you. It just never crossed my mind. Go grab your stuff and your dog. We can grab a hot dog and you can go back to the house with Kes to get ready for work." My heart does a little skip as Denver pops a kiss on my lips and races back to the cabin. "Don't forget your guitar!" I holler after him.

He comes back minutes later with Missy and an overnight bag thrown over his shoulder as well as his guitar.

"Let's go then." I smile and grab his hand. As I lift it up to my mouth to kiss it, I see Denver's mom walking towards the truck. I try to let go of his hand but he's not having it.

"I'm not ashamed, or embarrassed, East. If you are, then that's something we need to discuss with Kes." He depresses the button to open the window and smiles genuinely at his mom.

"Hey, boys." She smiles at us, no hidden agenda in her eyes. "What are you up to?"

"We're going to watch East's girl play soccer and eat dodgy hot dogs." He laughs openly.

"I've persuaded him to play at the open mic night tonight, too." I call across him and watch her smile broaden even more.

"Oh, how lovely. I wish I could come along; it's been years since I heard him play. I'm looking after the girls for Cal and Josie tonight. I guess they're heading there, too. Oh, what fun you'll have, Denny! I guess I'll hear all about it when they get home."

"I'll video it for you, Mrs. S." I smile, holding back a chuckle.

"I'd just love that, thank you, East. Well, you boys go have fun." She reaches in and pats Denver's cheek and he nods at her.

We have got to the end of the long driveway before I bust out a laugh.

"Not one fucking word, East, or you'll never see me again! You do not get to hear or use that word again." Denver scowls. I'm not even sure he's joking, so I make a play of locking my lips up tight.

"Just once, please, baby?" I beg.

"No! No one ever calls me that, ever." Denver shoots me a look that makes my balls shrivel.

Okay, I guess he wasn't joking. I turn the radio on to ease the tension emanating from Denver, then reach over and grab his hand again. We travel the couple of miles into town in comfortable silence, I catch him singing along to a few bars of a song, and now get to add sexy singer to his growing list of many talents.

I pull into the school parking lot and look over at him as he scans the number of cars here, his eyebrows raised in surprise.

"It's an interschool game; a lot of these cars will be from the away team. Heavy pressure from competitive parents." I sigh and raise my eyebrows.

"Does that include you? Are you shouting offside at every opportunity along with all the other proud fathers?"

"I'm the black sheep of the fathers, most definitely persona non grata here. Not only a single parent, but a gay single parent. I may as well be selling drugs to these kids for the welcome I get." I shake my head ruefully.

"Fuck that! Let's go and get loud and cheer your girl on! They can't lay that shit on me!" Denver leans across the console and pecks my lips before opening his door and stepping onto the heated blacktop. "When will Kes be here?"

I smile at how easily he has stepped into our lives and how much he adds to it. We hear a shrill whistle and a catcall. We turn and spot Kes standing with an excitable girl, wearing sports shorts and a team shirt, hanging onto his arm.

"Daddy!" Ellie shouts and sprints towards me, smiling hugely. I open my arms and she leaps into them.

"Hey there, baby girl." I kiss her forehead and let her drop back to the ground. "Ellie, this is mine and Kes' friend, Denver Sinclair; he's come to shout you on." I lean down and in a faux whisper add, "he knows all about the offside rule."

"Wow! That's cool. Nice to meet you, Sir." Ellie holds out her hand for Denver to shake, then, when Denver clasps it, she pulls him closer, "Can you explain it to my daddies, they don't understand."

"It's nice to meet you, too, Ellie. I've heard lots of wonderful things about you from your daddies and I would be honored if you call me Denver." He winks at her. "And I'll try but I'm not sure I'll do a better job than you at explaining."

Ellie looks at me and smiles, "Am I okay to call him Denver, Daddy?"

"You are, Ellie, but only because he asked you to, and only when I am with you. We still keep the rule in place for other adults." I smile. "Let's get this game going then, Ells-bells."

I reach out for Kes' hand but we drop our hands back down, neither of us prepared to have PDA's without including Denver anymore. I step ahead with Ellie but glance over my shoulder to see Kes clasp hold of Denver's hand briefly and whisper something in his ear that makes him chuckle and blush.

Denver drops the back of the truck down and calls for Missy to jump down and I watch as Ellie's eyes light up; she's crazy about dogs. Her shriek of excitement has us all cringing, apart from Missy who whines and wags her tail frantically. We take a few more minutes to let Ellie get over her excitement before we head down to the field.

"This is a very pleasant surprise." Kes murmurs to Denver as we casually walk to the pitch. Ellie has raced ahead and I have maneuvered us so Denver is in the middle.

Denver chuckles, "Yeah, I'm surprised too, but after East took advantage of me this morning and cajoled me into doing something I really don't want to do, I thought I'd get some fresh air to clear my mind."

"Really?" Kes narrows his eyes, "what did he do?"

Denver tenses between us as he thinks he has fucked up: we haven't laid down any sort of rules regarding what we are comfortable happening between two of us instead of three. Does he think my blowing him is going to be a problem with Kes? I hear him mumble a 'fuck' under his breath before he comes to a halt.

"Y'know what, this is too weird, I can't be here. It's too family orientated; I don't belong here. I'll see you at work tonight." He looks at Kes, "I'm sorry." He shakes his head and walks away.

Kes looks at me angrily. "What the fuck did you do?"

"I forced him to agree to playing at the open mic night." I let my voice fade out.

"How did you do that? Or can I fucking guess already?" Kes keeps his voice low, considering our surroundings and the close proximity of every nosey soccer mom in town.

"I blew him." I mumble.

"Oh, for fucks sake! You know what's got him leaving, don't you?" Kes stares at me.

"Of course I do, and calm down. We haven't talked about what is acceptable to do when we aren't all together." I feel a complete ass.

Then I hear Ellie's shrill voice call out and a quartet of giggling girls, led by Ellie, race past us. "Mr. Sinclair?" She calls out and I watch as the retreating back of my lover halts. "Oh, cool, I thought you were leaving. You're not leaving, are you? Can my friends say hello to Missy?"

"Sure they can, Ellie, and I was just getting something out of your dad's truck. I'd love to see you score a goal today." He answers so kindly and crouches next to his dog so the small girls can fuss her. His eyes flash up to us and I mouth I'm sorry as my hand touches my heart.

"I'll go talk to him." Kes snaps.

Fuck! I'm a dickhead!

□ □ □

KES

As I get to Denver and the gaggle of girls cooing over his dog, a loud whistle sounds out and the girls jump up, saying their goodbyes and offering a few more pats to the dog. Denver's eyes darken as he looks at me.

"I said I'd stay and watch Ellie play but I'm sure it won't hurt her too much if I don't." Denver's voice is low and gruff; I can tell he's hurt and confused.

"Denver, please. If you're worried about doing stuff with East when I'm not there, then stop. It's not a problem. I'm sure you wouldn't mind if you thought I'd blown East when you weren't there."

"Of course, I wouldn't; but you're a couple. I wouldn't expect you to stop doing anything you wanted to do with each other."

I watch as he glances around to see if there is anyone around to hear us.

"But this afternoon it was you and East that were the couple, so why is that different?" I know what his answer is going to be but I want him to see that it's okay. Perhaps we should decide together if we are happy to fuck each other when it's in a couple. Up until now, this hasn't been a problem because we have had every night together.

"C'mon, Kes; of course, it's different. You two have been together for years and are in a monogamous relationship." His is stubbornness emerging again; he really hasn't grasped quite how much we need him with us.

"We *were* in a monogamous relationship; now there are three of us and we each have a say in what goes on. If you feel that East did something inappropriate with you this afternoon, purely because I wasn't there, then we need to talk about it. But I'm okay with it, I promise. Hell, Denver, I'd have your dick in my mouth at any chance I could, too. I wouldn't have used it to bully you into playing tonight. Which you now have a get-out-of-jail-free card to play, if you so wish, by the way."

"I told him, *if* there were any spots free and *if* we weren't rushed off our feet at the bar, I would consider it." Denver smiles this time.

"I hate to break it to you, but East sorts out the time slots and he will step behind the bar to help me just to make sure you get up there tonight." I smirk as he realizes he's been played.

But he surprises me and shrugs. "At least my dick got sucked, his didn't!"

I burst out laughing and throw my arm around his shoulder. I'm about to tug him to me when Denver stiffens. Some girly laughter gets close and I step away, the pain in my chest at breaking away from him hurts as much as the look in his eyes. *Enough of this shit, it's time to claim him as ours.*

I watch as Denver leans back against the door of East's truck and tips his head up to the sky, I know this secrecy is getting to him. Glancing around to see if there's anyone else about then, when it's clear, I lean into him. With my hands either side of his head, I kiss his neck. He shudders at my touch but I know he's still warring with himself.

"Look at me, baby." I croon against his neck before pulling away. "We can work it all out; it's early days for us all. I know you are still coming to terms with what your ex did by cheating on you, but this isn't the same."

"I know that. This feels more real than the last couple of years I spent with him. I feel so happy and complete when we are all together. I just doubt myself when we are apart, I don't feel enough for you. I know what you are going to say, I also know that you want to go public. I just don't think it will be as simple as that and that's when you could end up having to choose. And I don't expect you to pick me."

"Fuck, Denver. Don't think that. We can, and will, work it out." I look around again then drop a kiss on his mouth. "We need to get back; we can talk it through afterwards. Please, baby, trust us to pick you."

"Yeah, East said just about the same thing earlier. But I can't expect you to tear your lives apart because of me; not *for* me, but *because of* me. I get that we live in a small town, which a lot of the times means small minds. I won't have the good reputation you and East have built up wrecked; I feel way too much for you both to ruin your livelihoods."

"Denver, baby, please." I look at him as he steps down from us. "Look, trust me when I say I don't give a shit what people think. My ex—before I moved back here—was so far in the closet, he was in Narnia. When I moved back here after my brother died, I refused to ever deny who I was. I didn't care if I never had a boyfriend here; I just knew I would never hide who I was again. Catastrophically, it took my brother's death to allow my parents to love and accept me for who I am. Then I found East and I knew he was going to be mine; I knew I wouldn't hide a relationship again. We were so determined to be strong and brave together. And now we have you, another man so ready to be accepted and loved for who he is, not what he does. Are you going to forgive yourself and be happy,

Denver? Happy with us?"

I watch as he takes everything on board, digesting the information. Maybe it's a doctor thing, but it sets my stomach churning as he stares at me but then he smiles, and fuck me, it's a hot smile.

"Okay, I'm still here and I still want to be with you." He looks around then ducks his head and drops the smallest, shyest kisses on my mouth before stepping away.

"That's good to know." I take hold of Missy's leash and we walk back to East at the edge of the field. We walk as close as possible without touching.

East looks at Denver and gives him one of his heart-stopping, dimple-showing, bad boy smiles and nudges him with his shoulder.

"I'm sorry, Denver. I pushed you then. You don't have to play tonight if you don't want to."

Then the whistle blows again and the game starts. East sits back on the bench and watches his daughter play.

My mind wanders as I gaze around the stands, trying to work out exactly how much of a problem coming out as a trio will cause. The main one would be how it affects Ellie: she hasn't had any problems or issues with me and East. *But how will it be when she gets older? What about high school, is she going to be strong enough to stand up to any comments? Will she be bullied because of it? Shit, these are things we haven't thought of. Has East?* I'm not so sure he has.

Then, *what about Denver?* He's already thinking of going back to being a doctor again, and I want him to. Google gave me a huge insight to just how brilliant he is as a doctor and surgeon; he won't want to lose his skills or be behind on the latest medicine. East will be back at the bar when this job ends—until he gets another; he already has some other work lined up but it's not as full-on as the Sinclair job. *Will his business suffer again if we go public?*

My eyes stop on Denver's brother, Cal. I didn't think he would be here, but then, his kids go to this school, too. They are younger than Ellie but there are different games going on today and it looks like there's little league baseball going on over on a different field. He looks at me and gives me a nod but when he spies Denver sitting with us his head tips as he tries to work out why.

"Hey, Denver, your brother is over there, he's seen you. Do you want to go say hi?" I nudge him with my shoulder.

Denver sits up and scans the benches, raising his hand when he sees his brother. Pushing himself upright, he looks at me. "You okay to hang on to the dog while I go over?"

"Sure, we're not going anywhere." I've still got hold of her leash.

Right then, East jumps up and hollers: Ellie has scored a goal and our cheer is deafening. East turns to me and hugs me, then does the same to Denver. Smiling madly, he claps loudly and whistles out to his daughter. Denver joins in the applause, grinning hugely, neither of them aware of their open display of affection.

But I look at Cal again and he's seen it. A confused look flashes across his face as he stares.

"Did you see that? What a star! I guess it's ice cream time when she's done." East grins broadly.

"I think I saw what everyone else did, and that was you hugging Denver in just the same way as you hugged me. I think you may have just let the cat out of the bag." I feel my frown and I don't want to ruin this moment for East.

We turn to a still smiling Denver. "What? Why are you both looking at me like that?"

"Because everyone has just seen you two embrace." I explain

"So? It was a celebration. I don't think there was anything more to it than a happy man cheering on his child. Don't overcomplicate it." Denver rationalizes. "I'm going to say hello to my brother. Relax,

Kes; no one will think anything."

We let Denver past and watch him saunter away to speak with his brother. He's relaxed and I see them smile as he approaches Cal.

"Am I making it worse?" I look at East, my hand reaching out to him. I clasp his and make him look at me.

"No. Yes. Shit, I don't know. I know how confused he is, and how he is still so unsure of himself. I'd like to strangle that asshole ex of his. What went on over by the truck?" East's eyes flick to mine briefly but he's back watching Ellie race up and down the field.

I fill him in and then on what I'm now concerned about, but I'm not getting anywhere as East continues to only half-listen.

"We can talk about it later. Is he planning to come back with us after this? He rode in with you, so how will he get back?"

"He's got his gear and his guitar and is staying with us tonight." East speaks quietly.

"That's great, but what about after this: we always take Ellie for a burger and ice cream. What's he going to do then?"

"He'll come with us. Christ, Kes, chill; it's not like we're going to blow him in the diner! He's our friend." East growls, then hollers out to Ellie as she runs of at half time. It seems the subject is closed for now.

Chapter
Ten

DENVER

"This is a surprise, Den. Not the place I would've thought I'd seen you." Cal laughs.

"Yeah, spur of the moment idea. East was over at the cabins and mentioned it; I didn't want another day out there on my own so I tagged along. I'm sure there was the promise of a hot dog in there, too." I laugh easily, not bothered by what assumptions my brother comes up with.

"They're good people, they had to put up with some rough shit but they just stood up for themselves and proved all the haters wrong. How are you enjoying working at the bar? Bit different from your usual job?"

I chuckle, "Yeah, it really is. But it's not enough and I don't want to stay out of the OR too long or my skills will get rusty and I'll need to keep up to date with the advances that are constant."

Cal frowns. "You're not going back there again, are you? Shit, Den, could you cope with seeing Alec?"

"Fuck, no! I'm thinking of looking around here, not here in Cooper's Ridge; I need a bigger hospital than here, but I don't mind a commute. I'm liking my time here; the people are good." I look behind me and see East and Kes laughing as Ellie fusses over my dog. I smile at the sight and my heart warms for them. My perusing is interrupted by Cal's snicker.

"Oh brother, that is a huge can of worms waiting to be spilt." Cal has a look of realization on his face as he continues to glance between me and my boyfriends. *Wow! Are they my boyfriends? I guess they are.*

"I don't know what you're talking about." I try to brush him off.

"Denver, the smile you had on your face then wasn't 'oh, look at them with my dog, aren't they great guys.' That was an 'I've seen you naked' kinda smile."

"Fuck!" I growl.

"Add that to the victory hug, and I say you three have bumped uglies; I'd lay my last dollar on it."

"Is that all you have to say about it?" I scrape my hands through my jumbled mess of hair.

"What do you want me to say? You're an adult, with an incredibly analytical mind; I'm sure you've thought about the consequences for hour and hours. Like I said, they are great guys. Just be happy, Denver. It's time you enjoyed living, instead of working ninety plus hours a week." Cal shrugs and then surprises me again by pulling me in for a hug. "Go, be happy, Den."

"Oh!" I say as I turn to walk back to my men. "Mom says she's minding the kids tonight so you can come to the bar, open mic night apparently."

"Yeah, it's a good night. You working it?" He asks, still smiling.

"Yeah, I'll see you then. And, thanks, Cal." I hug him again then say my goodbyes.

As I walk back, Ellie rushes up to me and catches my hand, surprising me at her friendliness. "Your dog is the best. Daddy says you're coming for burgers with us, that's so cool. I get to choose how many scoops of ice cream I can have today, too. Are you best friends with my daddies? Millie is my best friend, she's eleven, too."

I laugh as the little firecracker continues to talk without ever seeming to take a breath.

"Hey, Ells-Bell, I think you're being called." Kes comes and meets me as we traverse up to the benches.

"Bye, I'm gonna score another goal!" Ellie skips off.

"You okay, it looked serious there?" Kes asks as the back of his hand skims mine.

"Uh, yeah, I guess." I chortle making Kes frown and East walk up to us. "It seems that the way I look at you is in such a way that it screams I've seen you naked." I carry on sniggering, the funny side of it overriding the fact I've just told my lovers we've be outted.

"Oh!" They reply simultaneously.

"In fact, the expression he used is that we've 'bumped uglies.'" I'm grinning so much they end up joining in.

"Is he cool with that?" Kes gets serious again quickly.

"Actually, he really was. He said you're both great guys and I should be happy. So, I am: I'm going to get living and be happy. Everything will fall into place when it's ready." I look at them, "I really want to kiss you both, but I can wait."

"Fuck!" Kes curses, "I want you two, so damn much!"

Ellie does exactly what she predicted and scores another goal, setting her team up as the victors. Her enthusiasm and energy is endless, I'm exhausted simply watching her. But we have great burgers and Ellie chooses three scoops of varying chocolatey goodness. East drops her at her grandmothers tonight but only because we are all going to the bar and it will be late; normally, it seems, Ellie stays with East and Kes on Saturdays and his mom stays till they get home.

We shower together, finally able to touch each other the way we want to. After mutual fulfilling hand jobs, we wash up and step out, hating that we haven't the time to satisfy each other further.

I run my hand down East's still damp back as he pulls underwear out of a drawer, then throws them to Kes, before rummaging again for himself.

"We need to make some space for you, I'm thinking of getting another dresser and we have room in the closet for your hanging clothes." East turns to me as my hand stills on his hip. "Don't you think?"

"Um, East. I think you may just be jumping the gun here. First, Denver hasn't shown any signs of wanting to move in here, second, we are not out as a triad yet, and, thirdly, we haven't asked him. Let's just take it one day at a time. Cal's understanding and acceptance doesn't mean that we are all ready to leap out into the reserved town of Cooper's Ridge or flaunt ourselves." Kes leans in and kisses East then straightens up and winks at me.

I carry on getting dressed but I'm smiling hard, I'm so fucking happy right now. Walking up to East as he finishes dressing with a scowl on his face, I kiss him sweetly. "I'd love to leave some of my clothes and maybe a toothbrush here, sweetheart." His wide grin proves I've said the right thing to pacify him—for now, anyway—I've learnt he's like a dog with a bone when he gets an idea in his head.

☐ ☐ ☐

The bar is full when we get there: at least three deep, waiting for service, at the tap and the tables are full. Kes only serves easy food on open mic night; he explained most people merely want nachos, chicken wings and sliders. Easy on the kitchen and the servers.

"It's just chips and dips tonight." Kes laughs as we walk through to the office.

I brought my guitar but, by the looks of it, I won't get to play. A small part of me is disappointed but there'll be other times.

We step behind the bar and get to work; there's no time for talking now. East serves for a half hour before setting up a sign-up sheet. He looks at me and winks, which worries me. *Has he added me?*

The first act starts up and it's good: a young girl as the singer while a cool guy plays guitar. They seem lost in the moment and they harmonize beautifully, the crowd here seem to like it and they get a couple of songs in before jumping down, smiling at the applause as they let the next have a turn.

I smile at Kes as we cringe at some of the karaoke but everyone seems to be having fun as tipsy girls belt out *I Will Survive* and *Girls Just Wanna Have Fun*. I look at the clock over the bar and I'm surprised to see it's already ten thirty. The bar is still busy but it has mellowed out as some of the crowd head off; I think the loud girls continued their bachelorette party somewhere else.

Then East's voice comes over the system and I look up: he's smiling and I see my guitar on a stand next to him. *The little fucker! I'll get my own back on him later.*

"Ladies and gentlemen, we have our very own Denver Sinclair up next, he's a shy guy so treat him nicely. C'mon over, Denver, it's your turn now." He grins and the crowd start to clap.

I look at Kes and he grins and points for me to get out from behind the bar. "Go on, Denver; show them how it's done."

I step up to the stage and give East a playful thump on the arm, making him laugh as he struts away.

Looking up at the still packed bar, I swallow hard: I haven't played to an audience for a long time, but they are a friendly crowd. "Okay, guys, I may be a little rusty but here goes nothing." I prop myself on the stool in front of the mic and strum the strings a couple of times then start.

The first line of Kings of Leon's *Cold Desert* seems to hush the crowd. As my fingers pluck the cords to one of my favorite songs, my eyes close as I lose myself in the lyrics, and I sing to myself.

I feel distant. Since Alec, I've tried to ignore how lost I've been— the lyrics suddenly become more valid in my new life here. The one where I have a chance to love and be loved, where I am worthy.

I play the last few cords then rest my hand over the strings and open my eyes. The room is utterly silent as everyone waits for me.

"Thank you very much." I cringe at the thought of being dismissed by silence, but the room erupts as cheers and applause ring out. Lifting my head, I see smiling, joyful faces as the audience applauds me. I see lights on cellphones as photographs or videos are taken, shocking me to a standstill.

A few moments later, I step from my stool and make my way off the stage away, but East is in front of me. Tears fill his eyes as he tugs me against him. Wrapping his arms around me, his mouth is on mine in a crushing kiss. My hands slide up to his hair and knot in the soft locks while we kiss for what seems like forever.

"Fucking hell, Denver. That was just… Fuck! Just amazing!" East kisses me again then lets me go. Kes comes from behind the bar and struts towards me, his face fierce as he stands by East, his eyes sparkle with what? *Pride, maybe?*

"Denver, I'm speechless. Come here, baby." Kes opens his arms and I step into them. Resting his forehead against mine, I feel his heavy breath on my lips as he tries to control himself. Then, like East, he kisses me. Slowly, lazily his mouth slides over mine as he pours his emotions into this moment.

We separate and I sigh. Around us, the crowd is quiet, eyes glued to the scene. It seems we have shown the whole town that we are a threesome. My eyes go wide as I wait for the sneers and hostility to happen, but there is nothing but smiles and some laughter.

I peer around and see my brother—laughing, but shaking his head at the same time—his cellphone held up, recording the whole scene. Kes saunters back to the bar and East takes his place in front of the mic, ready to announce the next act.

"Okay then, that show is over but you've gotta admit: my man is damn good." East laughs with ease as the crowd claps again, there's a few whoops and hollers but no one says anything else.

When I tread back behind the bar—my head full of the buzz of swarming bees as the high of what I've done, and then being so publicly claimed by them floods through me—Kes waits for me, concern coloring his eyes.

"You okay, baby?" His hand runs down my back, soothing my tension.

"Huh?" My head still reels but then, taking a deep breath, I relax. "Yeah, I'm good. I'm really fucking good." I smile and pop a kiss on his lips then get back to work.

The remainder of the night is fun: the singing continues and the laughter flows as easily as the alcohol. East closes the night down and thanks everyone for coming along. Kes leans back against the bar, looking out over the empty room. East squares up the last of the tables but I find myself back on the stool with my guitar.

Not playing anything specific, until a certain song springs to mind and Bruce Springsteen's *I'm on Fire* comes out of the strings. I'm barely humming along then start to sing softly. I glance up and Kes has East in his arms as they sway together. Not the hot, dirty grinding I know they do so well, but the sweet, slow dance of people in love, holding each other close as they listen to me serenade them.

When I finish, they pull apart and hold out an arm for me. Comfortably, I step between them and dance; there is no music but my song permeates their heads. Kes kisses me, his hands in my hair as he pours his unspoken words into me. This is love. This is him making love to me with only his mouth. When he breaks away, his blazing eyes lock onto mine, still telling me how he feels.

East twists me around, his fingertips run down my cheek and over the rough stubble on my jaw then he smiles. I see his eyes glistening with unsaid emotion and I'm sure mine are the same. I drop a small kiss on his parted mouth.

"Shall we go home?" I use the word home for the first time. Normally, I call it their place but after tonight there's nowhere else I want to be. The shit can hit the fan tomorrow, but tonight we have everything we need in each other.

I wait with East as Kes locks the takings in the safe and switches the lights off. East reclines against my chest and my hand is on his waist, my thumbs in his belt loops. Resting my chin on his shoulder, I kiss his neck. "Thank you, honey."

"Always, baby. Always." He murmurs back, then there's a flash and we jump. Turning, we face Kes.

"That was a beautiful moment: I needed a photograph. The first of our new life together, the three of us." He smiles and joins us, kissing me then East, "C'mon, I think we have some celebrating to do."

Why do I feel nervous now? Maybe because there's no turning back without getting hurt. Or, worse, hurting them; the thought of that is abhorrent.

"I can't understand why you were hesitant about playing tonight, baby. You were incredible, the whole bar went quiet. At least you've got a talent to fall back on if you don't want to be a doctor!" East bursts out laughing. "We should put you on one of those talent shows, I reckon you'd even get Simon Cowell to smile."

"Not a fucking chance!" I laugh. "Kes, get your man under control."

"Impossible. And he's your man, too, so good luck with that." Kes chuckles but blows East a kiss as he drives us home.

We pull up onto the drive and the atmosphere in the car changes, electricity pulsing between us. East licks his lips tentatively as he feels it too, and, when I look at Kes, his eyes have darkened.

"Let's get inside." My voice sounds rough, heavy with need.

East and Kes head for the bedroom while I let Missy out for a quick pee in the garden. As I wait for her to finish her check of the garden's perimeter, always guarding, I wonder what Kes and East are up to in the bedroom. I call my dog, itching to be back with them. She comes up to me and I lock up behind me.

Kes and East are naked, sitting propped against the headboard. Slowly, they stroke each other's dicks.

"Damn, you look good!" I exclaim as I strip off my clothes, "Looks like I've got some catching up to do."

$$\square \ \square \ \square$$

KES

I watch Denver pull his tight, black work T-shirt over his head; the muscles in his stomach contract and tighten, making his six-pack even more distinguished. I want to map every square with my tongue. He has no idea how beautiful he is. Watching and listening to him perform tonight was incredible. There was no way I was letting that go unrecognized, my feet moved of their own accord toward him. Stopping as I observed East kiss him so passionately, without a care who watched, I knew I had to have him too.

Carelessly, we claimed him as ours, not caring who knew. What happens now is beyond or control. As long as we stick together, that is all I need.

Denver gazes at us as he lowers his zipper and lets his pants slide down his legs. Kicking off his shoes then stepping out of his pants, he bends to remove his socks before sauntering towards us. With his thumbs in the waistband of his tight boxer shorts, his erection proud and straining against the black fabric, he lowers them, letting his dick slap against his stomach before crawling up the bed to reach us.

East reaches for him and, with his hand curled around the nape of his neck, he pulls him closer, claiming his mouth as I reach out and grasp his dick with my free hand.

"Fuck me, claim me, own me." Denver moans as he separates from East.

"Oh, baby, we can do that. You're going to fuck me, while East fucks you." I groan as he slides his tongue languorously up my neck only to scrape the sensitive skin below my ear with his teeth.

Moments later, I watch as Denver and East rip into the foil of the condom wrappers and roll them down their dicks, covering them generously with lubricant once they reach the base.

"Lie back down, Kes, I want to look into your eyes." Denver whispers.

Shuffling down the bed, I grab my legs and pull them up to my chest. Denver grabs the lube and pours some onto his fingers and over my exposed hole. Working his fingers—first one, then adding a second into my hole—he gasps as East copies the action on him. *I'm not going to last once he's inside me.*

Then, slowly pulling his fingers out of my body, he lines his dick up to my needy pucker. Nudging, he pushes against me, breaching the tight ring of muscles before gliding deep inside. His balls touch my ass as he fills me completely.

I know the moment East enters Denver, I watch as his eyes roll back in his head and a shudder reverberates through his body and into mine as his dick swells and pulses.

As our rhythm steadies, I look at my two men and realize we are not fucking: we are making love. I am as in love with Denver as I am with East. As they pick up speed, my body reacts, my orgasm bursting from me, splashing over Denver's chest as well as my own. My cry is hushed by Denver's mouth as he stiffens and comes, the heat of his release burning through me. Then East cries out loud and climaxes, his hips still pumping into Denver as he pours himself inside him.

"I love you." My voice is hushed but heard by both men. I don't differentiate, I simply know I love them equally. East mouths the words back at me, Denver closes his eyes.

East pulls back first and Denver groans as East eases out of him. Flopping down to my side, he pulls off the condom and drops it in the waste bin then leans over to kiss me. Denver withdraws from me and repeats East's action and lies down on my other side. Lying still, he doesn't say a word. I look at him and see his eyes are tight shut. Looking at East with panic, he props himself up on his elbow and reaches across me to him.

"Hey, Denver; you okay, baby?" He trails his fingers down Denver's arm but moves it away when Denver flinches.

"I think I'm going to head off home. Shit! East, can I use your truck?" He moves and sits up.

"No." East answers him angrily.

"Oh, okay. No problem, sorry." Swinging his legs to the edge of the bed, Denver stands and walks towards his randomly discarded clothes and picks up his boxer shorts.

Seeing East is about ready to blow a fuse, I need to step in and defuse this situation. Putting my hand firmly on East's arm, I hold him back.

"Denver, what's going on? Why do you want to go home?" I speak quietly then walk to him. "Have we done something wrong?"

"No, no. It's me, I'm sorry. I think I'm getting in too deep here,

I'd be better at home tonight." His shorts are on and he pulls on his pants.

"No! What the hell are you talking about? We have had the best evening, and just had amazing sex, and you want to go home. I don't think so." East can't hold his tongue and stands next to me.

"Why do you think you're getting too deep, isn't that what people in a relationship do?" I'm genuinely confused.

"I'm not sure you need me in your relationship. You have each other, you love each other. And I already have too many feelings for you both. If I don't step back, I can see myself falling for you. You don't need that complication and I don't need the rejection. So, while it has been amazing, I'm going to cut my losses because, like I said, I'm getting in too deep." His eyes roam from me to East and, with a painful smile, he turns away. "I'll carry on working till you get a replacement or when you have East back, but it's best for my heart to stop this now."

"What about my heart? Or East's? Don't our hurting matter to you?" I ask.

"You have each other." His voice is devoid of any emotion.

"We want you, too." East snaps, and I nod.

"Kes, you told East you loved him while it was me inside your body. I told you I would be the third wheel, I won't be the toy in your games."

I flinch as if he has struck me. "I wasn't just speaking to East."

It's Denver's turn to wince but he doesn't back down. "You need to think about that between you. I'll see you around." He turns and walks out of the room. I hear him call for his dog but he doesn't come back.

"Is he for fucking real?" East shouts. "Fucking hell! How is he going to get home, it's gone 2am?" He starts pulling on his clothes.

"Where are you going?" I roar.

"To fucking stop him!" He bellows and then leaves me standing naked and alone.

What the fuck! I grab my jeans and tug them on, ready to go with East, but he's already down the driveway and races his truck down the road before I can call out. *How the hell can this have gone to shit so quickly? How can he not think I meant him too?*

I go back in and shut the door. When I get back in the bedroom, I pick up my cell phone. I'll call him; I don't expect he'll answer but I can leave a message. Swiping the screen to open the phone, I press his number. I hear it ringing, not in my ear but in the house. Wandering out of the bedroom, I keep it ringing to use the sound as a guide. As I walk into the kitchen, I notice the backdoor is open.

Stepping through the doorway, I make out the outline of Denver, huddled on a bench further down the garden, Missy is glued to his leg. The light of his cellphone twists in his hands as he turns it over and over. Breaking the connection, I observe as he runs his hand down his face. *Is he crying or frustrated?* I know he hasn't seen me but his dog has and I approach cautiously; I don't want to startle him.

"Den? Denver?" It's the first time I've abbreviated his name and I like the sound of it but the scowl on his face shows his distaste at the name, or maybe at me. As he lifts his head, I detect the pain etched on it.

"Did you mean it?" His voice sounds tortured, painful as he speaks.

I immediately know what he means, what he asks. "Yes. Yes, I did. I do."

My phone rings and it's East. "It's okay, baby. He's here. Yeah, well, I hope so. Come home."

"Did he go after me?" The pain in Denver's voice rips through me.

"Of course, he did. I'm pretty sure he feels the same way I do." I sit next to him but keep my hands to myself. We hear East calling out our names as he tears through the house. Denver gives Missy a command and she races down the garden to the house. The outside light comes on as East runs to us. Without waiting to hear from Denver, he pulls him off the seat and crushes him in his arms.

"You pull that shit again and I'll beat your ass so damn hard!" Then he kisses him, it takes a moment or two but then Denver wraps his arms around East and kisses him back.

Damn! Why didn't I think of doing that? I stand behind him and embrace them both as Denver lets go of East with one arm and reaches behind to clasp onto me.

"C'mon, let's go back inside." I release them. Keeping Denver between us, I hold on to his left hand as East takes the right in his and we amble back to the house.

"Do you still want to go home, Den?" Again, I use his shortened name; his eyes tighten as I speak. "Am I okay to call you that?"

East sniggers and Denver shoots him a look. "Not a fucking word, Brookman!" Denver snickers at him.

"What have I missed?" I peer between the two men but they bite their lips. East seems to be holding back a smile that may break through, but Den looks hurt.

"No, I don't mind you calling me Den. I prefer Denver, but I'm used to it being shortened." Denver scowls light-heartedly at East.

"So, Denver. Would you like one of us to drive you home?" I ask, still unsure of his feelings.

"No, but I understand if you would rather I went home." He looks at us miserably.

"No way! You're staying with us. If I have to tie you to the bed, I will." East growls at Denver.

"C'mon, I'm exhausted and we have Ellie again tomorrow." I walk past Denver and trap his hand in mine, tugging him along.

"I'll lock up." East calls out.

◻ ◻ ◻

EAST

Denver is under the covers, in the crook of Kes' arm when I enter the room, and seems to rest his head on his chest from what I can see, which isn't much.

Kes simply smiles as I strip out of my clothes for the second time tonight. I'm bone weary now and want nothing more than to lie with these two men who, unlike Denver, I know I'm in love with. I understand his caution—he's only recently come out of a relationship he thought he was loved in. So to have the courage to enter this highly unusual relationship is bound to make him freak out. I think it's only because Kes and I have had the chance to discuss our feelings about Denver, and to us wanting him with us that has made it seem so much more realistic, more viable to us.

I never thought we would be more than merely the two of us and Ellie, and it hasn't been the need to add someone else to our dynamics, it has been about wanting. *Him. Denver.*

"Come to bed, baby." Kes whispers, making me smile.

I slide in the bed and immediately Denver reaches out to me. I wrap my body around his as he lies into Kes' body.

"Do you really feel you love me?" Denver voice is soft, nervous even.

"I *know* I do, I can't even tell when it hit me, I just know the feelings I have for East, I now have for you. I'm trying not to overthink or complicate it, but it's there and I won't ignore it." Kes speaks quietly but with such determination, there is no doubting his

129

words.

"Denver, you drive me crazy. We do everything to reassure you of how much you mean to us and I have realized that it's not us you doubt but your own worth. Now is the time to cut that shit out and get used to us not only loving you, but being in love with you, too. Now I've said that, I've got one more thing before I fucking pass out. I want us to get tested; I don't want anything between us in any part of our lives." The room is deadly quiet and I stay silent, letting them absorb my words and I let out a breath when they whisper in agreement. "Good, now can we please go to damn sleep?"

I feel Denver's body vibrate as he chuckles but he whispers goodnight and I'm soon out of it.

□ □ □

I wake up, my legs stretching out into a space that should be occupied by Denver. Opening my eyes, the bright sunlight blinds me as my sight adjusts to the daylight. I'm alone in the bed, not something I'm happy about. Laughter comes from the kitchen, and then the rich aroma of good coffee permeates my nose. *Time to get up.*

Dragging a pair of sweats on, I stumble out of the bedroom and down the hallway to the kitchen. Kes has Denver pinned against the table and devours his mouth. Denver's hands on Kes' ass squeeze the tight globes through the soft fabric of his shorts.

"Hey, as much as I'm enjoying the show, I think I'm being neglected here." I smirk and step close to Kes, trapping him between us.

"You were fast asleep, baby. We haven't been up long but the coffee's ready." Kes leans back, turning his head so I can kiss him.

"That's good to know, but I'm hungry, so let's get cooking." I take a step back, Kes and Denver moving with me. "Come here, Denver." I grab his hand and tug him close. "Kisses, please."

I get a smacker on my lips and a slap on my ass.

Preparing breakfast, we discuss what to do for the day; Kes and Denver are working tonight, so we have the day together.

"I need to go home at some point: I didn't bring clothes for tonight, and Missy could do with a run along the lake. Do you want to come with me?" Denver looks hopefully.

"Sounds good. Is it okay if I bring Ellie? I feel guilty for not having her here last night."

"Of course, I'll call my mom to get some food together and we can picnic with her, if you'd like. Would she like that?" Denver looks happy at the thought of being out with us all today.

"I'll call her and we can pick her up on the way." I look at Kes and he's in agreement with me.

To say my girl is excited is an understatement: when we pull up outside my mom's, she's already waiting and hopping up and down. Getting out of the truck, I walk up to her and she throws herself at me.

"Do I get to play with Missy all day?" She shrieks jubilantly.

"As long as Denver says it's okay, then you can. Let's go and say bye to Gram." I catch hold of her hand and we walk into the house. "Mom?" I call out.

"She's in the kitchen." Ellie says.

When I walk in I notice there's something she needs to say to me, I know my mom when she gets a certain look in her eye.

"Go and get your swimsuit, hon; you might want to splash about." I watch her as she races down the hall and stamps up the stairs.

"What's up, Mom?" I know she's heard about Denver, I'm only wondering how much she will want to know from me.

"Another boyfriend, East? Isn't Kes enough for you?" There's a smirk there, I'm sure. My mom has always supported me, and I could never have managed Ellie and been able to work if she hadn't stepped in. I know she loves Kes and is happy for me.

"Kes is as wonderful as always, but, Mom, have you seen Denver Sinclair? He's amazing, not just to look at," I wink and she laughs. "He really is a good man and it seems that he wants to be with us as much as we want him. He's special, Mom. As special as Kes."

"Be careful, East. The rest of the town aren't as open-minded as I am. Remember that Ellie has to grow up here. Don't make life harder for her than having two dads already is."

"Mom, Ellie is always my main priority. This is new, but it's real and it will work. The rest of the town can bite my ass: this is my life and I will spend it with the people I love and who make me happy. Ellie will never have anything more than loving parents. I'm not expecting Denver to assume another father role but if she likes him then I'm good with them spending time together."

I hear Ellie racing down the stairs again and comes in, waving her swimsuit.

"I'm ready to go!" Ellie jumps up and down and attempts to drag me to the door.

"I'd like to meet him soon, East." My mom requests and I nod back.

Denver and Kes are talking as Ellie wrenches open the back door. They turn around to greet her.

"Hey there, Ellie, are you looking forward to this?" Kes asks

"I've got my swimsuit; daddy says I can splash in the water. Does Missy like the water, Denver?" Ellie asks but she looks at me, checking she's okay to use his first name. She beams at my nod of approval.

"She does, Ellie; she would spend all day in the water if she could." Denver smiles and she grins back.

I slide in next to her, "Right, buckle up, Ells-bells, then we can get on our way. Denver has sorted a picnic, too; we have to pick that up from Mrs. Sinclair."

"I like Mrs. Sinclair, she's always so friendly." Ellie smiles at Denver. "She let me read Harry Potter by myself when I was only eight."

I sit back and get ready to have my ears ringing by the time Ellie goes back tonight; I don't think she's going to stop for breath.

"That's excellent, Ellie, I love Harry Potter." Denver answers, "What house would you be in, do you think?"

"Gryffindor! I would be just like Hermione!" I watch with pride at my daughter and with admiration to Denver for being able to speak with her so comfortably and enthusiastically. I think falling in love with him has been very easy.

We pull up outside Denver's parent's home and he jumps out to go grab the lunch his mom will have ready. Kes twists around and looks at me.

"Everything okay with your mom?" His question is loaded with unspoken words.

"Yeah, she's extended an invitation to all of us." I smile, letting him know she's heard about Denver and seems okay with it, so far.

Denver comes down the steps with a basket and a serious look on his face. But, when he opens the back door, he hands the basket to Ellie and smiles.

"You're in charge of the lunch, Ellie." He smiles sweetly at her but doesn't look at us.

Fuck! His mom has heard, too, and it hasn't gone down well.

"You okay, baby?" Kes asks with a worried look on his face.

"Yeah, it's all good." Denver murmurs back. I see Kes reach over and clasp Denver's hand but I know Ellie can't. We need to talk to her about this before she goes to school tomorrow.

When we pull up outside Denver's cabin, we clamber out. Missy was quick to capture Ellie's attention and they race to the water's edge.

"Be careful!" Our three voices ring out at the same time.

We smile and chuckle as Ellie turns around and rolls her eyes at us. "I know, Daddy!" She steps back from the water all the same.

"Talk to us, Den. That wasn't a happy look on your face." I grasp his arm and haul him up to me and plant a kiss on his mouth.

Chapter
Eleven

DENVER

"Hey, Mom; thanks for doing this." I burst into the kitchen and grin, then I see her expression. "What's that look for?"

"Two of them, Denver? Don't you think this could cause you a lot of trouble?" Her voice is full of concern, rather than disapproval, but I can see she is confused.

"It could, but I'd like to think that most people will keep their noses out of my business and keep any opinions to themselves. These men who make me happy? Who don't look at me as a deadbeat workaholic?" I snap back. "I don't need your approval, Mom."

"I'm not disapproving, I'm just playing the devil's advocate here and making sure you have all thought this through. My fear is, if it goes wrong, that it will be you who gets hurt again. East and Kes have a good relationship; do you want to be the one that could break them up?" She smiles simply.

"I think this really is between the three of us; let us be the ones that worry. This may be something that goes nowhere. But, consider this: it could be the best thing that ever happens, not just to me, but to all of us." I pick up the basket she has prepared and peek inside. "Thank you for this, I'll bring the basket later."

"Denver, I want you to be happy, be careful."

"Yeah, I know you do. But, for the first time in my adult life, I feel wanted. Let me know what's best for me." I reply, feeling crass but determined.

I finish repeating my conversation and look at my men and smile. "So, she's thrilled with me right now."

Kes links his fingers through mine. "Y'know it will be okay, don't you?"

I laugh dryly, "We all know that's not true. This could be a serious fuck-up and could get a shit-load more grief from the town than you ever had before. But it also could be a storm in a teacup and be over with in twenty-four hours, but I'm in. I want this and I want it with both of you. I'm big enough, and certainly ugly enough, to take whatever shit is thrown at me and if it all goes to shit and we don't make it through together, then I've had the time of my life and it will be a damn good memory."

Kes and East smile broadly at me, Kes kisses me and East wraps me in his arms.

"Are we going to go for a walk, or are you going to stand there kissing all day?" We break apart when Ellie's shrill voice interrupts us.

"Yep, we're going for a walk, and I'm sorry for the delay." I call out and we head off to the trail. Kes is holding my hand and East walks on to catch up with his daughter.

"She's a great kid; not much fazes her." Kes laughs, we are walking a few paces behind them and can hear her chatter.

"Why we're you kissing Denver? Is he you're boyfriend now, too?"

"He is, baby girl. Are you okay with that?" East asks quietly.

"Is he going to live with you as well? I'm not sure your bed is big enough for all of you." I can see the concentration on her pretty face as she tries to work it all out.

"He doesn't live with us yet, but I hope he will soon. Don't you worry about our bed and remember the rules we talked about, please." East lets go of her hand and smooths his hand down her long, blonde hair.

"I remember. No talking about what happens with you and dad at home: it's private but not a secret." She intones seriously. "Do I call him daddy now too? Because that's gonna get confusing real quick."

"No, sweetheart. You can just call him Denver when we are together." East flashes us a grin over his shoulder, fully aware we have been following their conversation.

"That's cool, I like him, he's nice." She reaches for his hand and drags him forward.

"I like him, too." East grins like a loon.

I look at Kes and his grin matches East's. He pulls me close and, with his lips brushing mine with a featherlight touch, declares, "It's true, you are nice and I like you, too."

"Only nice? I wasn't nice last night when my cock was buried deep in your ass." I whisper back.

"No, that was way beyond nice. I can't wait to feel that again."

"Hmm, I'll see what I can do." I kiss him properly then we race to catch up with East.

"It seems busier here tonight than other Sundays, don't you think, Kes?" I look around the bar and see a good thirty or so more people than I've been used to over last month I've been working here.

"I think we have become something to watch and report back on. I think they might be expecting more of last night's action."

"They know it's not a live music night." I reply as I fill another jug of beer for a rowdy crowd in the corner.

"No, Denver-baby, I think they may be waiting for more from the three of us." East barks out a laugh as he slides off the barstool and offers to take the beer over to the thirsty group.

"Oh?" Then I realize what he means. "OH!" I blush dark red at the reminder.

"Hell, baby. Don't look like that or I'll have to give them what they're waiting for." Kes jokes as he walks behind me, pinching my butt as he goes.

"That's not going to happen." I mutter. Alec was not into holding hands or kissing in public, or basically touching when we were out, so these two, hands-on men are something very new and very different to what I'm used to. Then, and not for the first time since I was dumped, I realize I don't have to be the quiet one: I can touch my boyfriends, I can joke and mess around with them. It's not them who are unusual; it's him, Alec. Well, his new husband can be the subdued one now. And hell, I'd never marry a man I knew was cheating on his partner. He'll be more than likely to do it again; he got away with it once, so why not again?

When Kes walks past me again, I twist round and grab him. Dropping a chaste kiss on his mouth, I leave him speechless before a goofy grin spreads over his face. East high-fives me when I turn back to the bar. The wolf whistles and catcalls that follow make me grin rather than blush. *Time to be the man I want to be, not the man I thought I should be. I'm thirty-one and allowed to be affectionate and flirty with the men I go to bed with.* I shake my head and laugh at the plural, *men*.

East doesn't stay long tonight; he needs to be back at the ranch early tomorrow. I know he'll wake up when we get into bed but I don't expect anything more this evening, it has been such a full-on weekend. I'm beat myself but at least I can lie around in bed tomorrow morning, and I have the next few nights off. Most of the crowd thin out at around the same time as East, making closing up quick and easy.

"You look ready to drop, Den. Go, sit down, I'll finish the rest." Kes runs his hand down my arm but I shake my head.

"Nah. C'mon, we'll be out of here quicker if we both do it." I lift the stools and chairs so the cleaner can wash the floors tomorrow while Kes finishes cashing up and locking the day's takings away.

I brought my truck back with me tonight: I need to be able to get around without relying on East or Kes to get me home, even if I'm happy to be staying there while working. I plan on being back in the cabin tomorrow night; there's a few things, ideas I need to work through by myself. I'm not ready to live with them yet and I know that I need to get a job in a hospital again soon: I miss it. Not the long hours, but the job; I want to be saving lives again. Not in a 'hero' way, simply the thrill of fixing someone who could have died otherwise. The joy of completing a difficult, but successful surgery.

I pull up next to Kes and jump out and pace to a waiting Kes.

"The lights are all off: he must have gone to sleep." Kes comments.

"He must be beat, too. Ellie's a great kid, but her energy levels are off the charts."

Creeping into the house—so as not to wake him up—Missy ambles towards us, wagging her tail sleepily.

"Come on, girl; let's get you out for a pee." I stroke her soft fur and walk to the back door but she ignores me and climbs into the basket East bought for her and settles down. "I guess she's as tired as we are."

Kes yawns and wanders down to the bedroom while I fill up Missy's water bowl and check the doors are locked. When I make it into the room, Kes has stripped off and climbs in next to East, his eyes already closing. Shucking off my clothes, I leave them on the leather chair in the corner then climb in on East's other side. His warm, relaxed body stretches against mine as he mumbles but doesn't wake. Tucking my front to his back, I drift into a deep sleep.

"Fuck! Shit" I wake up to East trying to disentangle himself from between me and Kes and swearing quietly as he does it. It seems like all our legs have tangled together in the night. This is new to me, too: Alec hated cuddling at night. He said it was too hot, that I would be breathing on his neck all night. *Asshole!*

"East, honey, hold up; let me move first, then you can get out." I move to the edge and slide my legs from his.

"I didn't want to wake you, I'm sorry." He leans in and kisses me softly. "Although, I should be pissed you didn't wake me when you came in."

"We weren't awake long enough ourselves. Kes was out as soon as his head hit the pillow." I climb back under the covers as East heads for the bathroom. I hear the shower start up but sleep pulls me under before it turns off again.

"Bye, baby, see you later. Take it easy this morning." East drops a kiss on my forehead and I hear him speak equally as quietly to Kes.

The next time I'm woken up it's a much more pleasant experience as wisp-like strokes graze up and down my spine. Goosebumps break out over my skin as the fingertips reach the top of my ass. Twisting my head to the side, I blink my eyes open. Kes has his head propped up on his hand and a gorgeous, lazy smile spreads across his face.

"Morning, Den. Time to wake up, baby." Leaning down to kiss me, I roll over so I'm on my back as his mouth sweeps over mine.

"What time is it?"

"Playtime, baby." He whispers into my ear then nips the lobe playfully before licking the sting away. I still beneath him, making him stop. "What's up?"

"Are you sure we should?" I'm not sure this is okay. I know what he said after East blew me when we were alone, but sex is something else completely.

"I'm really sure we should, don't you want to?"

"It seems strange without East; I don't know if he'd be happy about it?" My dick screams at me for cockblocking him.

"I promise you, it's okay. Would you mind if I made love to East when you weren't here?" He goes back to kissing my neck, making it increasingly more difficult to say no. I really don't want to stop him.

"No, of course not. But it's different for you two." My voice fades away as I see him frown.

"It's no different, Den. I promise you." He looks around. "Do you want me to ask him?" He grabs his cellphone.

"No, of course I don't." I mumble, embarrassed.

"Well, it looks like I don't need to anyway." Kes grins and turns his phone to me, a text message on screen.

I look at it and grin as I read his message.

***Don't spend all morning fucking each other,
I want some ass when I get home.
Xxx***

"So, can we play now?" Kes smirks.

"Hell, yeah; we can play." I laugh.

Kes moves down my body and I soon stop thinking about anything but Kes and what his mouth is doing to me.

□ □ □

EAST

It's been a week and I'm finishing ahead of schedule—which is awesome, because I qualify for the big bonus I worked into the deal with Denver's dad. This is really the last place I want to be this morning, not only because of the hot men I left behind, or because I've had to leave them in bed together again. We've managed to persuade him to stay with us every night, ignoring his moans that, maybe, we should have a night apart. *Why the fuck would we want to do that?* None of it bothers me as much as being under the scrutiny of Denver's mother. She has been great to me and my team since day one, but I'm not sure how she feels about me. I haven't seen her all week and, now it's Friday, I'm hoping to get away with it again.

Denver said she was fine when he dropped the picnic basket off after our afternoon out, she even waved to Ellie from the porch. I head down the track to the last three of the cabins; the fixtures have finished being installed, so I'm here earlier than usual. I want to inspect the building work before I'm ready to do the walk-through with the boss. The buildings have been inspected and have passed the regulations with distinctions, and the wiring and plumbing is all certified.

Each cabin is set in its own, secluded space; privacy is guaranteed here, necessary for the ones with hot tubs on the raised, decked area. I like the two-story ones the best: the views from the main bedroom at the front are spectacular. The visitors will be spoiled for choice with what to do here.

After an hour of running through my itinerary for the day I hear a car coming down the graveled track. I walk out to greet whoever has arrived but stand still when I see Denver's mom stepping out of the vehicle. She raises her hand and gives me a tentative smile. My heart pounds as it picks up pace, *what does she want to say?*

"East, I know you're busy but can you spare a moment for me?" Her voice sounds nervous, which doesn't help mine one bit.

"Of course, Mrs. Sinclair. What can I do for you?" I'm fully expecting her to tell me to leave her son alone.

"I'd like to talk to you about your relationship with Denver, if I may?"

"I'm not sure it's appropriate. Maybe this is something you should be discussing with Denver."

"The man who turned up here three months ago was heartbreaking to see, he was so lost. His whole life had shattered around him, leaving him lost and broken. But then he started to change and he became happy again. And that, I know, is because of you and Kes. I don't have to understand the whys or wherefores to know that he is better with you." She looks at me and smiles.

"Thank you. He really is very special to me, to us. I can't imagine not having him in my life. I know it must have come as a shock, it did to the three of us, too, but it's good. We are good together."

"I saw that." She tries to hide a small smile.

I look at her in surprise. "What did you see?"

"Apart from the smile he had all over his face on Saturday when you went off to see Ellie, Cal came over last night and showed me the video of Denver playing his guitar. I saw him lose himself again in his music and that hasn't happened for a very long time. But I also saw him with you and then with Kes. That was something very special, you did that for him. You have brought him back to life and I can only be grateful for that. I don't think life is going to be easy for you, East. Staying happy and in love is hard enough with just one man to love, so I can only imagine what you have to work through with another man added in." She chuckles this time and I can't help but smile.

"He needs to get back to work though, East. And I only hope that you will both support him in his decision and be prepared for the long hours he will have to work. But being a doctor is the only job he has ever wanted and known, and he is also very good at it. His staying away is a shame to the patients he could save. Let him find his way back there, that's all I ask."

"Mrs. Sinclair, Denver has our full support in anything he chooses to do. I agree that he should be back in a hospital, but he is the one to make that choice and only he knows when he will be ready."

A truck drives around the bend in the road and I see my team turn up, ready for the busy day ahead.

"I think that's my cue to leave. Thank you for listening to me and I wish you luck. Don't hurt him, East; he is too good a man to be heartbroken again."

"I won't, I promise." I smile and she nods before turning back to her car. I watch her drive away. *Well, that was unexpected.* I stroll up to the guys and give them their final jobs for the week, knowing they are happy with the work they have done. Even more so when I let them know I've been contacted by another ranch wanting similar work done. They wander off to do the final work, giving me a free moment to call home.

"Hey, Den-baby, how're you doing?" I chuckle as he yawns down the phone.

"Sorry, honey. I'm beat today, some fuckers didn't want to leave the bar. I hope we didn't disturb you when we got in?" I hear the worry in his voice.

"No, it was fine. But I'm really ready to be disturbed tonight." I chuckle.

"Hell yeah, you'll be at the bar tonight though, right?" Denver has told me how much he's missed me with them in the evenings, but, by the time I've finished up here and been to see Ellie, I'm ready to drop.

"I will, babe, you gonna play a bit tonight?" Kes and I have been working on getting him to do a short set of his favorite songs.

"Yeah, I think I might. I think it could be fun, until I get booed off the stage, that is." He sighs. There's something distracting him and I can't work out what, but his head hasn't been with us.

"That's never gonna happen: you'll be stuck there all night if the crowd get their own way." I need to get back onto the reason I called him. "Anyway, Den, I had a visitor here this morning. Your mom came to see me." The line goes silent, "Denver? You still there?"

"Shit, East; I'm sorry, hon. What did she want? I've spoken to her and she seems fine with us now."

"She is, baby; she is thrilled with how much happier you are now. I think she just wanted to clear the air." I reassure him.

"Really? What did she say?" He doesn't seem his usual self today.

I fill him in on what had changed her mind. "She's just watching out for you, baby."

"I guess it's a good thing. I think I'm making the right decision for me, don't you? Has she made you doubt me, us?"

"No way, Denver, if it was up to me, you'd be moved in permanently. But, I'm being good and letting you set your pace."

"I know and I appreciate it, not that you've let me go back to my cabin. I probably will tomorrow, when Ellie comes for the night." Again, he seems to separate from us.

"Why would you want to do that? Ellie loves you, and your dog; I think she'd be disappointed if you weren't there."

"We can talk about it tonight, but I think it's a heavy load to drop on an eleven-year-old girl."

"Let her be the judge of that, Den." I look up at Dean and need to get my head back into work-mode. "I've gotta go; Dean's needing me. Are you sure you're okay, baby?"

"Yeah, I'm still tired, East. See you later." Denver sighs, ending the call, and I get back onto the job here, still thinking of his quietness today.

At three o'clock, Mr. Sinclair drives down to the site: it's time to give him the tour of the buildings. I'm ready for him to pick up any issues he wants me to change. His smile is wide as he steps up to me, his hand extended.

"I'm so happy to see this today, East. You have exceeded my expectations by what I can see already; I'm eager to look inside." He claps his hand on my shoulder.

"I'm surprised you haven't been down and peeked, Sir." This does genuinely surprise me. The walk-round is slow as he casts his critical eye over every inch of each building. Surprisingly, my clipboard is not filled with notes but only a few, small changes I can have my guys on immediately.

"Congratulations, East. I'm thrilled with your work; you and your team have gone above and beyond my expectations. Let me know when you've sorted the few issues and we can wrap this up."

"I will have them done by the time we leave today." I smile and wait as he climbs back into the cab. *Am I going to get away with him not mentioning Denver?*

He slams his door shut and rests his arm on the open window. "Oh, one more thing, East. He's happy again, and I think that is down to you and your partner. Thank you for that, make sure he stays that way." He winks and drives away.

Fuck! I tip my head up to the sky and take a deep breath. I seek out Dean and he soon has the guys on the small changes; I know they are all keen on getting their bonuses, too.

I merely want to get home and get some loving from my men.

□ □ □

DENVER

I know it's today, everything inside me screams to stay away from my iPad, to leave social media alone. I have, since I got back here: I have not updated my Facebook page or been anywhere near Twitter. I know those one-hundred-and-forty characters can hurt me as much, if not more, than a whole email or Facebook post. I don't know why Curtis, a friend from the hospital, told me; *did he want me to hurt again, or did he just think I would be best knowing? Fuck knows!* But the two men I have in my life now seem so much more genuine than Alec ever did: their vibrancy, their enthusiasm, and their affection for me is so much more real than anything I ever had with him. I know they've noticed I'm distracted; my head has been all over the place. East gave me a strange look when I didn't even react to his joke this morning.

But today is his wedding day, and I hate that I care! I hate that I am fighting myself not to look him up, to see the photographs. *Why do I want to let him hurt me all over again? I don't need him, I sure as fuck don't love him anymore!* But a little piece of me wants to see how happy he is. To see what his new husband looks like. A perverse desire to prove that I really don't care runs rife through my mind.

Kes has gone into work and East is up at the ranch all day. My mother's conversation with East and then a further phone call to me has settled that issue. For now, at least; who knows what will happen if I give in to East's constant, gentle persuasion to get me to move in. I'm sure a fair few tongues will start wagging, but I can live with that when the time is right. I know we will have to discuss the sleeping situation for tomorrow night, when Ellie comes to stay. I think I'm going to have a fight on my hand over that one, too.

About to crack and swipe open my tablet, my cellphone rings. It's a number I don't know but, hell, there aren't many people that call me now I'm here, so I answer it.

"Denver Sinclair." I answer the call.

"Dr. Sinclair?" A man's voice inquires.

"It is. Who am I speaking to?" I'm beginning to regret answering now, I think this could have something to do with Alec.

"Hello, my name is Dr. Woodruff. Carson Woodruff."

Fuck! One of the country's top trauma surgeons! I have studied all his techniques and listened to his lectures for as long I can remember. He is one of the reasons I chose to specialize in trauma surgery.

"Dr. Woodruff, I'm honored to speak to you." I fumble through my sentence like a naïve pre-med student.

"I hear you have left Cedar Greens, am I correct?" He questions me.

"You are. I had a personal reason for leaving." My mind whirs as I try and work out why he is calling me.

"Are you looking for a new hospital? Or has your personal reason taken you away from medicine?"

I wish he would simply tell me why he has phoned me today. "I have not given up on medicine, I just have taken a break. I will be looking for a position more local to where I am now, in the very near future."

"That's very interesting, Dr. Sinclair. Would you be at all interested in a discussion regarding a position in a new team in a new clinical facility I am setting up now?"

I'm at a total loss for words. I feel like a goldfish as I open, then shut, my mouth as I try to form a coherent answer.

"Oh my! Yes, Sir, I most certainly would." But my words dry up as I think about leaving Kes and East. "May I ask where, and what, you're starting?"

"You may," I detect a dry chuckle from him. "It is in Charlottestown, and will be the regional trauma unit for, I believe, the area you are now residing in."

"Then I would be very interested in discussing this further with you. Just tell me where and when and I will be there." I feel the excitement of working back in a trauma unit, and in surgery, bubbling to the surface.

"That is wonderful news, Dr. Sinclair. I have been following your career over the last five years and your talent is exemplary. I will have my secretary contact you with further details. I look forward to meeting you soon. Good afternoon."

"And I also; thank you for calling me." I listen to the silence as Woodruff ends the call. *Wow!* Charlottestown is an hour's drive from here, so totally doable. This is so cool, I can't wait to tell East and Kes.

I open my iPad to check my emails and do some research on the hospital in Charlottestown. As I swipe the screen, I decide. *Fuck it! I'm going to look at Alec and be happy, knowing I'm in a much better place, with much better men. Men I'm so happy with—way happier than I ever was with him.* When it opens, I type in his name, ignoring the shake in my hand, and there, in front of me, is a photograph of Alec with his new husband. I can't help myself from opening the picture. Alec looks happy, happier than I saw him with me; maybe this is the best thing for him. I know I'm happier without him, but it still hurts, like, really fucking hurts! He cheated on me for long enough to fall in love, to plan, and start a new life without me.

Shit! I feel the burn in my eyes as tears build. These aren't sad tears; they are angry, humiliated tears. I have only cried once and that was when I arrived home, the rest were bottled up inside me for months. But… *No! Fuck him! And fuck his new fucking life! Christ, I'm angry! I need to get out of here.*

I stumble to the bedroom and look at the smooth, made-up bed. A bed that has given me nothing but pleasure and joy, and now it looks so inviting I could simply climb under the covers and hide. As I walk towards it, I falter. *No! There's no way I'm letting him in my bed.* If I lie here thinking of him, it takes away from everything good that this bed represents.

Turning around, I open Kes' dresser and pull out a pair of running shorts and a vest. I know he won't mind; in fact, if I run and then go see him, he'll probably love the sight of me sweaty in his clothes. My heart lifts again as Kes floods my mind, his scent, the sounds he makes when we make love. *Shit! He's right: I do love him.* Then East's face flits through my mind and the image of him falling apart under my touch: *yes, I love him, too!*

Calling the dog, we head out of the house and follow the route I've been on with Kes and soon get into my stride and I let my mind wander. Alec and Michael come back to me but I feel calmer about them now. They are welcome to each other: they happily hooked up and then dated, knowing that one of them was supposedly in a committed relationship. *What's that they say? 'Once a cheater, always a cheater'. Poor Michael; he's going to have to keep a very close eye, and short leash on Alec.* The knowledge raises a smile to my face as I run through the town and out to the countryside.

The loop turns back on itself after thirty minutes and I'm ready to get back and showered. Feeling much better now, I think about Dr. Woodruff and his offer—not quite a firm offer of employment but it sounded pretty, damn close to me. I look at Missy and she's still happy jogging alongside me, so I take a left turn at the crossroads instead of going home and head down to the bar, knowing Kes will still be there.

Seeing Kes working through some paperwork at a table in the window, I tap on the glass, making his head shoot up. A smile crosses his face as he stands up. Flicking the lock on the door, he opens it for me. Missy trips in and heads for the water bowl Kes keeps for her by the bar.

"Well, hello there." His eyes run over my sweating body and sparkle as he catches mine. "You look good enough to eat." His mouth bumps mine in a sweet kiss that soon turns into something more as his mouth travels over my jaw and down my neck. "Fuck! I love the taste of you."

"I needed to clear my head, I hope you don't mind me raiding your dresser." I murmur into his ear as he nibbles the base of my neck.

"Not at all; they look good on you." Kes looks me up and down again, stripping me with his gaze. "They'd look better on my office floor, though, I think."

"Then you'd better lock up again and lead the way." I moan as he bites me.

But there's another knock on the door and we break apart. Kes curses when he sees it's the delivery from the fresh produce supplier.

"I'm going to have to take a raincheck on that, baby." He kisses me again and groans in frustration as he pulls away.

"I'd better go then. Got some news for you when we're all together, too." I peck his mouth one more time and call my dog. Then I remember my revelation and think there's two things to tell them tonight, a smile creeps over my face.

"Good news?" Kes asks as he unlocks the door again. "You're smiling, so it's got to be good news."

I smile as the delivery guy looks between the two of us, still standing close enough to be touching. He blushes and looks at his clipboard.

"Ho, come in, Josh; Denver was just leaving." Kes smiles warmly at the young man.

"Er, yeah, hi. I saw you play last week, you were really good." His blush deepens.

"Thanks, Josh. I hadn't played in a very long time. I was very nervous." I try to ease his embarrassment. "I'll see you at home later, Kes."

Kes nods and smiles ruefully as we have been cockblocked.

I jog back to the house and grab the mail as I walk up the driveway. Dumping it on the dresser, I head straight for the shower. My cellphone buzzes as I drop it on the bed and when I read the message a laugh bursts out of me.

Keep your hand away
from your cock.
That load is mine!!

My heart thumps hard in my chest. *Yep, this is love!*

I have a long, hot shower and keep my hands off my dick but my mind is full of the things I want to do to him and East tonight. After snatching another pair of shorts from Kes, I walk out and am surprised to see a letter addressed to me in with the pile I'd dumped on the table. Picking it up, I wander off to make a sandwich, pondering why I've got something sent here. Then I remember our blood tests; this day is getting better and better. I know I'm clear but I still wanted that piece of paper. I go out into the garden with my results and my iPad, ready to start my research. Checking my emails again, I get excited when I see one from Charlottestown Hospital. Reading it through, I grab my phone and call the number for Rhys Parker, secretary to Carson Woodruff.

I expect to hear a male voice but it's a bright and breezy female voice that answers. After introducing myself, I hold back my laugh as she gets excited.

"Oh, Dr. Sinclair; thank you for calling so quickly. We are very excited to have you come along and see what Dr. Woodruff has planned for here."

We chat comfortably while we work out when we can meet and settle on Tuesday next week; I won't have worked the Monday night and am not on that evening either. By the time we end the conversation, I get the feeling the only way I won't be working there is if I choose not to take it. And hell, there's no chance of that; this is even better than Cedar Greens. Hopefully, the salary will support it too. Even though I won't be Chief of Surgery, I think the facility is offering a better service to a wider area. And if no expense is being spared on the redevelopment of the department, salaries will have been negotiated, especially if they want me!

Lying on the lounger in the late afternoon sun, a shadow falls over me and I see my men smiling down at me.

"It's alright for some, lazing the afternoon away in the sunshine while his men are out working hard all day." East stands with his arms crossed over his broad chest.

"I'll bet he hasn't thought of what he's going to feed us." Kes answers

"Trust me, Kes, I've been thinking of what I'm feeding you all afternoon." I bite on my bottom lip and watch his smile broaden.

"Have I missed something, *again?*" East grumbles.

"Nope, but Kes had plans for my hot, sweaty body this afternoon but we were interrupted before we could get anywhere." I laugh as I watch Kes palm his dick through his jeans.

"Who blocked you?" East laughs and takes over rubbing Kes' bulge.

"Josh!" Kes huffs as he nudges his hips forward. "Poor lad, he didn't know where to look. He really needs to accept his sexuality." He laughs.

I stand and brush my hand over East's zipper. "Did you see your mail?" I glance at my printed results and smile, they nod and grin. "Clear?"

"Clear" They say together.

"Me too." I grin. "Maybe we should be discussing this somewhere more private." I murmur as I lean into them.

"We should." Kes kisses East's neck as I slide my tongue over the seam of his lips. East parts his mouth, allowing me to slip inside the wet heat and I stroke my tongue over the sweetness of his. But Kes drops to his knees before we move and has my shorts undone and down to my ankles before I realize what he's doing, then he's attacking the button and sliding the zipper down on East's jeans.

With a dick in each of his hands, he draws us to his mouth. As his tongue flicks between our touching crowns, I moan and buck into his fist. The heat of his mouth as he engulfs me has me crying out; East covers my mouth with his and swallows my cries. Kes' mouth switches and he takes East deep in his throat and pumps my length hard, his grip tight as we fight for control. But when he sucks both of us into the hot, wet cavern of his mouth, we all groan loudly. Feeling him relax his jaw, he gives us a chance to pump in and out of him in turn.

I cry loudly as, on a deep plunge in, I feel him swallow and I come. East holds back, letting Kes take my load. I watch as it dribbles out of the side of his mouth and I scoop it up on my thumb. East clasps my wrist and sucks my thumb into his mouth. I pull back, shattered, and collapse on the lounger as East takes his turn but I want in and I kneel next to Kes, letting East swap between us. It's Kes who gets East's cum as he groans loudly, East's fingers lacing through our hair to tug tightly as he moans.

"Fuck!" We call and then our exclamations turn to laughter as we look at the wrecks of us; Kes' mouth is red and swollen but his smile is euphoric.

We stumble inside and head for the shower, showing Kes our appreciation.

"So, what did you have to tell us?" Kes asks as we get dressed, ready for work.

We share tender touches as we pass by each other. East slides his hand down my back as I bend down to pull some clean underwear out of my bag.

"You've got something to tell?" He frowns as I pull more clothes from my bag. "Any chance it could be you're tired of pulling your clothes out of a bag and are gonna move in?" He drops a kiss on my shoulder as he walks past.

"Ah, well, no. It's not that. There's two things, actually. I tug my polo shirt over my head but catch their concerned glances. "It's okay, I promise. The first is easy: I found out the other day that Alec's wedding is today."

"Is this why you've been withdrawn? Shit, Denver; why didn't you tell us? We would have helped you through this." Kes runs his hand down my arm.

"I didn't want to know; someone from the hospital, where I used to work, thought it would be kind to tell me. I have avoided all social media, I don't want to see him with someone else. Before you start, yes, I'm with you and I'm committed to us, but today has fucking hurt." I take a deep breath and reach out my hands to hold theirs. "But, when I saw it, I realized I didn't care; they are welcome to each other. It's not me who's going to be looking over my shoulder, or wondering why he hasn't called or is home late. All the things *I* ignored that now seem so obvious, are someone else's problem. Do I want him to be happy? Maybe, but I'm not going to think about him anymore. I'm sorry if I haven't been open with you, I just needed to get my head around it all before I told you."

"Den, as long as you are happy then we are, too. But, babe; don't bottle shit up anymore, share it with us, we might be able to help you." East leans in and kisses me softly.

"Okay, I'll try. I'm kind of used to keeping things to myself but, for you, I'll try." I give a smile. "Are we ready to go?"

"We are, come on. Don't forget your guitar." Kes calls to me smiling.

We climb into my truck and I start the engine. The drive is quiet, I think I gave them a shock but I feel better for sharing. Maybe they are right, and I need to stop keeping everything inside me.

As I pull up in the space reserved for Kes, he looks at me and frowns.

"What?"

"You said two things. You had two things to tell us, your only told us one." He stares at me.

"Oh, yeah. I've got an interview next week for a trauma surgeon position." I step out of the truck and look at their shocked faces. "You coming to work, or not?" I smirk and strut up to the door.

I hear the passenger doors slam and wait for them.

Chapter
Twelve

KES

I crowd Denver; the heat of his body radiating through me. Leaning down, I whisper in his ear. "I think that was slightly more important than your loser ex-boyfriend's doomed marriage, don't you?"

East pushes the door open and we tumble inside. The Friday night crowd has started to fill the bar already; it looks like we're in for a busy night. I smile at Shelley behind the bar as we walk through to the office, she waves a greeting but carries on serving.

East shuts the door behind us and folds his arms over his chest. With his brow cocked, he smirks. "Time to start talking, baby."

We listen as Denver tells us about the phone call from a doctor he has followed and admired for years and I watch as he comes alive. He is so enthusiastic and animated, I realize we have only had the watered-down version of him. Maybe the freedom he has felt from the closure with Alec has lightened him, too, but this is a joy to see.

"I've Googled the hospital and all the facilities it is offering the area with this new department. Taking the main trauma unit away from Masterton General is a huge deal; it will make it one of the five major units in the country. It's something I would regret for the rest of my life if I didn't take it." Denver's eyes sparkle with excitement.

"Why wouldn't you take it?" I ask, curious he would consider not accepting.

"I'm not sure. I thought, maybe, you wouldn't be thrilled with the thought of me working over there." He frowns.

"Hang on!" East interrupts. I know what he's going to say and I put my hand up to stop him but he brushes it aside. "You're not planning on moving over there, are you?"

"What? No! Of course not. I just will be back on shifts again. I'm not going to have to be as full-on as I was before, because I won't be in charge. Time runs away though; a major accident or disaster can have us on lock down and I'd be there for the duration." Denver scrubs his hands through his hair, making it scruffier than normal.

"Are you asking for our permission, Denver?" I query.

"No, not really. If they offer it to me, I will be taking it. I would like your support. It will be hard for me to begin with; it feels like I've been away forever." Suddenly he looks anxious, nervously chewing his bottom lip.

"Denver, you not only have my support, you have my admiration. I'm sure East feels the same." I look at him and he smiles, nodding his head. "You should be proud to be sought out like this."

I watch the tension fall from his body and he sighs. "Thank you."

"Right, no more fucking about. If you're going on shifts, you're moving your shit to our place. I'm not having you away from me any longer." East growls and, for the first time, Denver laughs.

"Let me get it first, East, then we can discuss it again." He drops a kiss on East's lips and walks out the door.

"What do you reckon?" East asks me.

"I reckon I've just lost my bartender." I smile then copy Denver and kiss East before walking out to the bar and an evening of work.

Denver is laughing with Shelley when I take my place behind the bar and they turn to look at me still smiling. But Denver's freezes on his face when he sees me. Shelley touches his arm and comes toward me.

"Stop looking at me like that: he's all yours and you know it." She scowls but is holding back a smile.

"I don't know what you're talking about." I mutter, going red.

"Yes, you do. You wanted to rip my arm off for touching him." Shelley laughs, "I don't think I've got the right equipment for him, where as you two have everything he wants."

"I'm sorry, Shelley, I didn't mean to." I bend down and kiss her soft smooth cheek. "Go on go home; you've been here long enough."

"Nope, I'm meeting the girls here tonight: we want to see you man sing and watch you swoon at his feet." Shelley puts her hand up and fakes a faint.

"Have I done something wrong?" Denver mumbles as I walk up to him, his eyes dropping down so as not to look at me.

"Baby, it's me: I was being a dick. I'm sorry." I lift his chin with my finger and drop a kiss on his parted lips. "I got a bit green-eyed at Shelley touching you."

This cracks him up. "You're kidding me?" He shakes his head. "You share me with your long-term boyfriend but get jealous when a girl touches my arm?" He carries on chuckling and turns to the front to take an order from a young girl. I watch as he asks for ID, she looks young but she takes it in good humor and hands it over, smiling shyly at him and he gives her a wink.

Green-eyed again, I walk over and wrap my arm around his waist, pulling him close.

"Typical, the gorgeous ones are always taken." She laughs and pays for her drink.

"Do you just want to piss in a circle around me, Kes? Or, maybe, make a T shirt for me to wear?" Denver shakes his head and walks to the cash register.

East joins us and shakes his head. "You weren't this bad when you weren't able to touch him. Chill Kes, he's not going anywhere."

But my gut churns. *He's not going anywhere yet, but what about when he gets back with his peers and all the cute doctors and nurses? Will he still want me, us, then? I'm not sure.* I fucking hope so, because it will hurt way too much to lose him. *I need to stop thinking like this, he says he's in and I have no reason not to believe him. I wish he loved us the way we love him.*

"I know, I know." I smile and grab him a beer but my gut still heaves. I do what I have to do and get my head in the game and get down to work. This is my bar, I dreamed of this for years and now I have it; thanks to a lot of hard work not only from me, but from East as well. I wouldn't have this place without him. I love him, not more than, but as much as: I love him and I love Denver. *Why am I the only one to acknowledge how much they mean to me? East says the words and I know he thinks them but is he in it as much as me?*

I wander around the room, talking to the regulars and making friends with the new faces; I'm good at this. *This is mine, so why am I suddenly so full of self-doubt?*

Suddenly, the room goes quiet and I scan around to glimpse Denver taking his seat on the stool in the corner of the room. My heart skips as he seems so humble when he looks over the people who have stilled.

"Hi, um… I seriously don't know what the hell I'm doing here, but my crazy man East has persuaded me to sit here for a couple of songs. Please, don't boo me but if you start talking louder than I can sing then I'll stop, I promise." Denver observes the faces of the crowded room as they drink in his every word. I watch as he blushes and drops his head.

"Okay, here goes nothing."

As I hear him strum the strings of his guitar, it's like everyone in the bar holds their breath. When the chords of Hozier's *Cherry Wine* come through the mic, I stop breathing in anticipation for him to start singing. I look over at East and I see his hand over his heart as he waits. He catches my eye and we make our way to, not the front, but close enough to watch the man we love become someone else, someone who, with every word, becomes stronger and more dominant. He's holding these people, strangers to him, in the palm of his hand. *How has he gone without this in his life before?* The thought of ever meeting his ex flashes through me; I would take him down.

He finishes his song and there is a moment of quiet before the applause starts, his shy smile plays across his face as he accepts the acknowledgement quietly. Then there is a shout from a woman somewhere in the throng.

"Kiss Me!" Laughter floods the room. "I mean, *Kiss Me*, by Ed Sheeran."

There are more chuckles but my eyes return to Denver as he nods and starts. I watch as his eyes search the room this time, he gazes at me and East as we stand against the wall. East has his arm around my waist but his other hand still rests over his heart.

The words Denver sings are aimed straight at my heart and I know that this unknown woman has unleashed something inside the three of us that I never expected. *Why have we got so many hours still to go?*

Denver moves seamlessly into another cover and I wonder how much of this is what he may have bottled up inside him as Imagine Dragons' *Smoke and Mirrors* comes across the sound system. *How can he make it sound so heartbreaking as an acoustic version*, words I've sung along to through the iPod but never really listened to until now? *Can he believe we are simply that, smoke and mirrors?* Neither East or myself are prepared to let him start another song but he beats us to it and fluidly morphs into another. It's a song I've heard before, the lyrics are so familiar then it hits me: Half Moon Run's *Need It.* I know I should listen to him sing amazingly, stunningly enough to make my heart hurt, but I'm not sure I can bear anymore.

It's time to stop this now. As soon as the last bars end, Denver looks across and I see every word he sang has been for us. We wait, quietly, impatiently, for the bar to cease the applause and calls for more and my heart melts as Denver suddenly becomes himself again and blushes and shakes his head.

"Okay, thanks for not laughing at me, but I need to get back to work now; I'm sure you're all thirsty." He smiles and I see the hearts of my patrons break as he steps away from the made-up stage, the crowd parts as he walks modestly to the bar.

Fuck! How much longer do we have to be here? I look at East and he rolls his eyes then readjusts his pants; damn, I'm with him there. *My dick is so hard!*

We make our way to him as he is stopped by so many of the people here who want to talk with him. Shelley hugs and whispers something in his ear and he laughs and nods before moving on.

By the time East and I are back behind the bar, Denver is already serving someone. I walk up to him and wait for him to finish then pull him into my arms.

"You are fucking incredible." I murmur softly in his ear, relishing the shiver that runs through him. Dropping a kiss on his temple, I get to work.

East drags Denver up close and kisses his mouth, a hard kiss that is intense but quick. "Later, Denver. Just you wait."

Four hours later, I close the door and lean back against it as I look around the large room. It's going to take a while to clear this up but by the rate East and Denver are working, I think they want it done quickly.

Denver looks at me from behind the pool table. "Hey! Get busy, Kes; we've got places to be."

I push away from the door and finish cashing up the registers; takings are up. I'm going to have to find a way of getting Denver to do a regular spot here. Is his work really going to stop us from seeing so much of each other?

"Ready?" East calls out and I nod. Denver stands behind East and has his arms around his waist, his chin resting on East's shoulder: the image is so perfect, my heart stutters.

"Yep, let's go."

□ □ □

EAST

Looking down as Denver slides into me, my eyelids flutter at the sensation of pleasure undulating through my body. Denver leans over my chest and kisses me, his length filling me completely. Bare for the first time, I feel every ripple, every pulse and throb through his engorged veins as he fills me

"You need to move, baby." My voice rasps as my need for more consumes me. Kes leans over me and kisses me too.

"You look beautiful together." He sighs and strokes my chest.

Groaning, Denver pulls back leisurely, the tendons in his neck stand proud as he controls himself. The punch of his hips has him filling me again. On and on, the pull and push inside me takes me higher and higher.

"I'm not going to last, baby. Fuck, I need to come." I plead as Denver keeps up the steady pace. Kes reaches down and grasps my painfully hard dick, his grasp is firm as he matches his strokes to

Denver's. When he kisses Denver, my balls contract and draw inside my body, signaling Denver to pick up his speed and he grips my spread legs. Faster now he punches his hips, forcing his dick deep inside me. I watch as his face contorts into something beautiful as he gets ready to come.

"Fuck! Come, East; come for me, sweetheart." He pants and I watch sweat slick down his taut chest as the fire builds in my body.

Kes kisses me again as I arch my back and come. I feel the splatter of my cum but the sensation is overwhelmed by Denver thickening as he fires inside me, the heat of his release so intense without the barrier between us. I feel every surge as he floods me, his tremors ratchet through me, sending another burst from my body.

I collapse into the mattress as Denver leans over me, his breathing labored as he comes down from his high.

Soft kisses cover my face and neck from both Denver and Kes, then the sweet drag as Denver pulls out of my body. Falling to the side, I see him struggle to control himself. His arm moves to cover his face but I pull it away and clutch his hand in mine, centering him back with us.

Kes moves to sandwich Denver between us. "You have no idea how beautiful you looked. I love you both. You have my heart." He speaks quietly but emotion colors his words.

"I love you, too." I reply before propping myself up and kiss Denver, then I lean further to do the same to Kes.

Denver looks at us, his smile sweet and shy. "I love you, I can't explain how much I love you."

"Fuck!" Kes hisses softly, then he's over Denver, his body caging him beneath him. "Really?" Den nods. "Thank you."

Denver pushes Kes away so he can shuffle back until his back rests against the headboard. His eyes closed, I see him struggling with his emotions. And, when he slowly opens them, they glitter with unshed tears. I push myself up so my hand can trace the line of his jaw and he turns his head to kiss my palm.

"I never thought my life was lacking: I had a job I loved, that I still love. I had friends and I had a man who was supposed to love me; I was happy. Then it all fell to pieces. My job suddenly felt strained when the people I thought were my friends kept a secret from me. When Alec dumped me, I just had to get away. Every thought was clouded by mistrust, my life turned sour in the space of ten, maybe fifteen minutes, so I did the best thing for me and ran away. I yearned to be back in a place that was safe for me. Where I didn't expect to meet, or know anyone anymore, except my family. Back to a place that was my home, that I had no bad memories of. High school was too far back to make me reminisce of highs or lows, here was where I needed to be, it called me home. There was nothing here to scramble my thoughts while I decided what to do and where to go with my life." Denver chuckles and looks down with a slight shake of his head. "Until you. Until you got under my skin, I watched how you are with each other. It made me realize that these things had either stopped or had never really been there for me and Alec.

"Then, when you kissed me… shit, the feelings that stirred in me. I didn't know what to do with them. I didn't trust myself to make a decision and take a chance; I didn't believe that a third person in a relationship was a good idea. Not in one as solid as yours. But you are demons, sorcerers: you tempted and seduced me into taking a chance."

"Hey! There wasn't a gun to your head." I joke and kiss him.

"No, there wasn't, but I still fought it. I wanted you, I needed you, both of you. I felt complete around you, so I stayed even though I fought with myself, and now I can't go back. My heart is clenched tight in your fists and I don't want to be without you. I *can't* be without you: for as long as you will have me, I am yours."

"And you love us, so when are you moving in?" I squeeze his hip, making him squirm.

"I think you might need to persuade me a bit more, I'm not sure I should yet." His eyes sparkle again, but this time with mischief.

"I can think of lots of ways to persuade you, what do you think, Kes? Got anything to nudge him to make the right decision?" I slide my hand down the hard muscles on Denver's chest and abs, then follow the path with my tongue.

"I think I might need a lot tempting." Denver sighs and shivers at my ministrations. It's my turn to take him; as Kes sucks Denver's cock, I show him exactly how much I want him here with us, forever.

"Fuck!" Denver groans as he comes in Kes' mouth and I come hard inside him.

Waking up on Saturday is always the best thing for me: no work and the fun of my daughter for the weekend. Today beats all other Saturdays hands down as Denver's body is pressed up against mine, his head on my chest and his arm over my stomach. Kes is crushed up to his back, still sleeping. Denver must feel me shift and he tips his head up, blinking sleep-filled, unfocused eyes.

"Morning, baby." I whisper and duck down to kiss his mouth.

"Hi." He murmurs when I lift my mouth from his.

"You sleep well?" I ask as my hand trails his arm.

"I did; I could get used to this." He smiles and squirms against me.

"Well, if you lived here, you would get this every day." I joke and laugh quietly as he rolls his eyes.

"Stop pressuring him, East." Kes grumbles as he wakes up.

Denver rests his head onto my chest again and chuckles, then twist around to look at Kes. "Don't worry about it, Kes, honey. I'll do you a deal: if I get the job in Charlottestown, I'll move in. Is that okay with you, East?"

"Hell fucking yeah! That's okay with me." I sit up and pull him to me. "Fuck! I can't wait." I kiss him then spring out of bed. "Okay, I'm going to shower; who's coming with me?" I grab my junk and thrust my hips forward, they laugh but get out of bed.

"Race ya!" Kes barks out and darts past me.

After mutual blow jobs and orgasms, we make breakfast.

"What are we doing with Ellie today?" Kes hands me a cup of coffee. Denver stills as he waits for me to answer, I know he doesn't think he should be here.

"I thought, maybe, we could take a walk with Missy then grab some lunch out. She wants a movie night, too." I look at Denver, gauging his reaction.

"I need to be at home today, East. You can take Missy, by all means, but I need to speak to my folks and get some research done, make sure I'm up-to-date with new medical publications, as much as I can before I go to meet Woodruff." He smiles and I see he's determined to stay away today, but I keep my gaze on him and shake my head.

"I don't want to do that, Denver. I want you to be with us." I know I'm being pushy but I want him here.

"I told you yesterday that I wouldn't be here. I'm sorry, East."

"Am I missing something here?" Kes interrupts. "What's going on?"

Denver's eyes break away from mine to look at Kes. "It's nothing, I just think it's too much for Ellie to have to deal with, and now, with the interview on Tuesday, I really need to prep. I'm sorry, East, but I need to do this."

"Ellie thinks you're great. She'll be disappointed if you aren't with us." I grumble, knowing I'm being petulant. "I've been so busy at your folks' place that I haven't spent much time with you; Kes gets to spend his days with you, I feel like I'm left out."

"Oh, East, I'm sorry." Denver sighs and reaches for me. "How about I come back this afternoon, after you've had some time with her. I do need to do some reading up today."

"I'm so desperate for us all to be together the way we should be, I just want you with me, with us." Leaning forward, I rest my forehead against his as my hands tangle in his hair, "I love you, Denver, and I want to share that with Ellie."

"I love you, too, but baby steps, East; I don't want to rush this and fuck it up."

"That won't happen, I promise." I whisper against his lips. I feel Kes behind me as he runs his hand down my spine, planting a kiss on the back of my neck.

Then we are kissing, our mouths pressed together. Soon, three tongues tangle, eliciting a moan from deep in my chest, then Denver pulls away.

"I need to go, I'll call you later. Have a fun day." He kisses us individually and walks out of the kitchen and back down the bedroom.

Kes stands with his arm around my waist and his head resting on my shoulder; I know he isn't happy about this either, but he is better at keeping his emotions under control. It's a few minutes before Denver walks out again, his bag slung over his shoulder. Missy trots up beside him and sits by his heel.

"I'll call later." Denver smiles but his eyes are tight as if he finds it difficult to leave.

"Okay, baby." Kes replies, I can only nod.

"I hate this." I mutter as the door closes behind Denver.

"We have to let him do this his way. He loves us, East, of that I'm sure. So, c'mon; let's get your girl and have fun.

□ □ □

DENVER

"So, what do you think? Is this the sort of environment you can see yourself in?" Dr. Woodruff has spent the last three hours, well... I think the words are 'courting me'. The whole set-up is amazing; the Medevac is based here, making it *the* trauma center in the area. The operating theaters are state-of-the-art, out of this world and the ER is well set out and spacious; the promise of staff-to-patient ratio is higher than I've worked with before. The whole place has me buzzing with excitement but I'm not showing all of my hand yet: we need to discuss position and salary.

"I think you have organized something incredibly special, I like what I see very much." I smile genuinely.

"Then, maybe, we can continue this conversation in my office. Rhys will be there also." I don't know why he mentioned her, *is he concerned about being alone with me?*

"Will she?" My eyebrows rise, questioning him.

"Yes, she has the package I've put together for you. If you are interested, of course."

"Did you doubt me?" I ask, curious to hear what he thought.

"No. No I didn't doubt you; you are one of the best surgeons in our field. I had reservations, in case you are still on your sabbatical, still having personal issues to deal with. I want you here, Denver; but I want you here one hundred percent. If you can't offer me that, I think I would have to pass you by." His candid reply surprises me but I admire his open, direct approach.

"My personal issue, as you call it, is over. I am actually happier now than I have been in years and I think working here could be the icing on the cake for me. I'm happy to talk terms with you, but I may drive a hard bargain." I chuckle as he laughs openly with me.

"Come along then, Dr. Sinclair." He extends his arm and we head towards his office.

Another hour later and I make it back to my car, my head reeling at the position and the salary I have been offered and accepted. My first thought is to tell Kes and East: I want to call them as soon as I am in my truck and heading out of the hospital grounds. I know that East will still be working—and I don't want to interrupt him—and Kes will be busy at the bar. He doesn't work an evening shift today but he will be there until at least five this evening.

I haven't stayed with them since Friday night. When I left on Saturday morning, I expected to be back that night after my shift at the bar but I decided to come back to my cabin. I needed a clear mind, I wanted to be prepared for this meeting today. Of course, I hadn't factored in my mother's enthusiasm and desire to talk over every aspect. At least it stopped her from questioning my relationship developments. I press the call button on my truck's steering wheel and call her. I don't plan to be back there tonight: I have plans to celebrate with my men, plans I have been dreaming up for days now.

"Hey, Mom, you okay to keep my dog tonight? I don't think I'll be home." I keep my humor in check, I know she will be desperate to know how I got on, but my smile is huge.

"Of course, Denver, dear. She's happy here with us." She pauses, I can tell she is holding her breath. "Oh, for goodness sake, Denver: stop being mean and tell me. How did you get on?"

"Okay, okay. It's awesome, it's like the job was made for me. They offered me a position and I accepted it, I start next week." I breathe out a deep sigh of relief at telling someone.

"Oh, Denver, honey. How wonderful for you, we will have to have a celebration dinner. Leave it to me, we can organize something for the weekend." Then she goes quiet for a few seconds, I wait for her to speak again. "Have you told Kes and East yet?" I know there is still some confusion as to how and why I have gotten into this relationship but she has done well to keep it inside.

"No, not yet. So, don't you go and say anything to East if you see him there. This is my news to share, Mom."

"Of course not, dear. I don't think he's here today, I haven't seen him. Well, I'd better let you go and get back to your driving. I'll see you tomorrow, and congratulations, Denver; you deserve this." Her voice softens as she says goodbye.

It's a night off for all of us, so, as I drive back into the town, I stop and pick up a bottle of champagne and some steaks: I want to celebrate with Kes and East tonight. We have all night to adore each other's bodies. I want to share my excitement at my new position and the possibility of moving in with them, if they still want me. The journey to Charlottestown will be considerably quicker from this side of town than the ranch, but I know that's not reason enough by itself but, add it to the two amazing men I will be sharing a bed with, it's a win-win for me. I start on straight day shifts to get used to the position and the environment, but I know from experience how those days can drag into night times; we can sort that as and when they happen.

By the time I pull up on the drive, the sun is setting and there is a mauve-colored sky, the shadows have grown longer but the air is still warm. I know it's only going to get hotter as the year progresses, before the winter snow covers the peaks and encourages the skiers to the area. But, for now, this is my favorite time of year. Both of the other vehicles are already parked parallel to each other and I slot next to East's, on the furthest side.

Suddenly, my stomach knots and I feel nervous to join them; has my absence allowed them time to reconnect without a third? I sit here, running over scenarios in my head. Most of them lead to me being alone again, but then I stop and decide I have to remind them of what they have. I clamber down from the cab and grab my overnight bag and groceries from behind the passenger seat, then, clicking the button on the fob, I lock the doors. As I reach the front door, I don't know if I should ring the doorbell or simply try the door and enter. Eventually, I try the handle of the door and it opens easily on itself and I step into the cool hallway. Dropping my bag by the door, I make my way through the house, I love the sprawling expanse as East has accommodated his growing daughter's needs.

I walk into the kitchen, the hub of the house, and notice the doors to the garden are open. I hear muted voices from the decked area. Stepping closer, I haven't made myself known yet and Kes and East are in deep conversation as I approach the doors.

"He will come back, East; we don't know how long this meeting is going to take, but Denver is not going to leave us, he loves us." Kes tries to soothe East but I discern the tension in it.

"He left us quickly enough on Saturday. Ellie was upset and I couldn't even guarantee her he'd be back this week. I know she was too young to remember, but her mother walked away and left her in a crib with two bottles of milk; she has issues with being left by people."

"I know you do, too, baby. But I'm not going anywhere and I promise you: Denver will come home." Kes leans over the side of his lounger to kiss East and the sight causes a tightening in my chest.

"I just worry that it was too good to be true. Did we give too much of ourselves, too early? Are we going to be good enough for him when he's back amongst all his peers? Fuck! Kes, what do we do? Maybe we should call him?" East pulls his phone out and looks at it nervously. "I'm afraid to, he may tell me he won't be coming back."

I shift in the doorway and Kes looks up, a slow, lazy smile spreading on his handsome features and his eyes flash like diamonds. Lifting my finger to my lips to keep him quiet, he straightens his face. East still has his eyes on his phone, allowing me to step unnoticed behind his chair. I slide my hands over his shoulders and down to his chest then lean over the back of the chair. Startled, his head shoots up, allowing me to kiss him.

"Hey, lover, how're you doing?" I murmur in his ear as he twists around.

"Oh, my god, Denver! Shit, I've missed you." East stands up and pulls me against him. I feel tremors running through his body as he calms his emotions. "Why haven't you called? Shit, I don't know whether to kiss you or tan your hide!"

"I'd rather you kissed me." I chuckle and tug him into me.

Kes step up to me, wraps his arms around me and nuzzles into my neck, his hot breath on my skin. East reaches up and cups my face and kisses me softly then pulls back.

"You scared the crap out of me, Denver. Don't pull that shit again." His hands fist the lapels of my suit and he tugs me against his chest. This time the kiss is brutal, his mouth heavy on my own as he consumes me, *fuck, this is a good kiss.*

As we run out of oxygen, East pulls away, his mouth swollen and glistening: he has never looked hotter to me. Kes twists me around in his arms and rests his forehead against mine as he hauls a huge breath into his lungs, I see the emotion sketched on his rugged face.

"Thank you, baby. Thank you for coming home." His voice is ragged but his kiss is sweet and tender.

Pulling away from them but keep holding their hands, I look at them and sense a mixture of relief and confusion.

"Why didn't you think I was coming back? I said I would be, after the interview." I look between them.

"Because you didn't even get in touch; you let Ellie down on Saturday and then you go silent on us. What did you expect us to think?" East is angry and turns away, pacing a few steps from us.

"Hey! Hang on, how have I let Ellie down? I only met her the week before. Don't transfer your own disappointment on her to guilt me. That's not fair on her, or me." Unexpectedly hot, I shrug out of my jacket and throw it over the back of a chair, looking at Kes to see if he feels like this, too. "I needed to get this right: I wanted this job so damn much. I had to prepare myself to interview with probably the best trauma surgeon this country has. I had to remind myself of my own skills, I had to brush up on the latest news before I could go. I'm damn good at my job and I wasn't going to lose this position because I was too busy fucking to do my research. I wanted to make you proud of me, for being strong enough to get back to work. I wanted you to realize I was doing this because of the faith and the love you have given me. I just wanted to make you proud."

My hands are on my hips as I gaze between the two of them, my chest heaving as I try and rein in my anger and disappointment. East has the decency to blush and look away, Kes looks heartbroken. I want to reach out to them but this is not my fault.

East runs his hands through his hair as he sinks onto the lounger and I see him struggling to get himself back together, Kes has his arms wrapped around himself as if trying to hold himself together. I realize I need to get this back to the sweet reunion it should be. I wait for East to turn back to face me then, with a minute grin, I look at them.

"Aren't you even going to ask me how I got on?" I smirk.

"How did it go, baby?" Kes asks softly and reaches for my hand. East looks at me expectantly, hopefully.

"I got it! I start in a week." I reply, holding my head high.

"For the fucking win!! Denver, baby, you are a star!" East jumps up then grabs me around the waist and lifts me off the ground. "I knew you'd do it."

As he lowers me again, he looks into my eyes, "I'm sorry, Den, I'm really fucking sorry."

Kes wraps his arm around my neck and pulls me in before kissing me. "You're amazing, you know that, right?"

I nod, suddenly feeling very emotional. They envelope me in their arms and we stand together, holding on tight.

"I think we need to go out and celebrate, don't you?" Kes claps his hands together as we nod. "Let's go and get waited on for a change: dinner and dancing sound good to you?"

"Can't we just go to bed? We can celebrate there, too." East interjects.

"I need to get out of this suit and into the shower." I pull at the shirt that is beginning to cling to my back.

"Now you're talking. Lead the way, baby." East laughs and squeezes my butt as I walk past him.

□ □ □

EAST

Clearing Denver's belongings from his cabin is giving me the best feeling in the world, this is as good as Kes agreeing to move in with me. It took me the rest of the week, constantly nagging and needling at him, but I got my own way. And it's happening today. Kes was arguing with him in the bedroom about the best way to pack up his books, but it's gone quiet and that means someone has shut the other one up.

I lean against the door frame and watch my men kissing. It looks like Denver's in charge, so I guess it was his way to shut Kes up. It looks like it could be going on for a long time, which usually leads to much more than kissing. I cough and they break apart.

"Is this really the best way to pack? Hell, just dump it all in a box and let's get outta here: you can finish that later, when we're home."

"Kes is being a pain. I told him to do just that, but he's too damn fussy." Denver grumbles and runs his hands through his messy hair.

"Kes, do as you're told and let's shift, or you'll be late for work."

"Fine, but if anything breaks it's your fault." Kes moans.

"Oh, honey, we'll make it up to you." Denver pecks his mouth again, then carries on dumping the contents from the top of his dresser in the box.

"I think we're done." Denver smiles thirty minutes later as he surveys the cabin.

"Then let's go!" I carry the last of the boxes out and drop them in the back of Denver's truck. When I turn back, they're at it again. "Hey! C'mon, guys!"

They laugh and saunter up to me, both smirking.

"You are in for it when we get back!" I groan but they laugh and climb in the cab of the truck.

As we drive past the bar, there's a young guy looking at the ad in the window. His hands scrub through his hair then he knocks on the door.

"Stop, Den." Kes requests.

Denver pulls into Kes' designated space and Kes gets out. The windows are down, so I can hear what's being said.

"Hey, you okay?" Kes asks the guy.

"Um, er... yeah, I guess. I was just looking for the owner." The guy has a deep voice but it sounds sad.

"Hi, I'm Kes, The Last Drop Inn is mine, I'm the owner. What can I do for you?" Kes smiles then turns and looks over his shoulder at us. "I was just driving past and saw you, are you interested in the position here?"

"Yeah, I am. I've done bar work before." He stands taller now and I notice he is a good-looking man, tall and slim, but looks a bit down on his luck.

"Okay, are you local? I'm don't sure I've seen you around." Kes sounds kind but the young guy flinches.

"No, I've just moved here. I'm Mal... I mean my name is Carter."

"Okay, Carter. We open at twelve but I won't be here till three, can you come back then?"

"Yeah, sure. Thanks, Kes. I'll see you then." He turns away and wanders down the street.

Kes gets back in the cab and frowns. "He looks like he might need some help here, what did you guys think?"

"I agree, that isn't a happy, young man. You gonna help him?" I ask and, knowing Kes, he will have him under his wing in no time.

"I guess, I mean I have lost my favorite bartender." He winks at Denver.

"Oh yeah, you've so lost me. C'mon, let's go home and I'll let you find me again." Denver grins and bites his lip.

Oh, it's game on! I reach across and skim my knuckles down Denver's zipper, feeling the nudge as his hips reflex against my touch. Turning my hand over, I cup his junk in my palm and give a gentle squeeze, smiling when I feel him thicken. I watch him swallow hard and his speed picks up, in a hurry to get us home.

"Somewhere you want to be, Den?" I murmur, my hand still on his package.

"Yeah, inside you, you bastard." He groans. Kes laughs out loud, rubbing his hands together.

"What about all my stuff?" Denver grumbles as I drag him into the house.

"That can wait. You two have teased me enough this morning, so, let's get naked. Your gear can wait." I kiss up the side of his neck as we make it into the bedroom. Kes shuts the door behind us as he tugs off his T-shirt before joining us.

□ □ □

We walk into the bar minutes before three o'clock. Denver is working today, so he gets behind the bar and Kes heads to the office. I take a seat at the end of the bar and Den hands me a soda; I'm going to get Ellie later, so no beer for me. As she's been at a sports event at another school, she's late coming to me today.

The bar is busy this afternoon, it's another week before the Easter break and that's when the town starts to fill up; the cabins on the Sinclair ranch are already booked up, which makes me very happy. I know I did a great job on them and my bonus was well deserved, the debt we got into when we set up the bar is now almost gone. Another job like that one should get us in the clear. Kes is working extra hard here, too, and the open mic nights are bringing in a bigger crowd. I give Denver some of the credit for that but he refutes it and hasn't played for over a week now, maybe I could persuade him.

Right then, the door opens and the young guy from earlier walks in, looking about anxiously but Denver smiles at him.

"Hi, you here to see Kes?" He asks, his smile widening. *God, I love his dimples!*

"Um, yeah. Is he about?" He asks nervously, as Kes walks out of the office and looks over.

"Hi, Carter, do you want to come this way?" Kes greets him with a smile. "You okay here, Den?" Denver nods and goes back to serving.

"He looks like there's a story there, don'tcha think?" I glance at Denver.

Smiling sadly, he nods. "Then, maybe, he's come to the right place. You fixed me."

"I hope Kes doesn't have the same plan for him, I don't think our bed would fit a fourth!" I wink when I see his shocked face.

"That's really not what I meant." He growls, flushing bright red.

"Oh, baby, I know that; I'm messing with you." I reach over the bar and cup the back of his neck to pull him towards me. "I'm sorry." I whisper against his lips before I kiss him hard.

"Have you finished accosting my staff?" Kes' voice breaks us apart. Denver runs his thumb over his bottom lip, a motion I have always found incredibly sexy. His eyes are still dark as he blinks at Kes.

"Don't blame me: East started it." Denver pouts, making Kes laugh as he walks behind the bar and kisses Denver as I did moments ago.

I hear a gasp and I look at the new guy as he witnesses Denver being kissed by both of us, red staining his pale cheeks.

Kes breaks away and, a smile lifting the corner of his mouth, looks back at us. "Carter is coming in to take your shifts, Den. Carter, let me introduce you to my boyfriends: this is East, he's trouble, so watch him."

"Hey! That's not fair!" I cry indignantly.

"And this is Denver. He'll be working here tonight, too, so, if you need anything, you can ask him." Kes has his arm draped over Denver's shoulder as Den reaches out to shake Carter's hand.

"B...b...both of them are your boyfriends?" He stutters as he shakes Denver's hand, his face bewildered.

"Yes." We say in unison and laugh.

"Do you have a problem with that, Carter?" Kes asks, his eyes narrowing slightly as he questions the new guy.

"No, no, not at all. I'm sorry." He blushes again.

"Don't worry about it, both of them are all bark and no bite." Denver eases the tension. "Come on, let me show you around." He steps out from behind the bar and over to Carter.

As they walk away, I hear Denver talking about the place and what goes on. My heart swells at the kindness he shows the sad, young man. I look at Kes and raise an eyebrow.

"What's his story, Kes?"

"Not sure yet, but he needs a place to live and some friends. I'm going to let him take the apartment above here. There's definitely something there, but it's not time to find out yet."

"I'm sure we will." I look over and see him smiling tentatively, then Denver says something we can't hear and he smiles properly and lets out a laugh. *Damn, that boy's gonna break some hearts around here*, I'm not sure if they are going to belong to the men or the women.

□ □ □

DENVER

Jesus, this feels surreal, alien yet so familiar: the hospital smells and sounds like every other I've worked in. The bustle going on around me—that to a patient looks so haphazard, so random—makes perfect sense to me. I take another step inside and a petite, dark-haired, young woman barges past me.

"Move, or you'll get mown down!" She barks as I quickly side-step to avoid a gurney charging past me.

Instinct takes over and I immediately assess the patient. My cursory glance troubles me but they are gone before I can take a closer look. Striding up to the nurses' station, I wait patiently for the young, male nurse to finish his phone call before giving him my name.

"You need to book in over there," he points to the reception kiosk at the front of the department. "I can't do anything until you've booked in." It's at this moment that he looks at me and a look of—

what? Horror? Embarrassment?—crosses his features. I'm not sure, but he recognizes me.

"Crap!" He mutters under his breath as a pale red tint flushes up over his neck and face. "Doctor Sinclair, I'm really sorry. We're rushed off our feet this morning, which is not normal for a Monday morning, but it is an emergency room after all."

"It is indeed, so, maybe, you could show me where I'm going, so I can get to work." I smile kindly, so as not to make him hate me. Nurses run every department, not that we like to admit it: piss one off and your life could very quickly be made very difficult.

"Of course, it's this way. We are so excited to have you here. You really have come at the right time, too; we need someone so focused to really make this place come alive." He blushes again.

"So, Callum," I look down at his name badge, "how long have you worked here?" I ignore the 'so focused' comment, because I am no longer going to live and breathe hospital life this time around; I have so much waiting for me at home. *Was I really that bad, though? Probably.*

I listen as he fills me in on his time here and about the department and hospital. He is very enthusiastic, something I admire and appreciate. Soon, we stop in front of a door and Callum knocks on it twice.

"Come in." I hear the voice of Carson Woodruff and smile as Callum pushes the door open.

"Dr. Sinclair is here, Dr. Woodruff." Callum smiles and lets me enter, then turns to me and says his goodbye.

"Denver, excellent to see you here. Let's get you to work." Woodruff stands and shakes my hand.

And, oh boy, did he mean it.

The dark-haired woman scowls again when I enter the room and I'm sure I hear a sigh of 'him again' but I smile nicely and step aside to let Carson walk past me.

"Ah, Connie, excellent. Let me introduce Doctor Denver Sinclair, he's me when I'm not here. He may be me when I am, but who knows?" He lets out a chuckle to the joke only he is privy to.

"Shit!" She exclaims and sends daggers my way.

Whoa! What's going on here?

"Hi, Connie, nice to meet you. Um, I'm sorry about earlier." I know an early apology is always good, especially to a resident. I see her relax and a smile tentatively crosses her face.

"Nice to meet you." She replies and smiles this time.

"Okay, tell me where I need to be and I will disappear from under your feet." I joke.

It's five hours later before I finally get to sit down and grab a coffee. I grimace at the forgotten taste of coffee machine 'coffee.' Callum shoves a mug of something that smells and tastes so much better in front of me, making him my friend for life. I pull my cell phone out of my pocket; I've had it on silent all morning but have felt it vibrate a couple of times. A huge smile breaks out and I laugh as I see a photograph of East and Kes, with Missy at their feet, and they are holding up a good luck banner.

Callum looks surprised at my laugh, I chuckle again. "A good luck message from home." I tell him, not giving any more away.

"From you wife?"

This makes me snort, and shake my head. "No, I'm not married." I swallow the last of my coffee and stand up. "Thanks for the drink."

The rest of my shift is busy and I get lost in the bustle, surprised when another unknown face approaches me. Looking up from the tablet I'm updating some patient notes on, a man, about twenty-five years old, smiles at me. He's about six-foot tall with neat, dark hair—a total contrast to my messy hair after eight hours of running my hands through it—and confidence exudes from him. This guy knows how good-looking he is.

"Hi, it's Denver, isn't it?" The unknown man inquires, "I'm Chase Fielding, one of your junior doctors, coming to take over for the night. Have you had a good first day?"

"Hi, Chase. It's great to meet you, and yes, I've had a very good day. I think I've made the right decision." I shake his proffered hand.

"Better than Cedar Greens?" His eyebrows rise, but then he recognizes the shocked look on my face, "I've been following your work; I'm quite a fan." He blushes a pale pink color.

"Yes, I think I'll be happier here than I was there." I wonder how much of my life there he has been following, but he seems genuine enough. "Okay then, I'm off home. I will see you tomorrow. Good luck and my number is on the board, if you need me."

I get back in my truck and start the engine, my mind full of getting to my men; it's Monday, so they will both be at home. My heart races, I can't wait to tell them all about my day but, more than that, I'm excited to have a home to go to, one that is full of love. The distance passes quickly and I pull up on the driveway shortly after leaving my first day behind.

There are no lights on inside, but it's not too dark yet, and everything is quiet when I push open the front door. I need to get out of these clothes and into the shower; I haven't had to scrub in for surgery today, so I'm wearing the smart, black slacks and white button-down shirt I put on this morning and I can smell the hospital on them.

Without checking the kitchen or the garden for my men, I undo my shirt as I hurry into the bedroom. Not bothering to turn the light on, I continue to strip out of my clothes as I walk into the bathroom. I flick the shower on and wait for the water to heat up, then I sense movement behind me and turn.

"Hi." I whisper my greeting to the two men standing in the doorway. I watch them as they gaze at me, their eyes roaming over every part of my naked body.

"Hey, baby, how was your day?" East asks as he flicks the button on his cargo shorts, then he pulls his T-shirt over his head.

"We've missed you, Den." Kes copies East's actions and soon they stand naked before me.

"I missed you, too. I need to get the smell of the hospital off me." I step under the water, tipping my head back to let the water sluice over my hair and over my face.

I feel two sets of hands stroke my chest and waist, the tender touch sending a shiver over my body, and I moan when a mouth captures my nipple and sucks gently.

"I think we can help you there." East murmurs against my neck, then his teeth scrape over the heated surface.

I hear the pop of the body wash bottle opening and feel Kes' hands soaping my body, caressing every inch of my torso, never going quite low enough. My dick is hard and proud against my stomach. I nudge my hips forward, making Kes laugh but his hands stay stubbornly clear and continue to soap me. Gliding over my hips and down my back, his soapy hands cup my ass, then a finger slides down my crack and up again before being replaced by East's cock. A moan escapes me.

"Stay still, Den. Let us look after you." Kes whispers against my lips. "Tell us about your day. How did it go?"

"Are you kidding me? I can hardly remember my name with your hands on me and East's cock rubbing up my ass crack." I moan as his hands slide over my ass. "I'll tell you later."

I capture Kes' mouth and plunge my tongue inside, dueling with his. East sighs behind me and kisses across my shoulders and up my neck. Breaking away from Kes and turning my head, East takes my mouth. His teeth nip my lower lip, making me moan at the tug and sting. Kes moves down my body, sucking on my nipple, letting his teeth scrape over the hard nub, then travels down further until he kneels in front of me. His teeth grazing over my hip make me buck forward, then I feel his hot breath over my dick. But he's not touching it and it's killing me: I want to thrust deep in his mouth. I feel his smile against my skin as he moves over to my other hip, leaving kisses over my taut flesh.

East releases my mouth and runs his hands up my ribs then hooks them over my shoulders, holding me in his strong grasp as Kes finally moves closer to my dick. He dodges my thrusts and glides his tongue down my groin, licking the soft skin in the crease at the top of my thigh.

"Fuck!" I moan and let my head rest back on East's shoulder, the sensations running through my body overwhelming me as Kes runs his nose over my sac before sucking one of my balls into his mouth. His tongue swirls over and around the sphere before releasing it, only to do the same to the other. I'm panting, unable to control myself as I mewl and surrender to him.

As his tongue moves up to the base of my dick, I know I'm not going to be able to hold back. Sweeping up my length, he licks and sucks until—finally—his mouth is over the head. Flicking his tongue out, he laps at the precum weeping copiously from the slit. Stabbing his tongue in the hole, he ultimately sucks the head into his mouth. Swishing over the ridge before he takes me deep, his tongue is flat as he opens wide and lets me into his throat.

Kes' hands light on my ass and he separates the cheeks; East's cock is in the crack again but he slides it lower and I feel it against the tight pucker of my hole. Lifting one of my legs, Kes drapes it over his shoulder to give East easier access to his target. Kes still sucks on my dick as East nudges against my hole, pushing back, I allow him entry. The tight sting as he pushes past my ring has me gasping.

"You feel so good, baby. So hot and tight around me." East whispers in my ear as he goes deeper. I feel every pulsing vein as he fills me.

"I'm not going to last. Fuck, Kes. Finish me!" I beg for release. Kes sucks me harder and grips my length, pumping his hand up and down, taking me higher and higher. East is still in my ass, I know he's waiting for me to come before he pounds me.

"Come, baby. Give it all to Kes." East croons as he holds me still.

My balls pull up inside me as my orgasm shoots down my spine. I want to punch deeper into Kes' mouth but I'm being held so tight, I can only hand it over to Kes. Then East pulls back slightly and nudges my prostate, and I come. My hot release pours into Kes' mouth. I feel him swallow around the head, gulping down all I can give him. My body sags but Kes stands and supports me as East lets me go; his hands grip my hips and I know he's going to fuck me hard.

"Fuck me, East. Take me hard." I want to feel every part of him. Kes kisses me as East starts to pound inside me.

"You look beautiful, Denver; I love watching East fuck you. I know how tight your ass is and I know how it feels to be buried in you." Kes keeps up his dirty talk as East picks up speed and I know he's not far from coming when his hands grip me harder as his dick hardens further. And then he pours inside me.

"Fuuuuuuck!" East cries then bites into my shoulder; his hips still pumping as his orgasm rockets through him.

East slipping from my ass makes me moan again. I look at Kes and see he has one hand wrapped around his dick.

"Let me, honey." I whisper and get down on my knees but, as I lean in to take him in my mouth, Kes shakes his head.

"Stay like that." Kes continues to stroke himself. I love watching him do this: his fist is tight around his long shaft as he leisurely strokes then picks up speed. Kneeling in front of him, I know he wants to come over me, to mark me. My chest heaves as I wait expectantly then, as Kes cries out, his cum fires from him, splashing my face and neck. Leaning in, I capture the head in my mouth. Sucking and licking over the sensitive head has him bucking into me as I lap up the last of his cum. Resting back on my heels, I look at the two shattered and spent men and a giggle bursts from me.

"Shit, you guys. I only wanted a quick shower." I stand up and wrap my arms around them, kissing each individually. "Do you think I can get washed up now?"

"So, how was your first day? East chuckles as he reaches for the body wash.

"It was good, it was good to be back. The people seem friendly." I answer, stealing the bottle from him. I think of Chase and wonder what he knows about me.

Chapter
Thirteen

KES

I watch as Denver strolls through the bar door, and I'm not the only one. Men and women alike peruse him as he walks, unaware of his admirers, with his eyes fixed on me. A smile breaks out over his rugged features and he swipes his hand through his blond, messy locks. He looks tired but after another long week at the hospital it's only to be expected.

"Hey there, handsome, what can I get you?" I wink and lean over the bar towards him.

"A kiss and a beer; I'm in dire need of both." Denver leans in to meet me and presses his lips against mine. I swallow his sigh as our lips part and the tips of our tongue touch briefly, before he pulls away.

"You okay, Den?" I ask as he frowns.

"Yeah, it was a rough night, last night. I'm sorry if I woke you when I got in." His hand scrubs down his face, he still looks half-asleep.

"No, it was fine; I felt you but I don't think either of us stirred. You wanna talk about it?" I hand him his beer and stroke my fingers over his knuckles as he takes it from me.

"Hell is what it was. It was touch and go for most of the whole surgery; we ended bringing her back twice before we were finished and it's now up to her to survive. Twenty-two months old and battered by her stoned parents. She's alone now and it's up to social services from here on in; I'm going to be monitoring her progress; I feel she's going to need someone fighting for her."

Denver looks at me and I see the sheen of tears in his tired eyes. "She's so tiny, Kes." He shakes his head, trying to clear his mind.

"Den, do whatever you need to do to keep her safe." I look deep into his eyes. "What else is on your mind?"

"Nothing for you to worry about, honey; the rest is just work shit and an over-eager resident. His familiarity is bugging me. He keeps mentioning my old hospital and my time there, and it's bugging the crap out of me."

"Have you checked him out? He's probable just keen and happy to be working with you. You follow surgeons you admire, he may just be doing the same." I don't like the thought of someone hassling him with his past. "Is he causing trouble?"

"No, and he's a good doctor, he's just over familiar, too friendly. D'you get what I mean?"

"I do, but you're here now, so let's not talk about work." I smile and pop another kiss on his mouth, then move off to serve someone.

I watch Carter as he smiles at Denver and starts to talk. I think he's settling in with us, he moved into the apartment above here. He's keeping himself private and we are not going to push him for information but, as he comes out of his shell, he will start to talk, I'm sure of it.

East turns up next and casually lays his arm over Denver's shoulder, dropping a kiss on his temple, then calls for me and kisses me, too. I see a few glances from some of the patrons; the town is beginning to fill up with tourists and I'm not sure they expect to see three men together in this small town. The ladies all seem to smile but I notice a couple of shocked expressions from the men. One man grimaces but his partner nudges him and he looks away.

The bar is filling up and I'm looking forward to handing over to Shelley when she comes in at six. The bar goes quiet and I look up to see what's going on, surprised to see Denver sitting unobtrusively in the corner with his guitar. East is with him and has a smile on his face: he loves to hear Denver sing.

What shocks me is the choice of song: something has seriously rattled him when he starts to sing *Goodbyes* by 3 Doors Down. East's head shoots up and he catches my eye; he, too, is rattled by the song and the poignant lyrics. The hairs on my arms stand on end and a shiver runs down my spine. We need to talk about this. I glance around the near-silent room and see one woman with a lone tear on her cheek. *What has gone on?*

The next song is almost harder to listen to as Shawn Mendes' *Never Be Alone* starts. Denver seems to be playing for himself, his head down, his words clear but quiet. The room looks frozen in time as no one moves or speaks. Then it's over and Denver finishes by putting his guitar down and picking up his beer. Taking a long slug, he empties the bottle. He stands and looks around the room before kissing East and walking out the door.

East's chair scrapes over the floor as he bolts up and races after Denver. Throwing my towel on the counter, I follow. "Carter, I won't be long."

When I get outside, East has Denver wrapped in his arms. Den's hands cover his face as his shoulders shake. I press against his back as we support him through his struggle, stepping back when I feel him straighten up.

"Fuck! Shit!" Denver has his hands in his hair, tugging on the strands.

"Talk to us, baby. Let it out." East strokes Denver's ribs as I run my hand up his spine.

"She had cigarette burns over her body; there wasn't a part of her that wasn't bruised." He bursts out.

"Okay, baby. What do we need to do to help?" East's practical voice penetrates Denver's anguish. He looks at him askance.

"What do you mean?"

"He means: what do we have to do to make her safe, to make her ours?" I reply.

"How? Why? Why would you do that?" Denver shakes his head, bewildered. "They would never let me have her. A gay man with two boyfriends? Who would trust us with a little girl?"

"There is always a way, baby. If you feel that much for her, we have to at least take the chance." East smiles.

"She may not even make it: she is critical and on life support. I will find out more next shift." He looks at us and shakes his head. "You're unbelievable, do you realize that? How did I get so damn lucky?"

"We're the lucky ones, Den. I've told you before: we are meant to be together. Why else would you have felt the call home?" I kiss his temple and let go of him. "I need to get back to work; I will see you at home, later."

They nod and East clasps Denver's hand before following me to the front of the bar. "Look after him, East. Whatever it takes." East opens the door of his truck and Denver climbs in—I'll get Carter to drive my truck and I'll take Denver's home.

□ □ □

When I get home, East is in the kitchen and I hear the shower in the bathroom as I walk past our bedroom. East smiles and carries on stirring the pan on the stove.

"How is he?" I ask as I kiss East and peek into the pan, the smell of his rich pasta sauce makes my stomach rumble.

"He's okay; he's stressed to fuck but we talked and he told me all about the little girl. Fuck, Kes, we need that little mite with us; she had a collapsed lung, for fuck's sake." East's hands shake with anger, the thoughts and memories of Ellie being abandoned by her mother surfacing again. "Why are there so many sick people around? Why have a kid, if you just want to use it as a punching bag? Den isn't sure if she has suffered any brain damage yet. The meeting with the social worker is tomorrow, she will know more: she had been monitoring the family and had tried to have her taken from them but it wasn't successful, so she was making regular checks. This time, there was no answer at the door but she could see them in the house so she tried the door and let herself in." East heaves a huge breath into his lungs as he controls himself. "She found her in the crib, hardly breathing."

"Jesus! What a horror story." I gasp.

"I'm sure we haven't heard the last of it yet. Den is going to call her when she gets in and let her know what we want to do. We may be able to get to see her tomorrow, too. But let's find out how well she is after Denver checks on her this evening."

Denver walks in and looks better, brighter. "Hey, Kes." He kisses me, then runs his hand over my ass. "Sorry about earlier."

"Hey, don't apologize. You were a hit in the bar: everyone was talking about you; how great you sound." I laugh. "I think they want you back again."

"Yeah, well, maybe. Look, I need to talk to you about what you said." He holds his hand up as I go to speak. "Let me finish, please. I don't know what it is about this child that has my heart tearing apart,

I intend to pursue fostering her. I don't want you to feel obligated to take her on because you love me. You may have never considered another child, and Ellie... well, she could totally flip out at the thought of sharing you."

I watch as Denver observes us and I never thought of him as so handsome, so put together, so perfect. I reach for him but he holds his hands up and keeps me back.

"We are so new in this relationship. I feel I may be asking too much of you to do this. But I need to." His voice is strong even though I see his hands tremble.

"Fuck that!" East wades in the only way he knows how and shows his hand. "That's bullshit. We love each other, all of us. We are a family and if you want to have this baby then we will have her. I can think of nothing more rewarding than watching, and being part of showing, a young child how life in a family really should be." East steps up to Denver and, even though he's pissed, his eyes soften as he gazes at our lover. "I've had one child abandoned by her mother, Denver. I can think of a million reasons why the authorities could fight us, but we are the ones in the right here and that little girl belongs with us." East clasps his hands around the back of Denver's neck and hauls him into his thick body, kissing him so powerfully that Denver almost loses his footing.

When they break apart, Denver looks at me. I smile a dry, half smile and nod at East. "What he said." I grin broadly now and tug Denver to me. "Yes: it's going to be scary. Yes: we are going to be tested. But dammit, Denver; don't ever doubt our commitment to you." It's my turn to kiss him and as my tongue slips between his lips, Denver's moan vibrates through my body. We lazily let our tongues tangle and dance with each other as I hold his hips hard against my own. His fingers lock in my hair, tugging on the band holding it back so that he can grab my hair in his fists.

"Let go of each other, for chrissakes! Denver needs to eat before he goes to work." East mutters behind us and sets some plates down on the table.

□ □ □

DENVER

I walk into the ICU and look for the charge nurse, smiling when I see her coming out of one of the rooms.

"Collette, how is she?" I look over to the room she exited.

"She's doing well; she's a fighter, that's for sure. But I guess she's survived the worst now. You going to check her over?" She asks, her shrewd eyes fixed on me.

"I am, but more for my own benefit than for a medical reason. I have handed her over to your team now. I have a meeting with her social worker in an hour, I want to be able to bring her up to date." My eyes keep straying over to the darkened room.

"She's still on the ventilator, she really is trying hard."

I can only nod and I walk over to her room. After squirting the anti-bacterial gel into my hands, I approach her. Her dark hair is still matted to her head and neck, but that may be more to do with the temperature in here than the neglect. The tapes and bandages covering her body bring a lump to my throat, the tubes and cannulas going in and out of her body causing a constriction in my chest. This is something that has never happened to me before: I have been affected by traumas I dealt with before, but never on a level as deep as this. My finger strokes down her cheek as she sleeps her sedated sleep as I listen to the beeps of the monitor and watch her tiny chest rise and fall.

She really needs someone in her corner and I know damn well I'm going to make it me.

After reading through her notes, I leave to get to work. As I walk through the department, I see the board behind the nurses' station is full but there are no major traumas so, after a quick hello, I head to my office. The long list of emails waiting for me when I turn on my computer has me groaning but I work my way through them, ruthlessly cutting through the junk, the medical reps and the after-dinner speaker requests. I'm not interested in getting back into that: my over-working was the downfall of my last relationship. My mind wanders to the memories of yesterday's love-making. The sweet kisses along my spine as Kes entered my body, the firm grip of East's hands as he held me in his tight embrace as Kes languorously slid in and out of my body. The feel of hands and mouths covering me as I climbed higher and higher, breathlessly crying out their names as I climaxed.

A knock on the door breaks me from my reverie and I palm the hardness growing in my pants, *thank god for white coats.*

"Come in." I call out and wait for the door to open. I smile when I see Miriam Salter, the social worker. "Ms. Salter, come on in."

Her smile and her eyes look tired, I think, of the horrors she must see every day. "Good evening, Dr. Sinclair, how's our patient today?" She drops her purse on the floor and sits in front of me, a thick file in her hand.

"She's improving slowly; still being ventilated and sedated, but the swelling on her brain is down and her liver function is good." We know, by the bruise on her back, she had been kicked in her lower back, causing damage to her liver. "What more do you know about her? Her name, for a start, would be good."

"She doesn't have one, or I have never been told it. The parents just called her 'she' or 'it'." The pained expression on her faces gives away her frayed emotions.

"And where are these dreadful people now?" My voice is strained and my hands are clenched tight.

"They are in police custody. They will be up before the judge on Monday morning. You will be called to give evidence, but I believe they are being compliant and have admitted the abuse. They have signed her over to the child protection services and we will be looking for a foster home and a forever family while she is still under your care." Miriam looks at me shrewdly, assessing my reaction.

"That's good to hear." I flatten my hands on my desk and look directly at this tough woman. "I want her. I mean…"

"I know what you mean, and I know you do. I could see that immediately, yesterday. Are you married? In a long-term relationship?"

"No, I'm not married. I'm gay and in a loving, committed relationship." I will have to divulge more, but I will wait until I'm asked.

"And your partner, how does he feel about it? This is not a quick decision to be made on sympathy; she is going to need a lot of support. Her speech is limited and she is not used to being fed."

"That won't be a problem, and, yes, they are both on board." I sit quietly while she contemplates my comment.

"You have more than one partner, Dr. Sinclair?" Her face gives nothing away.

"I do, I have two. Does it make a difference? I mean, we are in a loving, committed relationship. One of my partners has a daughter, she's eleven. She was abandoned by her mother when she was around a year old." I suddenly feel a chill in the air as the social worker looks down at her notes and makes a note.

"I think that this could be an issue, Dr. Sinclair. You have to realize that your relationship status is unorthodox. I'm not sure the authorities would feel it would be in the best interest of the child to be with three men."

"But this same authority left a child in a known abusive environment until she was almost killed. Please, tell me where the reasoning is in that decision?" I'm trying to keep my voice calm but I feel my temper rising.

"I will need to discuss this with my team. Please, don't think this is a no: this is no longer a decision I can make alone. Leave it with me for twenty-four hours." I think I see some pity in her eyes but I'm not sure, she may have already made up her mind and discounted us.

A thought jumps into my mind and I'm instantly ashamed of it, but I need to know. "Would it be an easier decision to make if I was applying by myself?"

"As a single carer? You would consider leaving your partners for her?"

"No." I shake my head. "I'm just curious of the workings of your department. Is a single parent better for her than three loving, caring parents?"

"Dr. Sinclair, you have to see that my hands are tied, I can't make this decision alone. Let me get back to you tomorrow." She collects her purse and stands.

"Fine, please call me tomorrow. I am on my last shift here tonight and will be away from work for three days. You have my cell number?"

She nods and leaves me alone in my office. I sit with my head in my hands, struggling with my thoughts: *did I really consider giving up Kes and East to look after a child? No, it was an errant thought, a curiosity more than a genuine question. I think. Fuck!!!*

I collect myself, ready to get to work. Looking at the clock, I see the meeting didn't take as long as I expected. But then, I didn't expect to be knocked down at the first hurdle.

The next eight hours go quickly as a steady run of patients arrive throughout the evening and night. When it's time for me to go, I happily hang up my coat again and leave. As soon as I'm on the monotonous drive home, I start thinking about the damaged, little, nameless girl and the unfairness of the world. One where children are born to people with no desire to have or care for them and where some of the best people are denied children. I'm not putting myself in that category, but I hurt at the cruelty of the world where women are unable to conceive and would make the most loving, nurturing parents and drug-filled, violent and hateful people can have as many as they want. How many LGBT families are out there, desperate to have a child but are frowned upon by old-school authorities?

I pull up on our driveway and realize I have done this on complete autopilot, so lost in thought, I simply pointed the car in the right direction. Tiredness washes over me and I need to be in bed. For the first time in weeks, I wish I was climbing into an empty bed; I'm not ready for the discussion I need to have with my lovers. I don't want to see the pain in their eyes as they are deemed unsuitable to care for a child so desperately in need of some love and affection.

Taking a deep breath, I climb out of the truck and head for the door. Creeping in as soundlessly as I can, I'm still not quiet enough to escape Missy's sharp hearing. She trips sleepily down the hallway, her tail wagging slowly.

"Hey, girl, whatcha doing up?" I whisper and scratch behind her ears. "Come on, back to bed." I walk her back to the kitchen and settle her down again.

Walking into the bedroom, I look at my soundly sleeping lovers. For once, they are not wrapped around each other but sprawled across the large mattress. I wonder if they made love last night. Is that why they are spread out? Shaking my head, I make for the bathroom and undress before turning on the shower. I wash quickly, ready to be asleep. Toweling off, I dump my clothes and towel in the laundry hamper and stumble, naked, to my bed.

"Hey, baby." East murmurs groggily as I climb into bed.

"Hey, sorry to wake you." I apologize.

"How is she?" East asks.

"Not good but better than yesterday; the swelling on her brain is reduced but still apparent and she is sedated and being ventilated still." I stop there, hoping he doesn't ask any more.

"What did the social worker say?" It's Kes who asks, woken by our muted voices.

"She wasn't prepared to commit to anything, she needed to speak to her colleagues." Please, don't let them ask why. But, of course, they do.

"What does that mean?" Kes asks quietly.

"It means that three men in a relationship don't stand a chance. Am I right?" East growls.

"Yeah, something like that. She's going to get back to me today." I yawn as I speak and let my head sink into the soft pillows.

"Get some sleep, Den. I'm getting up in a minute anyway. I'll be back here in plenty of time this afternoon." East swings his legs around and gets out of bed. I hear the shower start and then sleep takes me away.

□ □ □

EAST

I stand under the hot water, my head full of Denver's words. Words like sedated and brain swelling, words that should never be associated with an infant. *What the fuck am I going into work for? The guys don't need me there today;* there's plenty for them to get on with without my supervision. *I want to be here, I don't want to be left out. This is about all of us, a decision we all need to be here for. Denver thinks it's a no and, if that's true, he's going to need us both here. I don't want to miss out on this, it's too important.*

I switch off the shower and dry off. Grabbing my cell when I walk back into the bedroom, I fire off a text to Dean: he can manage today. I look at the two men in my bed: Denver has cocooned Kes as he spoons him into his body. My heart swells at the sight. *God, I love these men.* I climb back in and tuck in against Kes, smiling as he mutters nonsensically and kisses the back of my head. We drift off again.

199

"Why are you still here?" Kes' deep, sleep-laden voice murmurs in my ears.

"Are you complaining?" I chuckle as his erection presses into the crease of my ass.

"Never, just curious. What's going on?" He kisses the back of my neck, making me stretch into his body. "Fuck, East, don't do that to me; we'll wake up Den and he needs to sleep, he must be shattered." His mouth connects with my shoulder this time.

"Then, you'd better stop doing that then." I blame him.

"What are you blaming Kes for now?" Denver asks, his face still muffled into the pillow.

"Waking you up, baby. Go back to sleep." I answer.

"What? Why are you here? Shit! Fuck! Have we slept all day? Christ, we need to speak with the social worker." Den sits up then looks at the clock on the bedside table before he lies down again, groaning. "What's going on?"

"I was just asking East the same thing?" Kes answers.

"I decided today was too important a day for me to not be here. I know you will speak about her again and I didn't want to not be part of it." I grumble.

"That's amazing, East; thank you. I want you to be here for all of it, too." Denver reaches across and grips my arm. "You are amazing, East. Thank you." His voice is thick with emotion.

"Go back to sleep, baby; you need more than three hours."

"Nah, I'm good, years of practice. I'm the king of catnaps." He chuckles then leans into Kes' body. I'm not sure what he does but it makes Kes moan and nudge his dick against my ass again.

"Playtime." Kes whimpers as Denver grabs his dick.

Kes rolls on his back as Denver leans over him and kisses him, his hand lazily pumping up and down his cock. Not able to hold back, I let my tongue slide over the slit as a pearl of precum beads there, moaning as I capture his exquisite flavor.

"Fuck yeah, both of you. I want both your mouths on me." Kes thrust his hips up, fucking Denver's fist as I continue to tease the swollen head, sucking and licking the tip.

Denver releases his hold on Kes' thick, solid girth and moves between his legs. His hands slide under his ass cheeks and lift him off the bed. I open my mouth and take Kes into my mouth until he hits the back of my throat. Bobbing up and down, sucking him hard, my cheeks hollow as I tug hard.

Denver licks down Kes' sac and over his taint and I watch as he parts his cheeks and rims his tight hole. Another burst of precum bursts onto my tongue as Denver flutters his tongue over the quivering pucker before stabbing his tongue inside.

Kes goes rigid as his balls draw up into his body. We're not ready for him to come yet and we ease off, slowing our ministrations.

"No, No! Don't stop! I need to come." Kes' fists clutch at the sheets as he bucks his hips, desperate for more.

"Get on your hands and knees, sweetheart. East is going to fuck your ass and I'm going to fuck your mouth. You need to stay still and let us do the work. Are you going let us take you? It's going to be hard and fast, and you are only going to come when we do, all of us together." Denver looks long and hard at Kes, making sure he knows he means it. Kes hates having to hand over control but always comes like a train when he submits.

I let go of his dick and move so he can get into position. Reaching across to grab the lube from the drawer, I wait for him to be in front of me.

"Fuck, you look amazing. So eager, so needy. Your ass is begging for my dick, baby." It's my turn to have my mouth on him. I slide my tongue down his crack then, ignoring his hole, I scrape my teeth over the soft skin at the top of his thigh. Lifting my head, I see Denver stroking Kes' hair, barely running his fingers through the long soft strands. Kes' mouth is mere millimeters from Denver's poker-stiff cock; I see the gleam of precum coating the engorged head.

Flicking the lid of the lube bottle, I trail a stream down his crease to coat his hole, the cool liquid making him shudder. My finger follows the lube and circles slowly around his entrance before slipping smoothly into his hot, tight channel. First one, then a second; stretching him, ready to take me. Kes whimpers as his hips sway. Pulling out, I line my dick up and push inside him: long strokes in and out, before I bottom out and hold still.

"Open up, Kes; get that amazing mouth around my dick." Denver slicks the tip over Kes' full bottom lip then plunges deep inside him. "That's it, suck me hard."

As Denver pumps in and out of Kes' mouth, his hands knot in his hair to keep him still. I drag out of his ass and thrust hard back inside. Over and over, I pull out and plunge back in, feeling every ripple of his muscles as he clenches tight around me. With my hands gripping his hips, I pick up speed as I widen my knees to shift angles and hit his sweet spot every time.

"I'm not gonna last, Den, and our man here is about to blow." I feel the quiver of his muscles as his orgasm builds.

"Hell, yeah! I'm ready." Denver thrusts again and holds still as his back stiffens and he shouts out as he pours his release deep in Kes' throat.

I plunge inside him and cry out as Kes comes, his ass clenched tight around me as I fire inside him, flooding his ass. I collapse over Kes' back, covering him in kisses; Denver has his face held gently in his palms as he kisses him, the tenderness a welcome contrast.

I pull out and feel the rush of my release as I withdraw, then collapse down to the side. Lying on my back, I reach out for Kes and pull him against me. "I love you so fucking much, Kes, and you, Den.

I don't know what I'd do without you both."

Denver joins us, sandwiching Kes between us as we stroke and sooth him, bringing him down from a mind-blowing orgasm: his body still trembles as we run our hands over every inch of him. Whispering how incredible he felt and looked, Denver slides off the bed and goes to the bathroom. I hear water running, then he comes back with warm, damp cloths and cleans us up. Dumping them on the floor, we crawl under the covers and hold each other close. It doesn't take long for Denver to drift back off to sleep, leaving me and Kes to talk quietly.

Chapter
Fourteen

DENVER

Waking up in an empty bed is to be expected in the middle of the day, but I still miss that delicious slide of warm bodies rousing slowly together. I guess I got that this morning, though. Chuckling to myself, I clamber out of the tangled duvet and pull on a pair of sweat shorts. Fancying a swim, I forgo a shower and wander down to the kitchen.

"Hey, baby. You had enough sleep?" East reaches his hand out to me so I step into his embrace, letting his arm reach around my waist.

"Yeah, or I won't sleep tonight. You okay away from work?" I rest my head on his shoulder, enjoying his warm hand on me.

"Yep, it's all good. They have plenty to get on with. You wanna talk about what happened yesterday?"

"Where's Kes? I don't want to be saying it over and over." I sigh, frustrated at the result of yesterday's discussion.

"He took Missy for a run, he should be back soon. You want me to get you some breakfast?" East moves to the fridge.

"No, it's okay. I'm good for now." I scrub my hands down my face, trying to shake off the funk that's in my head.

Hey, baby, come here." East spreads his arms wide and I step in and lean against him as he wraps me in his arms, our bare chests touching eliciting a shiver from me. "It might not happen for us now, are you gonna be okay if she says no?"

"I think she already has said no. Her face when I mentioned two partners said it all, it closed down. I think, discussing it further was a way of getting out of telling me there and then."

We hear the door open and Kes and Missy come down the hallway. Kes takes one look at me and frowns.

"Has she called yet?" His face is a mask of worry.

"No, and it won't be good when she does. She called us 'unorthodox' and said that the authorities don't like that. Never mind that a little girl nearly died with her way more unorthodox parents. Y'know, they don't know her name, said they never mentioned it. Who the fuck does that?" I sigh as the pain in my chest builds.

"Denver, it's not our fault if they can't, or won't, see past the unusual to see what we have here is real. That we can offer so much; we can't make them change their minds and we can't change who we are or what we have." Kes scowls when he looks at me as the memory of me thinking about single parents and fostering flits through my mind. "What did you say, Den? Why are you looking like that? What did you say?"

Suddenly, his arms are folded across his chest and East's eyes are questioning me. I swallow and look at them.

"Look, it was just an errant thought, but I asked if they considered single people as foster parents."

"But, you're not single." Kes shakes his head. "Did you think of leaving us? Fuck! Denver. Are you kidding me?"

"I know I'm not and I didn't consider it; I just wondered if they discriminated against single people, too." I shake my head. "I didn't, I couldn't. You guys, you get me. You make me; I need you more than I think is good for me." I laugh dryly, "I couldn't be without you now, I thought you knew that, I thought you trusted me."

"We do, it's just a shock to hear you say that you asked that. Do you trust us to get you through this?" East softly asks and I'm nodding before he can even finish.

"Okay, now there's nothing more we can do about it until she calls, so what shall we get up to?" Kes rubs his hands together.

"I want to swim; I need to stretch my muscles out and it's too damn hot to run. Then, later, I fancy a beer: shall we go to the bar for an hour?" I stretch my arms over my head and feel the tension creaking in my back and spine.

"Naked swimming?" East waggles his eyebrows, making me laugh, not something I've felt like doing since yesterday's meeting.

I'm lying on the deck under the canopy, relaxing as much as my mind will let me, when my cellphone rings. Kes and East sit up from their loungers and look panicked.

"Put it on speaker, this way you don't have to retell it." East requests.

I pick it up and make sure it is her before answering. *Fuck, it is!* "Sinclair." I answer.

"Good afternoon, Dr. Sinclair. How are you?" Ms. Salter asks as if she gives a fuck.

"I'll be better when you tell me your decision, and you are on speakerphone, Ms. Salter, as my partners are here with me.

"Okay then, I'd better get on with it. I have had a long meeting with all of the relevant departments this morning and we have decided that we are going to place the child with a more experienced foster family."

"I wasn't expecting you to tell me any different. Although, I am surprised you are using the lack of experience as an excuse." I hear the bristles in my voice and East and Kes have moved to sit next to me, each with a hand on my thighs.

"But we would like to enroll you on our foster parent scheme, if you are still attracted to fostering. Or was it just this one child you were interested in?" Her voice is brusque, but I expected nothing else.

I know this is a massively loaded question but Kes speaks before I get a chance. "Ms. Salter, I'm Kester Dereham, one of Denver's partners. I think we are interested in bringing the right child into our home, just as much as you want to place the child with the right people. So, although we are bitterly disappointed in your decision today, we would be happy to work with you for another child to have a happy, nurturing, and most importantly, loving family to grow up with."

I smile and lean in to kiss his shoulder, but then East surprises me.

"Ms. Salter, I'm East Brookman, the other, significant partner. I have already had to deal with a child that has had to grow up with abandonment issues, as her mother left her in her crib one morning after I had left for work. I know we have so much to offer a child that, by not pursuing your offer, we would be letting both ourselves and a child down."

"So, Dr. Sinclair, it seems it's up to you to make a decision." She taunts me.

"I think my partners have said enough; you already have my opinion. Let's get this ball rolling." I smile. Even though I hurt for the loss of the little un-named girl, I can see some positivity coming from my disappointment.

"I think we need to set up an appointment to meet all of you together. This can wait until you are back in your office, Dr. Sinclair; I know how precious a doctor's time off is, I am married to one myself."

We talk for a few more minutes and then end the call.

"Well, what do you think of that?" I ask, still not sure if I should be angry or jubilant. I look at the two men I am so thankful for and wait, hopeful for a smile.

"I think it's playtime." East laughs as he grabs our hands and drags us into the house.

□ □ □

KES

It's been a tough week: Denver never got his three days off after being called in on the second day due to a multi-car pileup on the highway that kept him there for eighteen hours. I never consider the toll it takes on the medical teams when they have to deal with the gruesome act of life and death, until now. Denver has struggled to keep his emotions in place. Two of his patients didn't make it through their surgeries. One was a child, thrown from a car after not being restrained correctly in a car seat. East and I have struggled to find the right words to say as he became taciturn, showing a side we hadn't seen before, the side that closes off when he is focused on his work. This must have been how his life had been before coming back home; the role of chief surgeon is a heavy one to carry. At least he has a superior this time to turn to but still, he is withdrawn.

Add to it his disappointment from social services, and we are dealing with an unhappy man. It hurts to watch him struggle.

"What can we do?" East asks as we watch him drive off to work again. "He's exhausted."

"I think we're doing all we can. He'll be fine when he gets some rest, it's only three more days." I pull my black work polo shirt over my head; I'm working a double shift today. East is spending the day with Ellie, I think he's planning to talk to her about us fostering in the future, but it's his call as to when he tells her.

"Come on, I'll take you to work, then I'll be back before your shift ends." East pops a kiss on my mouth and saunters off to lock up the house.

□ □ □

Unlocking the door to the bar, I turn on the lights as I wander in and begin the set-up, my head still full of ways to help Denver get through this. Soon though, the bar starts to fill up with holiday makers looking for lunch and a break from the afternoon heat and I'm rushed off my feet. Unable to even take a break, I keep going. Carter works hard, he's proven himself to be a great worker and, although quiet, he mixes well with the patrons. The ladies love him but he never flirts back, simply smiles and accepts the complements they throw at him. He still hasn't told his story, maybe he never will.

I feel a hand on my arm and see East standing in front of me.

"Hey, baby. You okay?" His hand cups my face as he leans over the bar to kiss me.

"Yeah, it's been crazy busy all day. I hadn't realized how late it is. Have you eaten?"

"Yeah, Mom fed me. You want me to jump in for a while? Go do some office work or just take ten minutes."

"That would be great; I need to clear the tills." I wait while he walks around and grabs a towel, tucking the end into his back pocket. "Thanks, East." I squeeze his waist as I walk past.

Wearily, I walk to my office and start to cash up this afternoon's takings. Things are definitely picking up; the takings are high and it's only the start of the season. I check my cell for the first time since I got here and see a message from Denver

Crazy hectic here again
today, I'm going to stay over
and crash in one of the on-call
rooms.
Love you both
Xxx

I try to call him but it goes straight to his voicemail, which doesn't surprise me but I'm not happy about this. I know it's sensible for him to sleep there, rather than risk driving when he's tired out, but I miss him in our bed. I shoot off a quick reply and get back to cashing up. After thirty minutes, I'm done and can head back out to the bar. My cell pings again as I stroll out to the bar.

I'm sorry, I should be home
tomorrow. Not sure what
time. I'll call you.
Xxx

"What's that look on your face for?" East asks.

"What look?"

"You're frowning." His hand reaches out and his fingers smooth across my brow.

"Denver isn't coming home tonight; he says it's too busy. He'll call when he's on his way tomorrow. I hate him being away from us. It's not good for him to be grabbing a couple of hours sleep if and when he can."

"Kes, he's a surgeon; this is his life. We have to let him do it his way. We said we would support him and we knew he would have days like this. So, come on, we just have to look after him when he comes home." East hooks his thumbs into my belt loops and tugs me closer before kissing me. "I'm gonna shoot some pool with Cal, you okay here now?"

I nod and let him get back into the still crowded room.

Two hours later, we're closed and I trudge slowly, my feet and back aching from standing for so long. East drives and we get home quickly to a dark and silent house. East had been home and looked in on Missy to feed her so, after a quick fuss and a late-night pee, she's happy back in her bed.

"Come on, baby; you need to sleep." East strips me out of my clothes and bundles me into bed.

"I need a shower." I grumble but my eyes are already closing.

"In the morning, Kes." East slips in behind me and kisses the nape of my neck as I fall into a heavy sleep.

I feel sleep slipping from my body well before I'm ready to let it go and I snuggle deeper into the pillows, wrapping the duvet around my body. That's when I notice I'm alone in bed. *Dammit!* East is already up; I hate it when he does that, especially on a Sunday. We should be waking up together, swapping soft kisses and gentle touches. I hear him talking, so I decide to give up on sleeping and push the covers back, stretching before getting out of bed. I drag on some sweatpants and stumble through to the sound of East's voice, he turns as I walk up to him and smiles.

"He's here now, baby. Yes, he does. Very." East's eyes roam my body as I scratch across my stomach and look quizzically at him. "Okay, babe. I love you, too." East hands me the phone, "It's Den."

I smile and take the phone. "Hey, sugar; how are you doing? Did you get some sleep?"

"I got a couple of hours, I was just telling East that I'll be here a while longer but I should be home for dinner tonight. I miss you both." I hear the need for us in his voice and know it is echoed in mine.

"Oh, Denver, my love, we miss you, too. We'll see you tonight, I can't wait. We both can't. You have a job to do and you do it so brilliantly. We love you and we will see you tonight." I sigh as my need for him burgeons in my chest.

"Tonight then, lover." Denver's voice is full of promise.

"I can't wait," I rasp. East moved behind me, his hand running down my bare back and under my waistband to run his finger through the crease of my ass.

"What's East just done?" Denver barks out a laugh.

"Fuck!" I mutter. "He's got his finger in my ass crack."

"Tell him to get his hands off; nothing until we are together. You hear me, East?" Denver is laughing but I know we will do as he wishes.

"Later then, Denver." But as I am about to end the call I remember something." Hey, Den? What did you say to East as I walked in?"

I love the sound of his deep, dirty chuckle. "I asked if you looked fuckable. Look, I've got to go; kiss East for me, but keep your dick away from him."

I'm left with his baritone laugh, then a dead phone line. Turning to East and matching his smile, I check, "So I look fuckable, do I?"

"Hell yeah, but the doctor's order is for us to wait."

□ □ □

DENVER

Chuckling, I drop my cell back in my pocket when I hear a cough behind me. Turning, I find Chase is behind me, a smug look on his face.

"Can I help you, Chase? Do you need me?" I still get a strange vibe off this young doctor: he's too cocky, too familiar with me. He looks amused; I guess he overheard the end of my conversation.

"Um, sorry. Yeah, Dr. Woodruff is looking for you." He wants to say more, I can tell.

"Is there anything you need?" I ask.

"No, nothing." He walks away.

I get busy and carry on. I look at the clock and grimace at the realization I've been here over forty-eight hours. Wandering down to our break room, I decide I need a coffee to make it through the next six hours or so.

"You wouldn't think it of him, would you? But he said 'kiss East, but keep your dick away from him'. He's got two lovers. He was so straight-laced at Cedar Greens, always working, and had no clue his ex was always cheating on him. What do you think of that?" Chase's voice is a loud whisper.

Scooting closer to the door, *and* standing at the frame; if any of them turned, they would see me.

"I don't think it's any of our business, that's what I think." Callum retorts, making me like him even more, he's an excellent nurse.

"Oh, for god's sake, Chase; grow up! Who cares who he sleeps with? He's an amazing surgeon and I want to learn as much as I can from him." Connie turns and sees me, her eyes go wide but she doesn't acknowledge me. Pausing, she waits for me to speak.

"So what if he's got two partners, it's still got nothing to do with you. And you should've walked away when you realized he was on his cell." Callum answers.

"All I'm saying is, he's far too uptight for a man that's fucked by two men. Hell, if I had two women, I'd be permanently fucking smiling." Chase turns around and sees me standing in the doorway. He blanches and I see him swallow hard.

"Get back to work, Fielding." I know better than to say anything when I'm this angry. I watch as he saunters past me, exactly like I thought: he's a cocky bastard.

Finally, it's time for me to go home. Tired through to my bones, I want nothing more than to climb into my warm bed. I have seventy-two hours away from the hospital and want to spend it with Kes and East, preferably in bed, but I know they still have to work. At least, we have three nights together.

Both trucks are on the drive as I pull up, which sends shivers through my weary bones; the expectation of some lovemaking gives me my energy back.

I can't see them when I walk through the house but I'm not sure where they are, even Missy seems absent. *Maybe they're in the garden?* Then I hear East, and it seems like they are arguing. This is new; I've not heard them do more than disagree with each other. I step further, ready to find them and defuse the situation but my blood turns to ice and I freeze.

"You have to be fucking kidding me. Shit, Kes. This was your idea. You're the one that started it all." East sounds angry and confused. *"You said it would be a great idea, and it is. I still want it."*

"I was wrong, I don't love it the way I thought I would. Yeah, it felt like a good idea at first, but it's damned heavy work and I'm not sure if it's worth it now." Kes' words cut through me like a knife; I can't believe what I'm hearing.

"You said you loved it. That it was perfect! I still fucking love it and now you just want to throw it away, because you've changed you mind? Well, fucking unchange it, because I'm happy with it. It suits, it works. It's perfect."

"I'm sorry it's not right. It's not Denver; I'm just not seeing it working with him."

That's all I need. Turning around, I stumble back to the front door and walk out of it. I don't even think I shut it behind me. I get back in my truck and drive away, my head full of the words that have me crippled, broken and hurting. Nothing Alec did or said is as painful as this. I drive out of town and head for my old cabin; I know it doesn't get used. I pull up outside the cabin and sit vacantly behind the wheel, looking out over the calm water but see nothing but the two men who made me feel so alive and so loved. I hear nothing but the words from Kes.

"I'm not sure if it's worth it now."

Why am I even surprised? I couldn't keep one man in love with me: how could I ever have thought I could have two? My chest constricts as my heart bursts under the pain. Gasping for breath, I stagger to the cabin and, pushing the door open, I fall inside. I manage to hold myself together until I get under the scolding water where I can persuade myself that my gasp is from the heat of the water; no matter, I know it's from the pain of my broken heart. My chest heaves as I cry out my anguish, tears flowing freely down my cheeks as I crumble. My knees, no longer strong enough to hold me up, give way and I slide down the tiled shower wall until I sit with my arms wrapped around my bent knees. I cry for what seems like hours, the water turning cold and it's still not enough to get me to stand and face myself again.

Eventually, my breathing evens and my sobs subside but the fractures in my heart remain the same. Huge fissures that with one tap would split open, leaving me wasted and worthless.

Slowly unwrapping my body from my arms, I stretch and stand up. Shutting the freezing water off, I grab a towel and roughly dry off, then my bed calls for me. I avoid looking at myself in the bathroom mirror—I can't look the image of a wrecked man. Crawling under the duvet, I bury in the soft pillows and close my eyes, expecting sleep to be a long way from me. But, whether it's exhaustion from too much work or my body's way of letting me silence the screaming in my head, I sleep.

There's a knocking coming from somewhere but my mind is still locked in sleep and the noises stop, leaving me to my dreams.

I'm running down corridors: long, stark white hallways, always turning. I'm searching for a door I know will get me out of here. There are voices ahead; I can hear East—he mentions my name—but when I call out, the voices stop. I keep running and calling out, then the walls disappear and I'm in a forest, but I know this one. I'm at the ranch, I can see them now. I can see East and Kes. I shout and they turn to me. I see someone else move from behind a tree and, oh god! It's Alec. They are talking to Alec. I shout again, calling out their names but they don't answer, they simply laugh at something Alec has said. Then, as I get closer, I see them take Alec's hand and they walk away together. Calling out one more time, I watch as East turns to look at me and he shrugs as Kes leans in to kiss Alec.

With a scream dying on my lips, I wake up, drenched in sweat and tears running down my face again. My breath hitches in my throat as my rapidly beating heart slows down. Turning my head into my soaked pillows, I wail again, despair and pain racing through my body and soul.

Doing nothing more than turning my pillow over, I close my eyes and let sleep lull me again.

Chapter
Fifteen

EAST

This morning has been hectic, with me and Kes racing around, wanting to get Denver's surprise ready for him when he gets home, which, looking at my watch, should be anytime now. I hope he makes it and there are no more emergencies; he must be exhausted. It's been nearly three days since he went there. Walking out of the spare room, I look at Kes and see him frowning.

"That's weird. Why is the door wide open?" He walks over to shut it. "We can't have closed it properly after dragging all the gear in; you need to fix that latch, babe." He winks.

"Cheeky fucker! But, I guess, I should." I walk down to the kitchen and grab a couple of bottles of water from the fridge, handing one over to Kes. "It feels strange without him; we have all meshed together so simply, I never thought of anything like this for us. I never wanted more than you and Ellie, but Denver just fits with us." I sigh, "I wish he'd fucking hurry up and get home."

"Yeah, me too; my balls are turning blue." Kes grumbles, then chugs half the bottle of water in one go. "Come on, babe, let's finish this. I've got work in a couple of hours, and you need to get to see Ellie. Have you told her about the fostering yet?"

"Yeah, I talked about it yesterday. She was good about it, she says she wants a sister, there're enough men in her life." I laugh, "I guess she's right about that, any boyfriend is going to have to be brave to call on her with us all around."

"That's great, because I know she has to talk to the social worker, too."

We carry on our idle talk as we work and, soon, we're done. The cream walls are showing off Denver's achievements and some of his artwork, too.

"Okay, we're done, I'm going to shower and head off to the bar. You gonna send Den a message to tell him where we are?"

"Yeah, I'll call in to see you when I've finished at my mom's." I grab my cell and my jacket, shouting out my goodbye.

When I arrive at my mom's, Ellie sits on the porch reading a book; I love how she seems uninterested in the latest technology, preferring a book over an iPad and Facebook. I know it's only a matter of time but, for now, I'm happy.

"Hey, Ellie babe, whatcha reading?" I step the three wooden steps to the porch.

"Harry Potter, it's the last one and it's so exciting." Ellie jumps up and hugs me then leads me inside, jabbering on about Dobbie and trapped dragons.

I talk about the meeting we had with the social worker and explain that we don't get to choose which child we have: they put the one who will thrive the best with us.

"Can I come and live with you when you get another one, or I'll miss out on everything?" Ellie asks, pushing her bangs out of her eyes so she can look at me.

"I don't know, Ells. I thought you like it here with Grams?" I'd never thought about it, but it's something we need to talk about.

"We're okay as we are for now, Ellie. This could be a long way off yet. Stay a bit longer with me, poppet." My mom runs her hand down Ellie's long blonde hair.

"I know, but I'll miss out, I know I will." She sniffs, making me think she may have given this more thought than I expected.

"I'll need to talk this over with Denver and Kes; it's their home, too." Reaching over to give her a hug, I wonder for the first time if she should have moved with me years ago.

"Okay, Daddy."

"I love you, Ellie. You are my world."

"I love you, too." Her arms squeeze around my waist.

I spend an hour helping with her homework, then we kick a soccer ball around till it starts to get late.

Saying goodnight, I head out to the bar; I'm not staying long, I need to get to work early tomorrow. A new job on the other side of town—someone wants a swimming pool in their back garden—it's a nice, quick job and pays well. Life really is on the up for us now, money seems to be steadily coming in and our debts are paid off.

I think of Denver and of how much our life has changed since he walked into the bar all those months ago. Glancing down at my cell, I frown when there are no messages from him. I guess he's still at the hospital. He's probably fallen asleep again in one of the on-call rooms.

The bar is heaving when I walk in. Carter gives me a shy wave as I weave through the mass of bodies. "Where's Kes?" I ask Shelley when I reach the bar.

"Office." She answers without stopping serving.

"Hey, baby, you okay?" I wander into his office and see him on a call, so I keep quiet.

"Okay, yeah. Thank you, I'll let you know as soon as I can." Kes ends the call and drops his cell on his desk. As he leans back in his chair, his hands run down his face.

"Hey, what's up? What's got you looking like that?" I move quickly around his desk and stand in front of him. Kes opens his legs so I fit between his knees.

"That was the hospital. I called to see what was happening with Denver, because I tried to call him earlier and it just rang, not even switching to voicemail."

"So, what did they say? Is he back in surgery, or just busy? I reckon he's crashed out asleep again." I have a feeling it's none of those things.

"No, he left about six hours ago. He finished his shift and left. I even got them to check to see if his truck was still there, but it's not. He definitely left the hospital at four, when his shift ended, and he's got three days off now."

"So, where the hell is he? Why haven't we seen him?" It's my turn to scrub my face as fear builds. "I suppose there've been no accidents on the road?"

"No, the hospital would have been involved and there've been no incidents." Kes stares at me, his face etched with concern.

"Maybe he's back at the house now and is fast asleep. He probably got in and collapsed into bed. I'll go back and check."

"Yeah, go do that. If he's not there, I don't know where the hell to look." Kes sighs.

□ □ □

I only have to look up our street as I turn onto it to see that Denver isn't home—there are no cars on the driveway and the house is in darkness—but I drive up and park. I'll check that he's not here; he may have had a problem with the truck and needed a tow truck. I know I'm clutching at straws and that he's not here.

My mind goes back to this afternoon, I think about what happened and the door being open. *He was here! Denver came home but left again. He left without saying anything or shutting the door. But what would make him do that?"*

I run through everything, then my heart stops. He heard us, he heard Kes say 'it's not Denver', he said 'it's not working for him!' *FUCK!!! He thinks we were talking about him!*

I race back to the truck and hurry back to the bar, our earlier conversation running on repeat, interspersed with how easily the words could be misconstrued. My pulse is racing as I pull up at the bar again and I rush through the crowds, back to the office.

I'm short of breath when I burst back in the room. "It's us! He heard our conversation. He heard you say it wasn't working, and it wasn't Denver." My hand is over my heart and I feel the pounding as it beats rapidly in my chest. "He's left us, Kes. He left because of what you said."

I watch as the color drains from Kes' face. "What are we going to do? I bet he's at his parents. Can you go over there?"

"Not tonight, Kes, it's too late now." I flop into one of the chairs and run my hands through my hair. "How are we going to get him back, he'll never trust us again." I lift my head and look at Kes to find tears flooding his eyes.

"I'll go to him tomorrow. I'll sort it, East. I promise." Kes looks devastated. I know how he feels.

□ □ □

KES

His truck is here, so he must be, but there's no answer and I've been hammering on the door. I don't have anywhere else to be, so I'm going to sit it out and wait: he has to come outside at some point.

It's been four hours and there's been no sight or sound from him. I've knocked again and again but silence is my only reply. I really thought I would've seen him by now, East has called about four or five times and I don't know what to say. He is trying not to blame me, that it's not my fault Denver ran away. He could've come in the room and it would have been sorted out straight away.

The longer I sit here, the more pissed and annoyed I become. I start hammering on the door again before realizing the futility. I need to get back to the bar this evening; I can't sit here any longer. He knows where we are when he stops his sulking.

But as I drive away, I know it's purely my frustration that is making me feel like this: it's not his fault. He was massively over-tired and is still bruised and damaged from his fuckwit ex, but I need an outlet and it seems easier than hitting something.

I walk into the bedroom and see Denver's clothes and toiletries hanging neatly in the closet and sitting tidily on the dresser and my heart breaks. Sitting on the edge of the bed, I give in to my emotions and tears flood my eyes and burst, running down my cheeks and dripping off my chin. *Is this it? Is this all we get of him? Fuck no! We haven't even started our lives together; we need to work this out. We need to be together, we work well. It's simple, I love him: I love him so damn much.*

When East comes home, he looks as wrecked as I feel. Walking into my arms, we simply hold each other. My head rests in the crook of his neck and I breathe in his scent, letting it anchor me, righting the world for a brief moment.

"No word then?" East whispers, his voice rough in his throat.

I shake my head. "I stayed for as long as I could; I have to get to work now. What time will you finish tonight?" I can't believe it's only midafternoon.

"I'll be home by six. I was thinking of calling around there, but I think we've tried enough today." East shakes his head in disbelief. "I thought he'd be back with us. I thought you would have explained and it would be sorted, but life isn't like that, is it?"

I can't speak through the lump in my throat, so I shake my head.

My shift in the bar is a curse as much as it is a blessing; the bar is full again as the vacationers keep piling into the town. The camping sites are packed and the ranches are heaving with occupants. For me, it's everything I've worked for.

By the time I close up, my head is spinning. I crave sleep but my mind is still fixed on the door of a cabin only a few miles away. It may as well be on the other side of the continent for all the access I have to it. Carter has been quiet tonight, he knows something is up and has had the sense to keep away. The serving girls have been kept too busy to gossip or pester me. Thankfully, it is Shelley's night off, so no third degree from her.

I climb into my bed and pull East's sleeping body against mine, wrapping my arms around his solid, warm body. I kiss his neck and close my eyes.

I carry on for two days, calling him but no longer staking out his cabin. I know he is due back at work tomorrow, so maybe he'll come around even if it's only to get his clothes. But there's nothing, no sign and no word. I'm ready to pitch up at the hospital, somewhere he can't ignore me, but I won't. I won't interrupt his professional life. I'm on my days off now and have no need or desire to go into work, East is finishing early and we are thinking of getting out of town. Somewhere different, somewhere to clear our heads, and to give us a fresh perspective on how to handle this. Unfortunately, life kicks a bit more dirt in our faces when East has a rush job after a burst boiler and a collapsed ceiling.

I spend the day in the house alone, doing the things I used to do before Denver. I clean out the pool and mow the lawns; all the garden work gets done before I head in to start on the house and the laundry. I need to keep busy, otherwise I will be back in the truck and out to the ranch.

East comes home and we decide to see Ellie together and take her out for some ice cream. Her constant chatter has my spirits lifted and we laugh along at her stories. At least, we got something right with her.

By the time we are in bed, I can't help but turn to East; I need to be close to him. I need to taste and feel him. Our kisses are heated and fierce as we claw at each other's bodies, desperate to give and take everything we can from each other. Entering him, I moan loudly, painfully.

This is good, this is real. I have a man who loves me deeply and passionately and, as I run my hands over his firm body, I revel in every ripple of his muscles and every sigh and cry he utters. It doesn't take us long to reach our climax. I lie over him and kiss him hard.

"We have this, East, we have each other." I whisper as I kiss him again.

"I know, baby, I know that. But who does he have?"

We clean up quietly and sleep wrapped in each other.

I wake before East; he gave himself the day off since ours was taken away from us yesterday. I gently disentangle myself from him to head to the bathroom. Returning, sleep comes slowly to me but, eventually, I drift off.

The weight of another day without Denver with us weighs heavily on me. East is silent as we go through the motions of our everyday lives; we talk mutedly and touch frequently but, at eight o'clock in the evening, my cell rings.

"Hey, Kes, I think you need to get to the bar. Your man is here." Carter speaks in his usual, quiet manner.

"We're on our way." I end the call and look at East, "he's in the bar."

When we walk in, the room is quiet. Everyone is facing the corner and a sound I know too well crushes my heart. I hear Denver quietly singing, but it's his choice of song that breaks me.

Chris Isaak's *Wicked Game* has never sounded so painful or so broken. East clasps hold of my hand and I feel him shudder at the pain pouring from Denver's heart.

Walking over to the bar, I see Shelley has her arms wrapped around her body as she holds herself together, tears pouring down her face as she listens. When she sees us, her face hardens and she walks over.

"You need to fix this, whatever the fuck you did to him. You fix it!"

Carter stands next to Shelley and I look at him for answers.

"He got here about four o'clock, he's only had a couple of beers and he's sat over in the corner ever since."

"How many has he sung?" East asks.

"This is the second, that's why I called you." Carter stares back at Denver as he sits oblivious to his audience as he sings to himself.

"What was his first song?" I really don't think I want to know the answer but I need to hear it.

"*Don't Speak*, y'know, the No Doubt song. He killed it man, there isn't a dry eye in the whole damn place. I don't know what's going on with you but trust me, I've been where he is now and I never want to feel like that again.”

I turn around to face outwards as the song changes and I know this, too, but only because Ellie plays it in the car and sings along.

He's sings softly, but it still sounds like a roar to me, as Troy Sivan's *Fools* pierces my heart.

I can't stand here any longer. As I push away from the bar, East is by my side. I glance once over my shoulder and see Shelley urging me on so I continue to walk to the secluded corner. My head has tuned out the rest of the lyrics; I know what is said and it hurts.

The people surrounding him are reticent to move away, so we weave between them until we get to Denver.

“Enough, baby. It's time to come home.” East speaks quietly and holds out his hand.

Denver's fingers still on the strings as he raises his eyes, showing exhaustion as well as pain.

Denver doesn't say a word, only looks back down at his guitar. Then, standing up, he pushes between us and walks away.

My hand reaches out to snag his arm but he pulls himself free.

□ □ □

DENVER

Driving into work was hard today; I spent every moment of the last three days in bed. I slept so heavily, as if my body needed to shut down. Not only from the pain of hearing Kes' words, but from the exhaustion of a nearly fifty-six-hour shift.

Hearing Chase gossiping about me frustrated me. I need to speak to Woodruff about him; I want to know why he was transferred here and how we can curb his need to tittle-tattle.

Pulling into my parking space, I feel empty. For the first time in years, I don't want to do this. Even after Alec made such a fool of me, I didn't let it affect my work, but now I'm not sure I want to do this. I shake my head and try and get in the zone, I know I can't let people down by letting my personal life affect me at work.

When I enter, I see Callum and he looks up and smiles his greeting but his features turn quickly to surprise. Leaving his work station, he walks up.

"Denver, what happened? You look shattered." He looks at me sympathetically.

"I'm fine, I just had a stressful couple of days, but I'm good. I promise." I smile and know it's not convincing but it's all I've got. It's seven in the morning and I'm here until three this afternoon, so I can do this. "I need to see Dr. Woodruff, is he in today?"

"Yeah, he's here already." Callum turns away as his name is called.

I walk off to Woodruff's office and tap on the door.

"Denver, to what do I owe this pleasure? Take a seat, please."

"Hello, Carson. I just want to ask you about Chase Fielding?" I hear the strain in my voice, so it's no surprise he can, too.

"Hmm, he's a strange one, for sure. He asked to transfer here, but I think I was doing his department a favor by taking him. He's a good doctor; he does have a cockiness about him that I thought would develop into confidence. What's he done to rattle your cage?"

"He could cause me some trouble: he overheard a private chat I was having with my partner, well, *one* of my partners. I have, or had—I'm not sure about that anymore now… but he then replayed what he had heard to Connie and Callum." I take a deep breath as I watch the look of shock on Woodruff's face. I don't know if it's at the admission of two lovers or of Fielding's indiscretion. "They both admonished him for telling tales, but it was the added tidbit that has me concerned."

227

"First, thank you for coming to me with this. I do know about you and your relationship with your boyfriends, and I am not at all concerned, what you do in your own life is of no business of mine or anyone else's. Second, I knew that you left after ending a relationship; I did not know the reason. I am concerned about Fielding gossiping about you. My question to you is: what do you want to do about it?" Woodruff leans back in his chair.

"I want it on record that I have reported his indiscretion. I would like to not have to work with him, but I know that is going to be nigh on impossible. But I would like him to be brought to account over his misdemeanors, even if it's just a verbal warning. I hope that would suffice, but how you deal with this is for you to decide. I just wanted to bring you up to date with the goings on here."

"I will be speaking with him, Denver. And, trust me when I say that you are more important to me than he is. We are a developing, and innovative department and I won't have it compromised by any member of staff." He smiles reassuring me.

"Thank you, Carson. I have to leave on time today; I've clocked up my hours already." I shake my head at the stupid rule.

"Then you'd better do what you are so good at. Thank you for your openness with me, Denver. I'll see you in a few days."

I don't see Fielding until I'm about ready to leave and he comes sauntering into our break room. His smug, know-it-all smile increases as he sets his eyes on me.

"Good afternoon, Dr. Sinclair. Did you enjoy your rest days?" He smirks.

"Good afternoon, Dr. Fielding. Yes, thank you. Enjoy your shift; I think that Connie has all the handover details." I turn and walk away.

"You look tired, have your boyfriends worn you out?" He asks casually.

"Be careful, Fielding. I've warned you once already." I walk away.

"Whatever, dude. Whatever floats your boat." He simpers.

As I drive away, I let my mind drift back to Kes and East; I've managed to focus on work and left them behind. But now they fill my head. Not the words I heard but the scent of their bodies, the taste of hot skin, the feel of hands on my body and the sounds and moans softly emitted as we made love.

Once again, I drive home in a daze and suddenly find myself outside the bar. I know it's Kes' day off so I stop. I need a beer; my guitar is still here and I want to take it with me.

It's crowded but I notice Shelley and Carter busy behind the bar, allowing me to get to the office. I know the combination on the door, making it easy for me to sneak in and out. Then, finding a quiet corner, I wait for the server to come over. I people-watch for a few minutes and see mainly new faces; these are the vacationers, here to trek and hike the amazing trails in the area. I'm guessing some of them are staying at my folks' place.

I feel a shadow loom over me and look up, expecting to see one of our waitresses but, *shit, no. It's Shelley.*

She looks me over. "You look like shit, and why aren't you where your men are?" Her eyes bore into me and I break apart. "Oh, honey, what has happened? He's not here today; I thought something was up when he said he wasn't even calling in today. He always comes over just to check, you know this."

"I can't talk about it. Can I have a beer, please?" I need a bit of time out, so I watch the groups of chattering friends as I wait for Shelley to return with my order. When she does, I sit back and drink slowly, surprised Shelley hasn't called him yet. I'm trying not to watch the door but my eyes keep drifting towards it.

Deciding to grab another bottle, I head for the bar. Carter serves me this time, with a nod of his head and a sad smile; I get the sense he knows exactly how I'm feeling. Walking back to my seat, I try to dodge a couple of young girls who catch my eye and smile.

"You gonna play that for us?" One asks, she gives me a little wink and smiles.

"I'm not sure, not really a good idea right now." I edge past them and take me seat. I have my guitar on my lap and I see people looking over, almost waiting for me to play.

My fingers make up their own mind and, without even thinking about it, I start playing, No Doubt's *Don't Speak* jumps into my mind and I'm soon lost in the painful lyrics and play for myself. As I morph into *Wicked Games*, I know I am ripping my heart out and I should stop but my fingers keep making the chords and plucking on the strings. The words are so fitting and my heart hurts, but my head won't let them go.

It's not until I'm halfway through Troye Sivan's *Fools* that I notice the hush in the room. Abruptly, people part as Kes and East stride toward me.

"Enough, baby; it's time to come home." East's words pierce my heart and I find I have nothing to say. Standing up, I move past them. Kes grabs at my arm but I pull free: if I let him touch me here, I'll break down and I have more pride than that.

I look at Shelley as I pass the bar and she blows me a kiss. I suddenly become aware of the total silence in the room: everyone is looking at, or between me and the two men striding through the room.

When I get outside, I lean against the door of my truck, my head clunking back on the window as I screw my eyes up to the sky. They weren't supposed to be here, now they have heard me pour my broken heart out to a hundred nameless people. Now they know exactly how much they have hurt me. And in any conversation we have, I fear they have the upper hand and will control it. I don't hear them, though; I thought I'd be crowded against my truck by now, their mouths on mine as they persuade me with their skills rather than their words.

I straighten up and open my eyes, squinting in the still bright sunlight. They stand on the sidewalk, Kes has his hands in his front pockets and he rocks back on his heels—a habit I know is a nervous one—and East's hands clench in and out of fists as they hang by his sides. They are wrong-footed, they don't know what to do. I guess the ball is back in my court.

"We need to talk." East says. I'm surprised it's him who seems to be leading; Kes is normally the force behind them.

"C'mon then, let's go talk." I see them exhale, as if they have been holding their breaths the whole time out here.

I press the button on my key fob and release the locks, "I'll see you in a few." I climb in, then wait for them to move away. East is driving and Kes looks at me sadly as they turn towards their place. Or, maybe, it can be our place again. *If* I want this again. *Why am I trying to kid myself? I want this; I want it so fucking much.*

I pull up next to them on the wide driveway and switch off my engine. I'm not sure how easy this is going to be, and I find it hard to get out of my truck. A small smile flits across my mouth as I remember feeling nervous months ago, when I came to talk about a job. I now know so much more and however much I hurt right now, I know I still love them. I know I still want them and, if East's words mean what I hope, they want me too.

Okay, here goes my pride and dignity: it's time to face them. I need to do it without breaking down, I can't cry any more.

My door opens before I can reach for it and East stands in front of me; he looks tired. I want to run my hand down his stubbled cheeks, feeling the heat build up in my eyes as tears threaten. Swallowing hard, I watch as he holds out his hand for me to take, a minute tremor shaking him as he hesitates to reach for me.

"Denver, baby, please." He beseeches me. "Please, come inside."

I nod and swing my legs around to jump down. I know he wants to take my hand or, at least, touch me, so I offer a small peace offering and let my fingertips flit across the back of his hand. I hear him sigh and my heart stutters at the need to comfort him. I know this is not his doing.

"Fuck! I've missed you, Den, I've missed you so fucking much." East pushes me back against the side of my truck and his hands cup my face, his eyes boring into mine. Then his mouth hits mine. His scent floods me, my brain stops working and I part my lips for him. As his flavor bursts onto my tongue, we groan. My hands clutch at his hips, keeping him pressed up hard to my body. Time stands still as we reconnect, our tongues tangle and dance until we hear Kes shout, making us break apart.

I brush the pad of my thumb over his swollen lower lip as he brushes his over my cheekbone. "C'mon, Kes needs to say something." His eyes are tender, no longer afraid.

"I'm sure he does, but am I ready to hear it?" I mutter to myself but East hears me.

"Let him explain, Den. He is hating himself so much."

"Okay, then. Let's go." I walk ahead of East, still not comfortable enough to hold his hand even though he wants me to.

Chapter
Sixteen

EAST

I trudge behind Denver, unclear on what Kes plans to say. I know how frustrated he gets when he is misunderstood, which is why he sat outside Den's cabin all damn day. He has been so quiet today, so withdrawn. I have tried to talk to him but he merely shakes his head and says he doesn't know what to do. Well, now is his chance; I am not ready to let Denver walk away again.

When I walk in, Denver is already striding toward the kitchen where I see Kes reaching into a cupboard and bring out three wine glasses. He turns away and walks out of sight but I know he's heading for the garden. Thank god, he's shut the door to the room that caused this fucking problem; I'm ready to burn the damn desk.

"I thought we could share a bottle of wine in the garden, is that okay?" He sounds nervous but Denver's equal hesitancy has me worried that this isn't going to be easy.

"I guess, but I need to drive so, maybe, I should stick to water." Denver stands in the doorway uncertain whether to walk outside or not.

"Don't walk away from us again, Denver; I'm not sure I could take it." I stand behind him, not brave enough to touch him again without his agreement, but I notice his back stiffens and his hand clenches at his side.

"You're not going back to the cabin, Denver. You live here, with us. It's where you belong." Kes bites at him and sloshes red wine in all three glasses.

I close my eyes, I knew it would go one of two ways and this is not the one I wanted. Before I can bring him up on it, Denver speaks, *oh shit!*

"Is this your explanation, Kes? Well, you've got me convinced. Do you want me to blow you just to make up for your lack of them in three days?" He turns and kisses me briefly but so sweetly. "Sorry, East; I love you but I don't work this way."

"Please, don't go. He's frightened. He loves you, Den, he just doesn't know where to start. Sit down, give him a minute to work it out."

He nods and steps outside. Kes is looking at the ground but lifts his head up when a chair scrapes over the floor. *Oh fuck, he's crying!*

"Denver, I'm sorry. I'm sorry for what you heard me say. I'm sorry they were so easy to misunderstand. How can I ever not love you? You own me, you and East are my soulmates. I hate myself, I hate that you heard words that would make you doubt me. I'm not good with words; I just say whatever comes into my head. They made perfect sense to me, until I played them over in my head. And I would have done the same as you, I would have walked away." Kes lifts his hand up to Denver but lets it drop again, still so unsure of what to say next. "I know you don't understand why we have found each other and I understand why you doubt yourself to be enough. But if you come home to us, I will tell you every day how much I love you."

"You did that already, Kes. That's what was so hard, why I couldn't walk in through the door and confront you, because Alec would tell me he loved me and look what he did. I know you and East are nothing like that bastard, but it was a candid conversation and sounded so real, so true." Denver picks up his glass and turns it in his fingers, I love the way he appreciates good wine. I smile when I see him take a sip, *maybe he will stay tonight.*

"I came to the cabin, y'know, the next morning. We knew you had left the hospital, I called to find out. It was East that worked out why you weren't with us. He wouldn't let me come out to you that night but I was there the next day. All fucking day, I hammered on your door, and you never answered. I expected a fuck off but not silence."

"Oh, I thought I'd dreamed that. Kes, I hadn't slept in nearly three days: I was exhausted, my heart had just shattered into a million pieces and my brain shut me down. I slept for nearly the whole three days off. I had dreams, nightmares, whatever they were. So, the hammering on the door was just part of the hell I was locked in." He raises the glass to his lips again.

I watch as Kes' eyes follow Denver's glass to his mouth and hear the sigh he emits when Den's tongue flicks out and licks a drop from the glass as he pulls it away.

"It seems that being unconscious for so long doesn't stop me from looking like shit, as my colleagues and friends pointed out to me today." He looks at me, then at Kes, "the question is, what do we do now?"

"You don't have to do anything, you have to let me make it up to you. To show you and East how fucking sorry I am. If you will let me. I love you, Denver, I really fucking love you." Kes lifts his eyes to mine, "you too, East, I've hurt you too and I'm sorry."

"I love you, too." Denver whispers.

"Will you stay?" Kes whispers in reply. I hold my breath while

Denver decides and with the most stunning, shy, hot, cute, whatever the fuck it is, smile, he nods.

"Yeah, I'll stay." Then his megawatt smile comes out as we crowd him, pulling him out of his chair. I let Kes kiss him first; I've had one already tonight.

"Hey, c'mon. Share, you bastard!" I grin at Kes and drag Denver from him.

We kiss for what feels like forever. Sometimes only two mouths, but more often it is all three of us. Denver leans his head back as we ravage his neck, I suck and bite on the soft flesh at the base while Kes licks up to the tender spot below his ear. Our moans become heavier and louder and I remember we are outside still.

"Come on, let's take this inside. I need more of you, both of you." I pant as my hands run over Denver's ass.

"God, yes." Kes moans, but Denver stills.

"What were you talking about, if it wasn't me?"

"Can I show you later, or, better still, tomorrow?" Kes asks. Denver nods and runs his hands over our dicks, making us groan.

Denver surprises me by taking the lead and walking away, the strut in his step is so confident when he looked so broken not an hour ago.

He turns his head and looks over his shoulder, "I need a shower."

I don't need him to say anything more, I race behind him in time to see him strip the last of his clothes from his lean, tanned body.

"Fuck! You are so hot!" I step closer as he straightens, his smile floors me. "Fuck! I love you." Pulling my shirt up over my head, I rapidly shed my clothes. My dick bounces against my stomach, my erection standing proud. I turn and see Kes hesitating in the doorway. "Kes, get naked, c'mon."

The shower starts and Denver frowns at us through the door. "Seriously, you two. I'm having to do this alone?"

This spurs Kes into action and he kicks off his shoes as I speed up to join Denver. Stepping into the shower, Den turns to me and the heat burning in his eyes has me hauling him up against my body. My mouth devours his. Pushing my tongue into his mouth, I stroke mine over his before sucking it into my mouth. Denver groans and his hands grasp my ass, kneading my cheeks, his fingers digging into the skin but it's not enough; I want his hands everywhere.

Kes steps in, sandwiching Denver between us, his mouth on Den's neck as his teeth scrape over the tender skin.

"You'd better not be at work tomorrow; I'm claiming you back, marking you as mine." He sucks the skin on Den's neck right above his collar bone, branding him.

"Let me wash; I don't want to do this here, I want our bed. I need to be back in *our* bed." Denver speaks breathlessly as we continue to cover him in kisses.

"I'll get it ready." Kes' rough voice, deep and full of lust, sends shivers over my body.

I grab Den's body wash and pour some into my hands. "I'm not quite so ready to stop touching your body." I murmur over his lips as my hands stroke his body, slick and smooth as the soap coats his skin. I roam the length of his spine and down the crease of his butt. As he leans into me, I murmur my love and devotion to him.

Moments later, Denver sluices the bubbles from his body and switches off the shower. As he steps out, I grab a towel and rub the soft fabric over him, absorbing the droplets of water. Then, taking his hand, I lead him to the bed.

"What do you want, Denver, what do you want from us?" Kes steps up to Denver. His hand slides over Den's hard cock and grips it tightly, pumping the solid length. Denver leans back against my body as my hands hold his hips.

"Everything, I want it all. Take me, mark me, claim me." He pants, punching his hips forward into Kes' fist.

"Get on the bed, baby." I whisper, "Lie down."

□ □ □

DENVER

My body aches for their touch, my dick dripping precum onto my stomach as I lie back. Kes runs his hand up my leg, his fingertips trailing lightly over my calf and knee. Shivers run over me as goosebumps stud my body. I wasn't going to turn our talk, Kes' apology and explanation into a stupid game. He's sorry. I miss him and East; they love me as much as I love them. Why should we hurt each other anymore? I want to be back where we were, happy and in love, it's that simple. We're not some chick flick that pisses everyone off, simply because they don't speak.

"Fuck, you are so sexy, baby." East leans over me and kisses me, so softly, so lovingly, then it morphs into more and I can't get enough. I tangle my fingers in his hair, keeping his mouth on mine as I moan.

Kes replaces his fingertips with his mouth and I feel the hot, wet kisses he covers my inner thighs with. I'm writhing in the bed, so desperate for more. An image flashes through my mind, one I would never have thought of, or even dreamed about. I want them both. I want them both inside me. *Fuck*, my dick swells and hardens even more. A burst of precum oozes from me and my ass clenches at the thought, the need.

"What's going on, Den, what has you squirming?" Kes' mouth is so close to my sac, I feel the heat from his breathe as he whispers.

"I want both of you." My voice is low and needy.

"You have us both, you have us for always." East kisses me again.

"No! I want you both! I want you inside me together. I need you both." My hands grab at them, unsure how they will react to my plea.

"Fuck!" East breathes out hard as he digests my words. "God, yes! I want that. Kes?"

Kes stills, his hands gripping my thighs tightly. Then, kneeling between my legs, he looks at me. I have never seen, and certainly never been on the receiving end of, such a scorching, hot look.

"Damn, Denver. Are you for real? You want this from us?"

I nod, my lower lip caught between my teeth.

"I need more than a nod, Den." Kes seems to grow in front of my eyes, his whole demeanor changes and, damn if he doesn't get even hotter.

"Yes. God, yes; I want this. I have been through hell these last few days, I need you to anchor me to you. I need to know that you choose me." I hear the raw emotion in my voice and I reach out to hold them.

Kes groans and ducks back down between my legs, his mouth immediately on me, taking me deep into his mouth. East sits up and leans over me, his cock weeping as he hovers it over my mouth.

"Take me, baby. Take me deep." His cock slides over the seam of my lips, making me open up to flick the bead of precum spilling from the tip onto my tongue. The sweet-salty flavor bursts on my tongue and I groan before lapping at his length then swallowing him.

Slick with lube, I feel Kes' fingers at my hole, I know and trust him to prep me well. I relax and let two fingers slide easily inside me. The need to have them and feel them inside me has my body relaxing, ready for them.

"You are so hot and tight, Den; you have to promise that if it's too much you tell us. I do not ever want to cause you any pain again." As he speaks, he slides another finger inside me.

"East, suck his dick, show him how much we love him."

East moves down my body, kissing every inch as he travels down my torso. Then I'm in his mouth but he doesn't take me deep; his tongue circles and surrounds the head before sucking on the tip. His teeth scrape over the tender, sensitive skin. Kes pulls his fingers back and I hear the lube cap popping open again. The cool gel smothers my hole as he pushes back inside, he's got to have four fingers in me now. I feel the stretch as it tugs and pulls on my tight hole. This is going to feel so good.

I feel my climax building inside me and my spine tingles. I don't want to come yet: I want to come when they are both inside me.

"Enough, Kes, I'm ready. Let's take it slow; I'm going to blow if East keeps sucking my dick." I bend my knees and spread my legs.

"Not like this, Denver: straddle East and lean over him. Take him first and I'll join from behind."

East moves like lightning and is propped up on a pile of pillows before I can form a coherent thought. Straddling him, I lean forward and kiss him hard. Kes pumps his fingers back inside me and I hear his moans and curses as my body accepts him. I feel empty as he withdraws but East presses his dick up to my hole, then he pushes upward and slides inside me. Kes has done such a great job of prepping me, East slips in completely, groaning as he goes balls deep. I lean further forward and capture his mouth. My tongue delves inside and duels easily with his.

My hips rock, forcing him to slide in and out of me. We moan when Kes adds his finger inside me, then another, letting me take the lead as he stretches me again. Moments later, his fingers slip out and, as East glides down but not out of me, I feel Kes nudge the head of his huge cock inside me.

"Hold still, baby. Just let him slowly in. Breathe, Den, you're doing amazing. This is going to feel so good. Take your time, take all the time you need." East's words wash over me as the stretch and burn consumes me. It's too much, but it's too good to stop.

"Fuck!" I cry out and Kes stills.

"Too much, Den? Do you want me to stop?"

"No, yes! No, fuck no, don't stop. Slowly, it feels so amazing, just go slow." I pant as my eyes screw tight shut and then he slips further in and the pain turns to pleasure. I can tell they notice it too, as Kes groans and pushes all the way in before holding still.

"You can move now, slowly; take it slowly."

Kes pulls back as East slides inside again. They push and pull, never too fast, but with every movement I feel myself climbing higher and higher. The feeling of them dragging against my tender muscle walls has me crying out. East holds still inside me, his head on my sweet spot and, as Kes slides in and out, the motion nudges East's dick against it.

"OhgodOhgodOhgod." Suddenly, my orgasm explodes from me, pelting East's chest as well as mine. Then one of them stills, I can't tell who until East cries out and his orgasm floods me first. The heat fills my channel, making my orgasm go on and on.

Then Kes roars and stills inside me and I feel him pulse and shudder, his orgasm mixing with East's, filling me with their release.

Then it's silent, apart from our labored breathing, as I feel both men softening inside me. I'm collapsed on East's chest as I gasp for breath and try to bring my emotions under control. Kes moves first, his dick slides from my ass and I feel the loss immediately. With another moan, he falls to the side of me. His hands stay on me, keeping the connection we desperately need.

East moves beneath me and I push myself up, giving him some space. As I move, I feel him slip from inside me and the rush of their combined release gushes from me. This makes me chuckle as I fall to the side of East. Sandwiched between my two men, I can't help or stop my laughter.

Kes props himself up on his elbow, resting his head in the palm of his hand, I smile at him and see a look of pure love in his eyes. His fingers slide down my cheek and he cups my chin.

"You are everything, Denver. I have never experienced anything like that before." He looks to East who is still collapsed, his arm flung over his eyes. "East, are you okay, my love?"

"You've killed me, Den, baby. I can't find the words to tell you just how much I love you. I never want us to be apart again."

"I can't believe we have just done that. The feelings coursing through me are so intense and so alive. I love you, too, both of you." I reach up to kiss Kes then turn to do the same to East. "Just one thing, though."

"What, are you hurt?" Kes panics.

"No, honey, I'm not hurt, but I've got a gallon of cum seeping out of my ass. Someone, please, go and get a cloth."

They burst into laughter and East rolls onto his side then gets off the bed. Moments later he's back with a warm, damp cloth and, tenderly, he cleans me.

"Fuck, Den. I think maybe a shower would be better." He laughs.

"I'm not sure I can stand yet." I admit.

East dumps the cloth in the laundry basket and lies back down next to me. I rest my head on his chest, grateful that he's cleaned himself too. Kes sidles up against me, his hand skimming my ribcage and down to my hip.

"Thank you." I whisper as the magnitude of what we have done hits me.

"It's us who are thankful, Denver. Thank you for listening, for forgiving me. I will never give you reason to doubt me again."

I feel sleep taking over me, and, even though we really should shower, I can't move. I feel safe and loved and whole again. Then, as

I slip under, the image of Chase Fielding flits across my mind. *I must tell them what has happened.*

□ □ □

KES

I watch Den and East sleep; they look so peaceful, Denver has his arm wrapped around East's body, holding him close. It's late but I'm too buzzed to sleep. I shift and slide out of bed, trying not to wake them, and slip on my shorts. I need coffee and some time to think. I can't believe we have him back. I'm nervous to show him our surprise and he will, hopefully, forgive me.

I take my coffee outside. The nights are warm, sometimes too warm, but it's a good temperature tonight. My head tips back and I stare up at the night sky and the stars. Gazing at the distant balls of fire, my head is still full of the sounds and scents of the three of us tonight.

Denver wanting us that way, trusting us after we broke his heart, is not something I'm ever going to forget. If we never do that again, I will remember every second of it. The taste of his sweat-drenched skin on my tongue as I lick up his back, the feeling of East's dick rubbing up with mine; it was unbelievable. I'm so happy we have never done this before, I think it's something every gay guy thinks about but never—and I mean NEVER—believes it will happen. My love for him only grows and grows. I close my eyes and go back to my thoughts.

"Hey, honey, what're you doing out here?"

Denver's voice startles me. With my hand over my rapidly beating heart, I smile and melt a little bit more as he bends over the back of the chair to kiss me.

"I couldn't sleep, I can't get how much I hurt you with my stupid words and yet you come back to us and still love us. What we shared tonight, Den, was just, shit... I can't find the words. It was something else, something so much more. I'm doing this really badly, it was more than, it was…"

"Everything, Kester, it was everything. It was all of what we each had to give. It taught me just how much we trust each other, and not to act like a fucking stupid kid." Denver sits next to me on the lounger. "I was at fault here, Kes, not you. I should've walked in and faced it, even if what you said had been about not wanting me. I shouldn't have run off and hidden. I'm sorry, too."

"Oh, Denver, my love. You should never hear those words said. I promise you now, I will *always* love you. Even when you're tired and crabby." I joke, trying to make him smile.

"Really, "he chuckles. "Even then? Wow, you must really love me." He smiles causes me to pull him close, making him lie next to me with my arm around him.

"Yep, even then." I run my free hand down his naked chest. "You are someone definitely worth loving. Your asshole ex is a fool, but he's the fool who brought you home to us. So, maybe, if I ever meet him, I should thank him rather than punch his lights out."

Denver laughs again. "Oh, Kes, darling, he'd run a mile from you with just one glance from you; you're so built and hot, you'd scare him away."

"Shit! What would he say about East, he's sporting some muscles!" I'm laughing when Denver pulls my face towards his.

"I would never let that fucker anywhere near either of you; I will take him out if he comes within fifty feet of either of you. You," he kisses my mouth hard, "You are mine."

His mouth hits mine again and I'm ready for him this time. My tongue teases over the seam of his lips, pushing for entry, pushing for control. I'm wrong, Denver is in charge as he rolls on top of me. His dick is swelling under the soft, cotton shorts he's wearing and, fuck, mine does, too. As his tongue invades my mouth and explores every area, my hands reach down and cup his ass cheeks, pulling him closer to me, letting me grind against him.

A long moan escapes me as he pulls back and runs his mouth and teeth over my chin and down my neck. I shiver as he licks over my Adam's apple then moves on to suck hard on the skin at the base of my neck, no doubt leaving a mark but I don't give a shit.

"Let me taste you, Kes, I want my mouth on you." His voice so low and raw, I groan loudly.

Moving down my body, he leaves wet, openmouthed kisses over my torso and down my abs. His tongue dipping into my navel makes me squirm, so he does it again. I feel his smile on my skin as he moves further down. As his fingertips dip under the top of my shorts, my hips push into him. Deftly, he pops the button and unzips me. My aching cock springs out to meet him, making him chuckle again. I love his laughter but, right now, I want his mouth so full of my dick he can't laugh.

"Fuck! Den, Christ, just get your mouth round my dick." I beg.

Silently, he leans over me and takes me deep in his mouth in one go, my back arching as the head hits the back of his throat. He quickly gets to work on me, his mouth skating up and down my length before his tongue circles the crown, then dips into the slit, licking the precum as it burst from me.

"God, you taste good." Den murmurs and takes me deep again, sucking me hard as his hand plays with my sac. I know I'm not going to last long, I feel my balls pulling into my body, but Denver tugs on them, making me curse. Then he adds a finger in his mouth and I know where he's going with that; I can't fucking wait.

I feel like I'm holding my breath as he releases it, waiting for him to slide it down to my ass. Then I feel it, as he swallows me again, he pushes inside me. Oh god, he slips so smoothly inside me. My chest heaves, the rise and fall centering me as he takes me higher. Then, as he strokes over my prostate, I know I'm a goner!

"Fuck! Crap! Yes, don't stop! Shit, don't stop!" I hear shouting but don't realize it's coming from me until I shoot my load and all I hear is panting. Denver's mouth is clamped around my dick as he swallows my load, *fuck, it won't stop!*

My dick softens at the same time my back hits the lounger and my tense, flexed muscles relax. Denver continues to gently, lovingly, lick and suck me as I come back down to earth. My breath hitches in my throat as I look down at him, he meets my eyes with my dick still in his mouth and I have never seen such a wanton, devilish, greedy, and smug look on his face before, but damn, it suits him. Keeping his eyes fixed on me, I feel spellbound as he lets his tongue slip around my head on more time. I see my release glistening on his tongue and, damn, I want that in my mouth. My hands grab him under his armpits to haul him up to face me.

"You just keep on fucking giving! God, how I love you." Before giving him a chance to speak, my mouth crashes against his. My tongue dives inside, overwhelming me with my own taste and I suck on his tongue. We groan and our hands grab and clutch as we devour each other.

As we break apart, both of us panting, I swipe my thumb over my swollen lips as Den uses the back of his hand to capture the last of my release before licking it from his knuckles.

"Christ, you're gonna fucking kill me! How can you be this damn hot?" I chuckle and pepper kisses over him. "You're one of the most respected trauma surgeons in the country, maybe even further afield. But you are the goddamn devil! That mouth of yours needs a fucking health warning on it!"

A faint blush stains Denver's cheek but that could be the adrenaline leaving his body—hey, he's the doctor, he knows what's going on.

"You reckon you can get some sleep now? C'mon, doctor's orders." His smile kills me.

"Yeah, I reckon I'm good now. I love you, Denver." I whisper into his ear as he leans in for another kiss.

"Yeah, but not as much as I love you." He looks at me now, his eyes delving deep into mine. "You saved me, Kes. You and East brought me back to life, not just the shit that Alec laid on me! You and East have made me want and need more in my life, you have given me more. You have made me human again. My life with Alec was numb, anesthetized as I took on more work to compensate; now I hate every extra minute I'm away from the pair of you. I have so much more to look forward to with you and East than I ever had with him. But, baby, it's bedtime, c'mon."

Denver stands up and holds out his hand, and it's so honest and open, I willingly accept it and let him pull me upright. My pants falling break the honesty, but only in a good way.

"Okay, Denver, take me back to bed." I smile and pop a chaste kiss on his parted lips.

"You going to tell how all this shit went down tomorrow?"

"Yeah, I promise to tell you everything." I'm led, in my sated, drug-like state, back to bed.

As we slide back under the quilt, East mumbles, "About time you fuckers got back here." He face-plants the pillow again.

"Remind me to tell you about Chase, too." Denver garbles as he falls quickly to sleep.

I wrap myself around him and sigh, *he's back. Thank god, he's back.* I let myself fall asleep, happy for the first time in days.

Chapter
Seventeen

DENVER

I walk out of the wide-open doors into the garden. Kes is cleaning the pool and East is on his ride-on lawnmower; the garden takes a lot of work but it's worth it.

I watch the muscles flexing, contracting as he sweeps the net through the water; he'll burn his back if he doesn't get a shirt on soon. I glance around and see his discarded T-shirt thrown over the back of a chair. Strolling over to it, I swoop it up and turn back to walk up to him.

"Kes, my love, you need your shirt on; you'll burn and then you'll be sore and I won't be able to touch you." I lean over the fence and kiss him as he reaches for me.

"You like me shirtless." He winks but grabs the shirt and pulls it on.

"I need to talk to you both, can you grab East and come inside?" I smile and run my hand through his hair, I love it when it's not tied back.

"Is everything okay? What's happened? Den, you've gotta give me more." Kes looks panicked and I smile at his pacing.

"Y'know I've mentioned the junior doctor, Chase Fielding, to you." I wait while they agree. "Well, he overheard me talking to you and now knows that I am in a relationship with both of you. I heard him discussing it with some other members of the team. Luckily, they acted sensibly and told him it was nobody's business and to cut it out."

"The little shit!" East mutters.

"Indeed. I don't care about them knowing; I never intended, or tried, to keep you a secret. I just think that my work and home lives should be separate. I'm worried, though, that you may not like anyone else knowing about us. I've spoken to Woodruff and he is going to deal with Fielding, although," I chuckle, "He knew about us already and isn't the slightest bit concerned. Which is a relief for me."

"Baby, I don't give a shit who knows. Hell, everyone that walks in the bar sees the three of us together. This is a small community and news spreads like wild fire, so I can't care who knows." East smiles and reaches out to clasp my hand.

"Anyway, I just wanted to get you up to date with what happened."

"You're right, Den. It's not like you're interested in him. I'm sure the little upstart will get bored of trying to bait someone who doesn't give a shit." Kes says.

Then he claps his hands and jumps up, "I think we've got something to show Denver, don't you, East?"

I laugh when they get excited and drag me out of my chair.

"Yes, we have, and I really hope you like it."

"What have you done? If it's dirty, then I think my ass might be out of action tonight?" I laugh and East's face lights up.

"Yours may be, but mine isn't." He winks as his eyes dilate and darken, and his Adam's apple bobs as he swallows hard. "Later, baby."

I let Kes take the lead, then I follow behind, my eyes fixed on his ass, high and tight in his snug jeans.

He turns down the side hallway, to a part of the house we don't use very often. There's a couple of extra guest rooms down here, so it's not an area I have come into very often. As Kes pushes open a door, I feel East take a place next to me as I look inside.

"What? What is this? Have you done this for me?" I look at them but then a shiver runs over me as I remember the words that hurt so much. "I don't understand what you were talking about if you have done something so thoughtful and kind, I'm confused." His hand wipes across his forehead as he frowns.

Kes walks up behind me, hooking his thumbs in my belt loops and pulling me against his chest. He drops a tender kiss on my neck before sighing.

"We spent all day looking for a desk and then we found this one. After dragging it in, I decided I didn't like it, that it wasn't you and I didn't see it working. I don't think I've ever said words I regret more. I love you, I love you more than I thought I would be able to. When you walked into the bar that first night, my heart ached, you looked so broken, East felt it too. I've said it before but it was you, you were calling out to us, needing us to fix you."

I twist around in Kes' arms to face him, his eyes bright with emotion. East steps behind me and sandwiches me between them. Sliding his hands into the front pockets of his jeans, he leans in and whisper in my ear.

"I love you, Denver, I always will."

As he moves again, we all kiss—three mouths always in sync, always together. I feel the heat rising and, as much as I hate it, I pull back.

"I reckon this desk needs testing out, don't you?" Kes whispers huskily in my ear, making goosebumps surface over my body.

"Fuck yeah."

□ □ □

Back at work, and with my head in a much happier place now everything is sorted at home, I breeze through my day. Nothing major happens and I'm able to get away on time. I've got East to myself for a few hours tonight before Kes finishes up at work, and I'm looking forward to spending time with him. Kes and I spent many hours together when I worked at the bar and East was out at the ranch, so it will be good to have some together time. I'm not sure he knows I'll be home when he finishes but I plan to make the most of it.

I get in and head for the shower, wanting to get the smell of the hospital off my skin. Chase didn't speak to me, leading me to believe he had been told to keep away from me unless we had to work together. I did catch him watching me though, but warily rather than with his usual cocksure manner. I soap up my body quickly and wash my hair, wanting to be in my office by the time East comes home; I want him on my desk. I want him begging for release.

I dry off and dress in my jeans, leaving my chest and feet bare and wander down to my office where my iPod is linked in to the music center and it's playing some of our favorite tracks, many of them ones I have sung for them. I hear the front door open then slam shut.

"FUCK!!!!" I rush to the door at East's shout and find him

barreling down the hallway to my office.

"East, honey. What's wrong?" I pull him into me and feel him shaking. Leaning back to look at him, I see how angry and upset he is. "Talk to me, East,"

I kiss his tense mouth, holding him close to me.

"I can't even think about it." East steps out of my embrace and runs his hands through his hair before knotting his fingers together behind his head. He looks at me and sighs before dropping his arms and stepping back to me. "I guess I should've expected it at some point, but I never thought it would hurt so much."

"Honey," I cup his face in my hands, "Talk to me, you're freaking me out."

East takes in a deep breath, holding it before exhaling as he tries to calm himself. "Kip fucking MacIntyre has just pulled out of his contract with me, he said… he called me a fagg…I can't even say it. He doesn't want someone like me on his property."

"WHAAAT!" I look at him horrified. "Who the hell is Kip MacIntyre?"

"He's just bought the Hartman ranch. He wanted a bunkhouse built. But not, apparently, by a cocksucking queer."

"I don't believe it. He actually called you that?"

"He's new in town, he didn't know I was gay when he booked me for the job. We organized it weeks ago, when I was recommended to him, so he hadn't met me until today. He saw us in the bar together, so when I turned up today with Dean and Ed, he went off on one. Calling me every disgusting word he could think of. I thought Dean was gonna thump him; I had to hold him back. We got in the truck and drove the fuck away."

"Did he sign the contract?" I'm so fucking angry, I don't know what to do.

"Yeah, he did. I'm gonna sue the bastard." Then, with a smile, East changes back to my man. "I think I can make his life very difficult for him, if I want to. He won't make many friends in this town if he starts spouting his homophobic shit: this is our town, we come from here. We have good friends and a kickass family that support me, you and Kes. I think he may be in for a shitload of trouble, no other contractor will want to deal with him when they find out why."

Then he looks me up and down, taking in my bare chest and wet hair. "Hmm, you look good enough to eat. Were you waiting for me?"

I take in his dark eyes and the slick of his tongue dampening his lip and my body fires up again but, somehow, I think of the asshole that has hurt my man and my anger flares up. Then East's mouth hits mine and he takes control, forcing my thoughts on nothing but him.

Pulling back, he cocks his brow at me, "Well?"

"Yeah, I was planning to do some very rude things to you on my desk, but I think, maybe, we should be working out what we're going to do about MacIntyre."

"I think rude things sound about perfect right now: we'll deal with that asshole later." He leans in and bites my neck, "Tell me about these dirty plans." He whispers against my skin.

"I'm going to blow you, then fuck you hard." I feel him shiver, "Take your clothes off, East." My voice is husky and filled with promise.

I step back again and lean against my desk, watching as he quickly kicks his boots off before shoving his shorts and briefs down his legs, kicking them off and out of the way. Next, his T-shirt is over his head and thrown somewhere in the room. He stands gloriously naked in front of me, his dick hard in his fist.

"God, I love your body. I can't get enough of it." I'm back up against him, my mouth glides over his warm skin, laying long, wet kisses over his chest and down to his abs. Tracing the defined muscles with my tongue before dipping into his navel, I drop down on my knees and bury my face in his groin. Inhaling deeply, groaning loudly as I take in the full scent of his heated body, my hands cup his ass, kneading and squeezing the cheeks. Then, letting my fingers slide up and down the crack, I head for his tight hole.

"Fuck, Denver, get your mouth on me." He pants as precum bursts from the head of his cock. Ignoring it, I slide my tongue up and down the deep grooves of his oblique muscles. The sharp, tangy taste of his sweat makes my mouth water as I lay open-mouthed kisses from one side of his hips to the other.

"I'm getting there, sweetheart. Just let me taste you, your skin is divine; warm and it tastes of honey." Languorously sliding my tongue over his skin, I nip the taut flesh with my teeth, making him shudder. Quickly slicking my tongue over the crown, I moan as his flavor bursts over my taste buds. Nipping his stomach one last time, I move back to his swollen dick, gliding my thumb over the head to smear the juices flowing from the tip over the engorged crown, my mouth hovers right above him and I feel the heat emanating from his skin; I blow a soft stream of air, cooling the heated, swollen head. I look up and see his eyes roll back in his head at the sensation. Then his hips jut forward, letting my mouth cover his length, and I take him deep in my throat. As my nose touches the short hairs above his dick, I hold still, his dick deep in my throat. East punches his hips forward and I let him fuck my mouth, pulling back to breathe before he repeats it. When I feel his balls start to pull up inside his body, I know he's about to blow, so I suck and lick up and down his length before sliding a finger up and down his crease, nudging against his pucker.

"Fuck, Den, yeah. Like that. Yeah, don't stop!" East widens his stance when my finger presses against his hole, then pushes inside. With my finger fucking his hole at the same speed as my mouth moves over his dick, I know he's gonna blow. He comes, his legs trembling as he shouts my name when he fills my mouth. I swallow his load, sucking him dry. Then, as my finger slides from his body, his legs give way. He slumps to the floor, panting hard. Leaning back on my heels, wiping my chin and mouth with the back of my hand, I chuckle at the dazed expression in his unfocused eyes.

"You've wrecked me, Den. Shit, that was intense." East wheezes. I lean forward to kiss him, knowing he can taste himself on my lips and tongue.

"My turn now, East. I want you on your back on my desk. Spread your cheeks; I want to see that gorgeous hole." I stand up and pull him with me.

I love how his eyes glint and I know he's going to give me a show; he doesn't disappoint. He sucks two fingers into his mouth and then, as he lies back and props his feet up on the edge of the desk, he slides them inside his ass. I can't tear my eyes away as his fingers glide slowly in and out.

"Enough!" Rapidly getting out of my jeans, I lean over and press my aching dick up to his hole. "Keep looking at me, honey; I want to watch you lose it all over again. I'm so fucking hard for you, I'm going pound your ass. You ready for that?"

Fuck, his eyes flash as he listens to me talking dirty to him and his dick twitches again. I push deep inside him until my balls hit his ass. Holding his knees up to his chest, I hold them still and fuck him. I wasn't kidding when I said it would be hard. My hips punch forward, faster and faster, with each thrust my cock pounds his prostate.

"Fuck yeah, I'm not going to last. Shit, East. Shit, shit!" Slamming hard inside him, my orgasm floods his hot, and oh so tight channel. My hips continue to piston into him as I ride my orgasm out. With one more nudge on his sweet spot, East comes again, not as much but my stomach still gets speckled with his cum.

Collapsing onto him, his arms wrap around me, holding me tight as my dick finishes twitching inside him. His smile floors me with its intensity when I reach up to kiss him. "I love you, Denver Sinclair. That was some thank you." He chuckles

"I love you, too, and that was only a small token of my appreciation." I kiss him softly.

Hearing the front door bang and Kes calling out to us, I feel East start to laugh as his head buries in the crook of my shoulder.

"East? Will you please tell me why I've got half the town clamoring for blood?" Kes marches into the room and looks us over. "What's going on?"

I slide out of East and grab some tissues from the box on my desk to clean him up before we pull on our clothes.

"Yeah, we had a problem at the Hartman ranch, and the homophobic dickwad that has bought it. I'm no longer his building contractor." East simplifies the situation, making Kes frown and rub his forehead.

"So, you thought fucking would be a good idea?" There's a faint smile on Kes' face.

"It beats going 'round there and punching the asshole." East shrugs. "He's broken our contract, so I'm going to take it up with my lawyer and let him deal with the compensation claim. Then MacIntyre can go fuck himself and his bunkhouse; I don't give a shit."

"Okay then. That makes sense of all the gossip: it's not gone down well and I think he may find it difficult to get anyone to work for him now." Kes shrugs. "Are you okay though, baby?" Kes looks East over then breaks into a smile and starts to laugh. "By the look of you, I think Denver did a good job of making you forget."

We both look sheepish but laugh along. "Yeah, I guess he took my mind of it." East chuckles.

□ □ □

KES

Another couple of weeks or so have passed and the summer weather is hitting its peak. Tourists and visitors continue to swarm the town, making my work hectic; I've never been busier or happier. My life has become so much richer and happier since Denver joined us. He works crazy hours and deals with atrocities I never wish to see, yet he comes home and is the most loving, funny and adorable man possible. My sex life has never been better as the three of us grow and develop our relationship. We learn so much about each other as we talk quietly into the night, Denver and East have made me fall so deeply in love.

☐ ☐ ☐

We have completed the foster care courses and have had the police checks, so all we can do is wait to see if, and when, we will be needed to care for a child. The only stumbling block we had is with Ellie's truculence over the possibility of another child entering our family. So keen and enthusiastic at first, she now stubbornly refuses to talk about it and storms about the house shouting that it's not fair. Although she has yet to share with us what it is that isn't fair, I think East simply puts it down to her age and he is happy when her anger disappears as quickly as it arrived and we get our girl back again.

"Don't you think she's a bit young for this?" East argues quietly with his mom over giving Ellie a cellphone for her birthday. She'll be twelve next week and we plan to let her have a party at the house, she's very excited about it.

I look over at Denver who is teaching Ellie how to play the guitar. We've been together for going on seven months and we are so in tune with each other, he lifts his head as I gaze at him. He raises his eyebrows, letting me know he can hear the conversation in another part of the garden, and shakes his head, a wry smile on his lips.

East looks at us and shrugs his shoulders, I think he's looking for back up but I'm not stepping in; this is between the two of them. I agree with East, but I'm not ganging up with him against his mother, oh no, no way.

Ellie laughs at something Denver says and my heart bursts to see them together. Denver was so hesitant to be part of the family unit, wanting to keep life as simple for Ellie as possible, but he had no need to worry. Ellie simply accepted him and, when some of the kids teased her about it, she just shrugged it off, never choosing to get dragged into the taunts or jibes. I know the two of them have talked about it but neither have divulged the content of their conversations. Ellie is as happy with Denver as she is with me.

I step up to the pair of them and Ellie smiles at me, her teeth covered with a metal train track of braces but she still looks pretty. Her long, blonde hair and her baby blue eyes making her look older than she is but her healthy, down-to-earth attitude stops us from worrying about boys. Although, it would need to be a strong, brave boy who dares to knock on our door.

"Listen, Dad, listen to what Denver has taught me." She stretches her fingers over the strings and then strums them; she's slow, but it's a definite tune. When she comes to a stop, we all applaud, making her blush.

"So, Ellie, what's the final count to the party, and what time do you want the clowns and bouncy castle here?" I hold back my grin but Denver must cough to hide his laughter.

"WHAAAT! No! No way! You do know I'm going to be twelve not six, right? There's no way I'm having that!" She looks horrified and hollers out to East. "DAD! Tell him, tell him I'm twelve and I don't have clowns and baby stuff at my party."

East looks up and grins at me then saunters over to us. "Oh, Ellie, sweetheart, it's already booked, we can't get our money back now. I'm sure all the boys and girls will love it, too."

Ellie hands Denver back his guitar and puts her hands on her hips and scowls, then turns her sweetness to Denver. "You know I'm too old for all that, don't you? Don't let them do this to me, I'll be laughed at. No one will be my friend."

"I'm pretty sure they're messing with you, sweetheart." Denver whispers to her.

She swings back to face us and, with a stomp of her foot, she flounces off. "I hate you, you know that, right?" She shouts at us, looking over her shoulder before storming out, flipping her hair dramatically over her shoulder as she goes inside the house.

"Did we just get our first 'I hate you'?" East looks at me and bursts out laughing. "Oh hell, this is going to get so much worse."

"Yeah, you wait till she gets her periods, then you'll know how horrible she can really be!" Denver speaks quietly as he strums on his guitar.

"Oh, we are doomed!" I groan and clap my hand on East's shoulder. "We'll let you handle that side of her."

"I'd better go and apologize, you coming too, Kes? You started it." East growls and holds out his hand for me.

"No way, you go first." I sit next to Denver and wrap my arm around his waist. We watch as East goes in search of Ellie. "You okay, baby? You're quiet today?" I drop a kiss on the top of Denver's shoulder.

"Yeah, I'm just tired, it was a long week. I'm happy to be off for a few days now; I need to sleep in a bed that is actually comfortable and for more than a couple of hours."

Denver spends a couple of nights a week over at the hospital and has managed to condense his shift into a straight block rather than traveling backwards and forwards every day. It doesn't always work out but we still get him in our bed more nights than we originally thought.

"Well, I guess it's good that we plan to stay in tonight and have an early night. Ellie isn't staying tonight; she's got a friend coming over for a sleepover tonight. Which means we can pamper you tonight, baby."

Denver sighs and turns his head to mine. "I think I like the sound of that." He kisses me softly, then more firmly, only pulling away when East clears his throat.

"She says you need to apologize too." He smirks.

I stand up and bump his shoulder as I walk past him, "Asshole." I mutter and he laughs louder.

Fifteen minutes later we are a happy family again; Ellie has forgiven us for teasing her and I think East has accepted that she will be getting a cellphone for her birthday from her grandmother. I watch them leave then take a wander down the garden and see East has Denver in a tight embrace, his hands gripping his ass as he whispers something in his ear. They both laugh then Denver lets out a moan, and that is a sound I never tire of hearing. I join them and run my hands down East's back and over his ass, he pushes back into my grasp.

"Ready to take this indoors?" I purr.

"Fuck yeah." East answers and moves from between us to stalk down the garden to the house. "Come on." His call makes us laugh and jog down to catch up with him.

□ □ □

"I don't know what you want me to say?" East looks at Ellie as she stares at him. "I'm not sure it's a good idea. Aren't you happy at Grams?"

"I am, but I want to live with you now. I'm not a baby, and Gram still thinks I am. She doesn't let me do anything my friends do."

I watch as East scrubs his hands through his hair and drag them down his face. Looking over at me, I give him a small smile of support.

"Ellie, it's difficult for us in the school breaks, you know that. We are all out at work; Kes works long hours, so does Denver. Both of them can spend the day sleeping before working a long nightshift again. You would still need to be with Gram through the day while you're out of school. It just isn't practical, sweetheart."

"You just don't want me here. I bet you wish I'd never been born. My friend Melody says that her dad stopped wanting her when her parents split up and he got a new girlfriend. She says you probably never wanted me anyway!" Ellie storms off, furiously tapping a message out on her month-old cell phone.

"What am I going to do?" East walks to me and I open my legs, letting him step in the space. I wrap my arms around him, resting my head against his stomach.

"I don't know, babe. She'll get over it. She's just turning into an adolescent and we have to put up with the tantrums and attitude for a year or so and then we'll get a better, happy Ellie again." I kiss his stomach as East runs his fingers through my hair.

"Maybe I'm wrong and she should be here." East looks for reassurance.

"East, I think she should have the stability of the home life she already has, and continuity is important. Talk to your mom, then maybe the three of you should talk together."

"What about you? She thinks of you as her father, too." A frown creases his forehead as he questions me.

"Babe, I will support you in every way; if you want me to be there, then that's where I'll be." I lean into him and kiss him. I feel the tension in his body ease away as my arms wrap around him, we stand silently in a comfortable embrace until my cell phone rings.

Looking at the screen, I see a picture of Denver smiling at me, "Hey, babe, what's up? You're not stuck at work again, are you?" I switch on to speaker so East can hear too.

"No, I'll be home on time, I'm on a break and I wanted to say hi and I love you." His voice is soft and full of emotion.

"What's happened, baby?" East picked up on it too.

"It's just been a tough shift so far, and I wanted to speak to you."

"Oh, Denver, we love you, too. Get home safely and we'll prove it to you." I tell him.

"That's good to know. Look, I'd better get back. I'll see you soon." The call ends and I look at East, his frown matches my own.

"Something's gone on, I wonder what?" I lean into East as he wraps his arm around my waist.

Chapter
Eighteen

EAST

"Something is up with Ellie." I look at Denver and Kes as we get the food ready to grill outside.

"What do you mean? She seemed okay last weekend." Kes says as he walks past me to the fridge.

"Mom says she's got all secretive and won't tell her who she's talking to and she's always on the damn cell phone. I knew it wasn't a good idea to let her have it. God knows who she's talking to all the time." I rake my fingers through my hair. "Maybe she should be living here, I can be more in control. It's not fair on my mom to have to put up with her being difficult. What do you think?"

"I think you should talk to her about it this weekend, but it's up to you, East. I love Ellie, she's a sweet girl, but she's going through puberty and she's going to be difficult and stubborn. She can't help it, it's her hormones kicking in."

"Oh fuck! Why didn't I have a boy, I'm sure I was never this difficult!"

"I bet you were; remember the whole going from I-won't-wash to spending an hour in the shower because you could play with your dick while thinking about the football team?" Denver laughs loudly. "I know I did, Kes was also one of my fantasies."

"I hope I lived up to your expectations." Kes laughs and walks out the kitchen doors to the garden, carrying plates and cutlery out to the table.

"Hell yeah, you did." I laugh and follow him out.

"Hey! What about me, didn't you fantasize about me? I'm feeling left out here." Denver pouts sexily.

"Oh, babe, you were all over mine!" Kes laughs and reaches out for him.

"Yeah, you are definitely the icing on the cake." I run my hand down Denver's back and cup his ass.

"I hate having to work this weekend, I want to spend it here with you." Denver sighs and sits down, picking up one of the breadsticks he carried out.

He only has to work one in three weekends, but I know he hates missing out on time with us.

"Well, Ellie has soccer tomorrow, so that's what I'll be doing and Kes is working the day shift too, so it's not like you'll get much time with us. And you love your work, Den."

"Yeah, I know but it's the silly season, when the roads get filled with tourists that don't understand the concept of slowing down on the smaller roads, and we get the aftermath of their reckless driving." He sighs.

"But that's why they sought you out, baby: they wanted the best." I smile

I love spending our evenings lazily like this. We usually end up making slow and sweet love and I can't wait.

Waking up, I stretch my back. Den left for work early this morning but kissed us goodbye before leaving us to sleep again. Kes is still sleeping so, leaving him to rest, I go to shower and get the coffee on. When I reach the kitchen, my phone buzzes and I check out the message. *Fuck*, I need to get to one of the sites I've just finished, there's a burst pipe and water everywhere.

I leave a note for Kes, if I hurry, I can be back to watch Ellie play, I head out to my truck, making sure I've got the tools I need and my phone, then drive off to the ranch. It's out of town and it's going to take me thirty minutes, maybe more.

As I drive down to the cabins, I see Todd Mathews, the ranch owner, waiting for me. He smiles and waves as I pull up alongside him.

"East, you're a life saver. I've turned the water off and, luckily, there's no one staying in it this week. Next weeks is booked up here."

I shake his proffered hand. "No worries, Todd. I'll get it sorted today and any work that's needed, I'll get one of my men out here on Monday to make good on any damage."

Reaching into the back of my truck, I grab my tools before following him inside.

"Shit, Todd; that's a lot of water. You have any idea how it happened?" I gaze at the mess of the kitchen area. The whole place is flooded, it's going to take a couple of hours to get it fixed.

"No idea. It's been fine; we had people staying but they left here about three days ago, so the cleaners were in and they never said anything." Todd replies.

I get to work: fixing the split pipe doesn't take long, but the rest of the room is a wreck and I start ripping the damaged pieces apart.

"How're you getting on?" A voice interrupts me and I turn to see Todd standing in the doorway.

"Yeah, just about done; I'll send Mike or Dean out on Monday." I stand up and look at my watch. "Shit, sorry Todd, I've gotta go. I need to pick up Ellie."

"Okay, East. Thanks so much for coming over, I appreciate it. I'm sorry it took up so much of your day."

I try to keep to the speed limit but I know I won't make it in time; the traffic is busier, so I switch and cut through some of the shortcuts the tourists don't know about and make it in the nick of time.

I pull up and park as close as I can get, but I'm still pretty far back. There's still quite a few cars, so I'm not the only one late to pick up my child. I switch off the engine and get out as I see Ellie; she's talking to someone I don't know. A woman, her face hidden by a baseball cap and dark glasses.

Then I see her reach out and get a hold on Ellie's arm, and I see my girl's eyes widen in panic.

"HEY!" I shout out and pick up speed, racing across the lot, but I'm a long way back. I see other parents looking over as the woman pulls on Ellie's arm.

A man gets out of the car they are next to and says something to the woman. Then one of the parents approaches as I still weave through the vehicles. They seem to be arguing but the woman still hasn't let go of Ellie. I feel like I'm running through quicksand; I can't get there fast enough.

A whistle blows and I see the soccer coach running, too, then I'm there and I grab the woman, yanking her arm off my daughter. We are surrounded by parents now and the woman is trapped, the man gets back in his car and races away. When she turns, she swings her other arm and tries to punch me but I'm quicker than her and dodge. I get to see her face for the first time, *Fuck!!*

"Stacey?" *Fuck! What the hell is she doing here?*

"East! Let me go!" She shouts. "She's my daughter, I want her now." Her voice softens and she looks back at Ellie, who looks like she's about to faint. "Come on, Ellie; you know it makes sense. You're grown up now, you need your momma, you don't want to live with your dad no more, you told me so. It'll be good Ellie, so much fun."

"You…you lied to me. You said your name was Melody, that you were the same age as me." Ellie's voice breaks and she starts to sob.

I hear sirens and I watch Stacey's face as fear washes over her. I want to pull Ellie into my arms, but I'm afraid to let go of this despicable woman. As the cop cars pull in, the crowd dissipates to give them room to get close to us.

As the first car comes to a stop, I look past it and see another car tear into the lot. *Kes.* I feel my body start to shake now that he's here; he will hold us up. *Fuck, I wish Denver was here.*

One of the cops walks up to me and nods. It's Conner Martinez; we went to school together so I know he'll recognize Stacey, too. "What's going on, East?"

"This woman tried to take my daughter against her will." I speak firmly, not even giving Stacey a glance.

"I'm her mother! I'm entitled to see my daughter!" Stacey shouts.

I've let go of her and have Ellie wrapped in my arms, her body pressed against mine. With her head tucked against my stomach, I feel her tears drenching my shirt. Kes reaches me and holds me before dropping down to speak to Ellie.

"See, this is what she's living with: two men! She should be with her mother, not with two gays." Stacey spits out.

"I think we'd better take this to the station." Conner says as another cop gets out to put Stacey in the patrol car.

"We will follow you. Do you need Ellie, or can she go to my mom's?" I ask but Ellie tightens her grip around me and I feel her shaking her head. "I guess Ellie is coming with me."

Right then, one of the moms comes over and says she has it videoed on her cell phone. The second cop takes note of everyone's names and lets them know they will be in touch.

As the crowd disperses and people get back to their own vehicles, I kneel and look at Ellie, her pretty, little, heart-shaped face crumples.

"Am I in trouble?" She sobs.

"No, baby girl; you're not in trouble. Come on, let's go talk Conner, you can tell him all about it." I kiss her forehead.

"I'll drive." Kes offers and we walk over to his truck. "I called Denver, he'll be on his way now."

"Thank you, baby." I pop a quick kiss on his mouth.

□ □ □

DENVER

"Go back to sleep, honey, I'll call you later." I murmur to East as he reaches out to me.

"Hmm, love you." He mumbles to me, still locked in his sleep fog.

"Love you, too." I kiss him again and then Kes reaches out to the space I occupied fifteen minutes ago.

"Bye, babe. Love you." Kes' voice is even heavier with sleep than East's.

"You, too, sweetheart." I drop a kiss on his head and watch

poignantly, wishing I was still there.

It doesn't take me long to get my head back in the game and, within an hour of being in the ER, I know it is going to be one of those days. Yes, I'm here 'til Monday morning but that doesn't mean I want to be rushed of my feet or swapping from one operating theater to another. I can deal with steady, I can deal with a rush of adrenaline before the calm takes over again, but I hate these feelings that today is not going to be a good day.

Today is going quickly but there's been a lull for a couple of hours, which always sets me twitching. It feels like the calm before the storm; at least, it gives me time to catch up on my emails and reports. Leaning back in my chair and stretching my back, I feel the creak as my spine straightens out. I need to walk around for a while, it's gone midday and I need a coffee and something to eat. Taking a wander through the ER again, checking everyone is happy with what they are doing, I make my way to the doctor's lounge, I know there will be something to eat in there. The refectory always leaves sandwiches and snacks for us over the weekend.

Chase Fielding is in the nurses' coffee room as I walk past. I've gratefully received the change in his shifts but knew I would still have to work with him.

"He's got two boyfriends, y'know? Can you imagine such an uptight bastard ever relaxing to take two dicks up his ass?" He laughs, unaware that no one else is joining him. Not because they have seen me, but because he's a complete dick.

"You really talk some shit, Chase. You spend an awful amount of time bad-mouthing a man who doesn't even give you a smile when he walks in. Are you jealous? Do you wish it was you he wanted?"

This makes me stifle a laugh but Callum lifts his head and sees me. For a moment, he stiffens but relaxes when he sees me smiling. Then, grabbing his coffee, he walks out. I pat his shoulder, if only to reassure him.

"Yeah right, I don't ever need to suck his dick. I'm on my way up here; Woodruff will have me over that asshole any day, I don't care how good he is. Whose dick did he suck to get to be chief trauma surgeon before he was thirty? That's what I'd like to know."

"I think there has been enough talking in here today. There's still patients waiting. Let's move it, please." I watch with glee as his back stiffens when he recognizes my voice. I wait as everyone else shuffles quickly past me. Most won't meet my eyes, but I don't care for them.

"You've moved from the doctor's break room to the nurse and auxiliary break room, why was that, Fielding? Were you not getting enough attention in your own break room?" I take a large step towards him and see his eyes widen as I stare him down.

"We were out of coffee in the other room." He stutters, looking over my shoulder, eager for an escape route.

"Now, listen to me, I'm only going to say this once. Stay away from me, don't talk to me, don't talk about me. If I hear you talking about my private life again, even if someone else tells me you are, I will ruin you. I will have you out of here so damn fast you'll think your ass in on fire." My voice is calm and I don't raise it; any passer-by would think this is a normal conversation.

"Do you understand me? You will never be as good as me if you waste your time here. You could learn a lot from me, but now I can't stand the sight of you and you are officially off my team."

"You can't do that! You don't have the authority. I'll go to Woodruff and tell him you're threatening me. You won't be the golden boy here then." Fielding crosses his arms over his chest and stares back.

"Off you go then, you tell him. I'd love to hear his reaction." I know that Woodruff will have his ass over hot coals. "No? You're not going to? That's because you haven't got a fucking leg to stand on. Now, get out of my sight."

I watch as he storms past me, his eyes blazing with hatred.

I shake my head at the trouble one man is causing me in my place of work, I love it here and really want him gone. My phone buzzes in my pocket, surprising me; I normally leave it in my office. I see Kes' face on the screen and swipe my thumb over it to answer.

"Hey, my love, this is a nice surprise." I smile as I speak.

"You need to come home, babe. Some woman has tried to snatch Ellie after soccer practice." Kes speaks rapidly, I can tell he's running.

"What? Shit! Okay, I'm on my way." I end the call and go and search out Woodruff. It takes me ten minutes to get out and onto the highway. I'm grateful for the huge, powerful engine my truck has but I really wish I had my nippy sports car right now.

I have luck on my side, the road is relatively clear and I make good time. Kes has messaged me, telling me they are with the cops at the station, so I drive straight there.

Pulling up on the other side of the road, I jump out and dart across. Racing through the doors, startling everyone inside the foyer, I look around frantically. I spy Kes at the back of the hall, he looks up and our eyes meet. Striding towards him without paying attention to the audience around me, I pull him into my arms. His head drops to my shoulder and I feel him shake. My hand cups the back of his head while the other rubs up and down his back.

"Thank fuck you're here." He sighs.

"Tell me what happened." We move back to the chairs at the edge of the room and I listen as Kes fills me in on everything that happened.

I can't believe what I'm hearing. "Stacey pretended to be another twelve-year-old girl? Jeez, that's sick! Poor Ellie, is she okay?"

"No, not even a little bit, but she will be. She thought she was going to be in trouble, poor kid." Kes shakes his head ruefully.

"How long will they be in there?" I nod to the room Kes says East and Ellie went into.

"I have no idea. East's mom is there too. And they have got Ellie's computer, so they can go through her social media sites. I had no idea there were so many of them. Christ! This is such a fucking nightmare."

Hearing footsteps walking towards us, I pay them no mind, my hands clasp Kes' tightly as he speaks quietly. When they stop in front of us, I look up and I know I look surprised because she smiles at me.

"Miriam, what are you doing here?" I look at her shrewdly, and she holds out her hand for me to shake.

"My department always gets called in where children are involved, it's just routine. More a support for the child really; we have the resources and staff available for her to talk through this and try to come to terms with what happened. I am not here to investigate you." The social worker explains

"I should think not! Shit, we've done nothing wrong." Kes splutters,

"I know that, Mr. Dereham. I promise, this is all to help Ellie." She smiles genuinely and I feel Kes relax as he observes her.

Abruptly, the door opens and East walks out with Ellie. Seeing me, she drops East's hand and runs the short space to me. I scoop her up like she's a toddler and hold her tight against me as her hands wrap around my neck and she clings to me.

"Good to see you, kiddo." I look at her and smile. "I'm guessing it's pizza and ice cream night, tonight."

She nods, still tearful but trying to smile. "Daddy has already said that. I thought I'd be in trouble." She whispers to me.

"No way, Ells-Bells, none of this is your fault." I drop a kiss on her head and put her back down again. I catch a look from Miriam, but I'm not sure what she's thinking and I don't care, my focus is on my family.

When the cop follows East, I am amazed that I recognize him: Conner Martinez! We were on the track team together. He looks good. There's another guy with them and he looks serious but smiles when he sees me. I'm sure I should know him, but my mind has gone blank; it will come to me.

"Good to see you, Denver, it's been a long time." He holds out his hand for me.

"Yeah, hi, Conn, shame it's not in better circumstances." I watch his face harden. He was always a cool dude at school, never one to blow his top; I see this has made him a good cop.

"We'll be in touch, East. Our guys have already picked up her accomplice; I think this will be an easy one, your man here will keep you up to date." He shakes our hands again then goes back into his office. We are left standing together.

"I thought I'd never see you back here again, Denver." The familiar man speaks and then it clicks, Daniel Mortimer. *Shit, he's grown into a good-looking man.* A tall, skinny, geeky guy at school is now a buff, built man.

"Hell, Daniel, good to see you again. What, are you a lawyer now? That's awesome. We'll have to meet up under better circumstances." I shake his hand, then, after he speaks quietly to East, he leaves.

"Shall we go home?" I suggest. "I'm sure you don't need to talk to Ellie today, Miriam. I think she's had enough questions for one day."

"That's not a problem; I will speak to Sergeant Martinez and get the paperwork over with. Mr. Brookman, please, call me if you or Ellie need to talk." Her smile seems genuine but her eyes dart between us, we are all touching at least one of us; we are a tight family.

□ □ □

It's nine-thirty and Ellie has fallen asleep, East is exhausted but still too riled up. It's been a tense evening, with East's mom only now leaving. We have discussed everything with Ellie and it has been decided that she is going to live here now—she will be at her Grams after school—and both parties seem happy with that. Mrs. Brookman finds it hard to deal with all the internet crap that went on; she knew nothing about it and is tired of it all.

Ellie is very unhappy, she had no idea that anyone would think of being so devious and calculated. She really believed she had a friend in Melody. But when she had wanted her to get in the car, Ellie said she wasn't allowed in the car because her dad hadn't texted her to tell her the change in plans. East is so proud of her for that—a simple rule that has worked when it's had to be Kes or me collecting her. Before her cell phone, he would call the school and they had a password set up so they knew it was him; something a lot of the parents do, apparently.

I walk into the den with a bottle of red wine and three glasses, Kes sits on the long, leather sofa, his bare feet up on the coffee table. East is stretched out with his head on Kes' lap and, when I get there, I pour us all a glass of wine before lifting East's feet plopping them on my thighs after I settle down. It's a comfortable room with a large TV, perfect for films and sports, but tonight the screen is black. Imagine Dragons are playing softly through the speakers linked up to an iPod.

"You okay now, sweetheart?" I run my hand up his leg and he lifts his head up then swings around to sit up.

"I don't know! I really don't know how I feel. One part of me wants to find that bitch and wring her scrawny neck, another wishes I'd never set eyes on her. But then I wouldn't have Ellie and I don't regret her, not once have I ever regretted having her." He lifts his wine glass and sips before continuing. "What sort of woman does that to a child, especially her own child? The cops reckon she was going to demand money from us, she's in deep shit with loan sharks and has a drink and drug problem. Yeah, she was gonna kidnap my kid, put her through fuck knows what, for a few grand." He sighs deeply again and his head flops back to the back of the sofa, his eyes screwed up tight as he tries to block the images of what could have happened from his mind.

"East, my love. None of the things you are imagining happened or are going to happen; Ellie is here and she's safe. Her mother is nobody to her, she doesn't know her and she sure as shit doesn't like her. Stop worrying about things that aren't important, that bitch isn't worth the oxygen she breathes, we all know it and now so does Ellie." Kes runs his hand through East's hair and leans over him to kiss him.

"Thank you." East whispers, he looks at me and smiles. "You dropped everything and came to us, Denver. I love you so much for that."

I sit upright and look at him confused. "What did you think I would do? She's my family, don't you think of me like that?"

"Denver, of course, I do. I needed you as much as I needed Kes. Ellie asked for you. I just wanted you to know how much you mean to us. We are family, the best fucking family there is. And we are going to watch that bitch go to prison for what she tried to do to us."

"Good job, because I'm not fucking going anywhere! You can't live without my dick!" I sit back, smug, and wait for the reaction.

Kes starts to chuckle first, East lifts his head again and gives me a grin, there's a sparkle in his eyes for the first time today. He laughs out loud, then pounces me, pinning me to the sofa. His eyes darken as he stares at me.

"Yep, you're right. I love your dick. Come on, let's go and play."

Chapter
Nineteen

KES

It's been a month since Ellie came to live with us and I had my reservations at first; we are used to being and doing what we want, where we want. And that usually means getting naked and dirty, but I needn't have had any worries. Ellie laughs when she catches us kissing or messing about, telling us we're gross.

Ellie had a few nightmares and was nervous if she had to wait for any of us, and, after a panic attack when she didn't want to go to soccer practice, Denver suggested her speaking to someone about it. It has been a great success, we don't ask her what she talks about with the counselor but it has helped her.

Another surprise is when she asked to move rooms, from the one close to our room to a bigger one next to Denver's office. It took a couple of weeks, and a small fortune in Ikea, making her a new, more grown-up bedroom for her to relax and become the girl she was before her hateful birth mother tried to wreck our lives.

We are having a few of her friends over tonight for a sleepover, this is something that is terrifying all three of us, Denver said he was going to offer to do another shift at the hospital to stay away. East threatened him with sleeping in the guest room for a month if he did. So, I'm standing by the grill, making hot dogs and burgers for the four girls messing about in the swimming pool.

I watch Missy race up and down the side of the pool, trying to catch the splashes. Denver lays on the lounger in a pair of cut off denim shorts and a bare chest and I can't stop myself from returning my gaze to his tanned body. I love him so much, I didn't think this sort of happiness existed, I thought I had everything with East and, if Denver had never come back to Cooper's Ridge, we would have had the happiest life. But, damn, that man makes a difference.

The doorbell chimes and Denver pulls himself upright, grabbing his plaid, cotton shirt from the back of the chair. Slipping it up his arms, but leaving the buttons undone, he goes to answer it. We're not expecting anyone else unless it's one of the girls' parents.

"Hey, girls, c'mon; food's ready!" I call out and East steps back from his lifeguard duties to let the squealing girls through the gate to grab their towels and wrap them around their skinny, long-legged bodies. Piling burgers and hotdogs on the table, I let them make up their own meals; the rest of the table is covered with chips and soda cans, and burger and hot dog rolls.

Seeing them happily munching away, I give them the instruction to stay out of the pool while I'm indoors, then walk indoors to see where Denver and East have disappeared.

I find them in the hallway and wander down, "Hey, who was at the door?"

Denver moves out of the way and I see Miriam Salter standing inside the door. I have no idea why she is here: she hasn't needed to speak to Ellie for a couple of weeks now.

"I was just explaining to Denver that I'm calling on the off chance of a chat with the three of you, but I can see that you are all very busy. I can come back another time, maybe tomorrow?" The flustered woman explains. It is strange; she is always so calm and controlled.

"Well, if you don't mind either talking to us in the kitchen or in the garden where there are four giggling girls, you are very welcome." I smile and reach out to hold Denver's hand, he is sporting a frown and I don't know why. East walks past with the social worker and I pull on Den's hand, holding him back.

"What's up, babe?" I ask him quietly.

"I don't know. I don't know why she is here, and why she is looking so worried. Social workers don't normally look like that when it's a pleasant, drop-in visit."

"Well, we're not going to find out standing here. Let's go." I squeeze his hand and we hurry to catch up with them.

We find them in the kitchen, not wanting to interrupt Ellie's fun with her friends.

"She looks wonderfully happy here, East. How have the three of you adjusted to having her here permanently?" Miriam enquires.

"It's great, we're loving it. I've got used to the sinks clogged with long hair, damp towels dumped everywhere and cereal bowls left in just about every room she goes in." East chuckles but pride shines from his eyes.

"Yeah, it's all good fun; she gets her chores done without complaining too much and she's happy. That's all we want for her." Denver answers her, too; his hand still gripping mine like a vise as he tries to keep calm.

"Miriam, as lovely as it is to see you," I smile, "I'm sure you didn't come here just to ask about Ellie, why are you here?" I thought I might as well come out and ask or we could be tiptoeing about all night.

"Ah, yes. Straight to the point, Mr. Dereham. Denver, this

involves you the most here, but, obviously, it is not a decision to make by yourself."

Denver squeezes my hand so hard, I feel he might break it. Moving my other hand over it to loosen the grip, his eyes flash to mine.

"Okay, what do you need to tell me?" Denver asks quietly.

"The little girl that you looked after when she came in after being resc…"

"I know who you mean, you don't need to repeat it." Denver snaps. I know he still hurts over the loss of that broken child.

"Of course, you do, Denver, I'm sorry. Well, the foster family are going through their own troubled time at the moment and they feel they are no longer able to look after her. She has been well cared for and nurtured but they haven't been able to bond well with her." Miriam takes a deep breath and is about to continue when a loud shriek comes from outside and we bolt through the kitchen door.

Moments later, we are back inside and the girls have been asked to play quietly for a while.

"Carry on, please." East asks, Denver sits down with us standing behind him, each resting a hand on his shoulder.

"We would like to offer you the chance to foster her." Miriam sighs when she finishes.

Denver puts his head in his hands and cries, I feel the tremors running through his body as he silently weeps. A minute or two later, his head lifts and he looks at her, and then at us. His eyes beseech us and I know we already have our answer.

□ □ □

DENVER

"Yes." I look at the woman sitting opposite me and, although my heart is beating too fast in my chest, I remain angry with her. She should have been with me from the start.

"I know exactly why you are looking at me like that and, I can assure you, I have had this out with my managers this afternoon. We got it wrong: you should have been given the chance. You are the only person who has received a reaction from her. I'm sorry."

I close my eyes at the thought of her still locked in her own lonely world. East's grip on my shoulder tightens, reassuring me they are with me on this.

"When will we get her?" My mind runs as fast as my heart with the things we need to purchase. She can use Ellie's old room; thankfully, East repainted it after it was emptied.

"As soon as you are ready. I have a list of all the useful items we think you will need, we have a fund for anything you may find difficult to pay for."

I snort at that, like I need financial help. "That won't be necessary."

"Well, I don't like to make assumptions. Is there anything else you want to ask me tonight?"

"How is she?" My voice catches in my throat at the thought of her.

"Physically, she is well; all the healing went according to your plan. Mentally? That's a different matter altogether. Her assessments show that she is suffering from no apparent brain damage but she still doesn't speak or make eye contact. And, as before, she hasn't cried. She eats well and sleeps all through the night, but she isn't affectionate yet. I'm hoping that you will make a difference for her in that matter."

Another shriek from the garden breaks the somber atmosphere. East loosens his grip on my shoulder and goes outside. Kes sits next to me and clasps my hands, he smiles, looking excited.

"How do you feel about this, Mr. Dereham?" Miriam enquires.

"I feel the same way as Denver: she should've been with him, with us, months ago. But, I'm prepared to overlook that because I only have her best interest at heart, and Denver's." He looks shrewdly at her. "Tell me, what made us your first choice, this time around?"

"Two reasons. The easiest one to explain is the closeness of your family unit after the attempted abduction of Ellie. This gave me a massive foot in the door when I wanted to prove to them that you are the right people to be looking after, and fostering, children that need love, unconditional love."

"That's only one, one reason." I reiterate when she looks at me questioningly. "You said two, two reasons."

"Yes, the second one was my own battle to fight. I have been fighting for same sex fostering and adoption for twenty-five years now and I refuse to give up when there are children desperately in need of caring and stable homes, regardless of the gender of the parents. I didn't push myself hard enough when they looked at a threesome, a triad, however you choose to name yourselves as a fully functional, affluent family; I let you down. Now I have the chance to save a sad, lonely child and put her with the right people, her forever people. I just hope you will prove me right."

"Miriam, you had us right at the start. Now it's time to make it right for my little girl." I push up from my seat and grin. "You need to give me that list, I'm going to need to go shopping tomorrow."

□ □ □

Lying back on the bed after the quietest sex we've ever had, East runs his hand over my sweating body, his touch so soft and loving my heart swells in my chest. Kes' body is pressed up against mine as his breathing regulates.

"Fuck! That was intense." I whisper. "You can do that to me any time you want." Both of my lovers took me, each easing to me separately. First East, his eyes fixed on mine as his body pumped slowly in and out of mine. Every stroke grazed the most sensitive part of me, taking me higher and higher but not letting me peak. As East reached his climax, I felt him swell and fill me, the fire in his eyes burned through to my very core as his love poured into me. Feeling East pull away made me moan at the loss but soon Kes filled me, lying on my side as his chest pressed against my back, his mouth close to me as he whispered his love in my ear. His breath, as hot as the fire inside me, washed over me, making my skin pebble as his thrusts increased in tempo. East's hand gripped tight around my cock, pumping in pace with Kes. The burn in my body devouring me as I came in East's fist, my cries swallowed in his kiss as Kes' climax filled me.

"That was amazing, baby. I love you so much." East kisses me deeply, consuming me.

Kes chuckles silently behind me, his laughter resonating through my body makes me smile against East's mouth.

"I guess we should get some sleep; we've got masses to do tomorrow. Are you excited? I'm nervous and eager for her to be here." I am excited, but nervous about the imminent leap into fatherhood.

"I think it's going to be a challenge, but one I'm ready for. I'm hoping it will be a rewarding one." Kes is always so honest when he speaks, so open.

"What will you do about work, Den?" East questions.

"I'll take paternity leave, it's available for up to two months. I doubt if I'll be away that long but I think I will take advantage of it for as long as she needs me. I know you two will be with me every step of the way; I'm going to need your support and your knowledge of how to look after a child. I don't want you to think that she is mine, she is definitely ours." I sigh at the thought of our child.

"You know what we didn't ask?" East says.

"What?" I thought we'd asked everything we could.

"Her name. We don't know what they have called her."

"Shit!" Kes chuckles again.

"It doesn't matter: I know what her name is going to be." I've always known what I would call my daughter. "Her name is Phoebe."

East holds my trembling hand and Kes has his arm around my waist, both anchoring me, keeping me centered. The house is child friendly, locks have been put on cupboards, the fridge, even the toilet seats. Plug sockets have covers on them and everything precious and breakable has been moved to higher surfaces. The bedroom is ready and the shelves are full of books and toys, the bed is made up, and the dresser and closet are full of clothes. We have done it; we are fully prepared for our little girl to come to us, to come home.

The car we have been waiting for pulls up on the driveway and I suddenly feel sick.

"Oh god, here we go. Are we ready?" I ask.

"Baby, you've got this. You are ready, we are ready. Relax and enjoy this moment." East murmurs.

Ellie has the camera on record and is ready to film us starting our new life. She has been amazing, so enthusiastic, and has helped us pick her clothes and toys. I look at her standing out on the front grass, beaming at us.

Then the car doors slam and I look over. Miriam has my child in her arms and I see the wide look on the toddler's face as she looks around. Then she spies me and, for both of us, the world stops; her eyes shine and something I never allowed myself to hope for happens.

A small, shy, smile appears on her face as she squeals, fidgeting in Miriam's embrace, desperate to move. Tears building in my eyes as I leave East and Kes, rushing to her as her arms reach for me.

Plucking her from Miriam, I lift her away and embrace her for the first time. Looking down at her, I see her gazing at me. Lifting her hand, she touches my face and I realize I'm crying, tears run down my face as she watches me.

"It's okay, Phoebe; daddy is so happy to have you home." Leaning down, I kiss her soft, light brown hair, loving the feeling of her in my arms.

When I look up, everyone around me is crying, Miriam most of all.

"I have never seen anything like this before, that little girl is yours, Denver. She always should've been with you. I'm sorry I let you both down."

"Nothing matters anymore, Miriam; she's here now and she's ours." I look at my boyfriends and they step quickly up to me, careful not to crowd but eager to be with our daughter.

Phoebe looks at them then shyly ducks her head under my chin.

"She knows who her daddy is." Kes laughs and strokes her arm.

Epilogue

One year on

DENVER

"Fuck yeah, right there! Don't stop, oh fuck, don't stop!" East begs, my cock plunges hard in and out of his ass as he kneels upright, his back against my chest. With my arms holding him up, Kes teases his cock with his tongue, flicking against the engorged head then leaning in to suck the tip. Every time his balls tighten and draw up in his body we stop, leaving him panting and cursing us.

"Are you ready to come, my love? Are you ready to shoot your load into Kes' mouth? Do you want me to fill your ass?" I whisper into his ear as he bucks against me, desperate to make me finish him.

"Fuck! Shit! Let me come!"

I wrap my hand around his weeping dick and pump it as my hips piston against him, thrusting me deep inside him. "Come, baby, come!" I let go of his dick as Kes wraps his lips around it. I feel East's orgasm as his ass grips my cock, drawing me deeper inside him. My climax fires from me, exploding deep in his channel. I bite down on his shoulder as I come.

Kes sucks hard on East's sensitive cock before releasing it. He kneels and captures East's mouth, kissing him hard, his mouth still full of East's release. Then he leans forward to kiss me; tasting East on his tongue, I suck it.

Kes catches East as I release him from my grip and we slump down on the bed, East mewling as my dick slides from his ass.

"Fuck! That was hot!" East sniggers as he wraps his brain around the sensations he experienced.

"Hell, yeah." I pant.

"Daaaadddy!" I hear the cry of my daughter and bury my head in the pillow, to hide my laughter.

"Perfect timing." Kes groans.

☐ ☐ ☐

I can't believe the change in me, in my life. I never knew happiness of this kind truly existed; in nearly two years, I have become a new man. I have a job I love and that I'm good at. Woodruff stepped down, giving me the Chief of Trauma title, which I love. Kes has Carter as full-time manager at the bar—and we have had the pleasure of watching his life unfold and become full of love and life—but has kept a few shifts a week there and has office days. East's construction company has grown, too, and he has two teams of men and a site manager in charge of the day-to-day work, giving East time to spend with Ellie and with us.

Ellie is at high school, and is a confident and popular teenager and is still proud of her dads, including me. She takes all the comments in her stride; although, I heard one of her new friends tell her that her dads were hot and she gagged and screamed 'GROSS!!' at her and ran away laughing.

This year has been one hell of a rollercoaster ride: Phoebe has been amazing and came on in leaps and bounds when she got here. Her walking was the first to happen, it took about a month for her to pull herself up to stand; before, she would sit wherever we placed her. Poor Missy was the object of her desire so, when the dog moved away, Phoebe decided to follow her. The first few steps were wobbly but she soon got the idea.

We had her in the pool every day, strengthening her legs, continuing the physical therapy she had been having before she came here. So, once she started, there was no stopping her. Her speech was next and I almost cried when she said 'Daddy' for the first time. Speech therapy has helped her, too, and she is quickly catching up. So, we have a three-year-old that is acting and behaving like every other child that age.

Today we woke up before Phoebe, which gave us the time to torment and tease East; I thought our sex life would suffer as our family grew but if anything, it got better. We know now to take advantage of every private moment, and have become the kings of stealth when we've needed to. Our parents have been amazing, and having three sets of grandparents has its advantages.

Like today, we have the day off and are spending it together at my parent's ranch, where Phoebe gets to ride one of our little ponies. Ellie rides well after a year, spending as much time as she can at the ranch—my mom has always loved Ellie and considers her another grandchild. And, tonight, we get to leave Phoebe with my parents and Ellie is at a school friend's. It gives us a chance to go out together, so we are heading into the bar this evening.

When I walk into Phoebe's room, she is out of her bed and is trying to get herself dressed.

"What's going on, baby girl?" I lean down and drop a kiss on her curls.

"Dressed, now, Daddy! My want dressed!" She pulls out another T-shirt and drops it on the floor.

"Okay, Phoebe, let's do this." In a few minutes, my little girl is dressed and ready for breakfast, and I'm being marched into the kitchen.

"Dada, look, my dressed." Phoebe beams at Kes who's already putting eggs and toast on the table for her.

"You look beautiful, princess." He grins and kisses her upturned face.

East walks in a few minutes later, with wet hair and a still slightly dazed look on his face; we obviously did a good job on him this morning.

"Eggs, Poppa. My got eggs." Phoebe smiles with a mouth full of scrambled eggs.

"So you have, beautiful girl. Did your daddy make any for us, too?" He asks, making Phoebe look at Kes.

"Did you make eggs, dada?" She asks.

Breakfast continues and, soon, we are ready to go out.

□ □ □

KES

We park up outside the bar and see it's filling up already, I've been looking forward to this. It's a night to have a few beers and maybe get a dance or two with my men. It's not an open mic night, but I brought Denver's guitar over a couple of days ago, it's been a while since he sang and I love it when he does.

We walk in and greet Carter and Shelley and the servers as we walk through to a section that has been kept for us. Denver stills as we reach our table and his eyes rest on his guitar before turning to me with a wry smile on his face.

"What is that doing here?" His eyebrow rises as he stares at me.

"I have no idea what you're talking about," I turn to East, "do you know why Den's guitar is here, babe?"

"Nope, no idea at all." East grins.

"I'll go put it in the truck then." Denver moves towards it.

"No!" We reply in unison.

"Please, play tonight, Den. You haven't played for us for ages." East pleads, giving Denver his cute, puppy dog eyes.

"Maybe." Den chuckles. "Buy me a drink and I'll think about it."

We sit down and order our drinks when Paris, one of our new guys comes over. Denver sits back and I see him relax as he looks around the bar; I know he has fond memories of working here. Even before we were together, he loved it here. He started to heal when he came here, the shadows lifted from his eyes and his smile grew as his confidence built.

I still hate the man who did that to him, even though I should thank him for sending Denver back home. But the urge to hurt him still runs through me. I know Denver doesn't think of him anymore but I hate that someone was so callous and heartless and so quick to break this beautiful man.

An hour later, the place is full and we are in a happy place. We've had a few beers and a lot of laughs when I see Denver lean over and lift his guitar up.

"You gonna sing for us, baby?" East asks as he runs his hand down Den's arm.

"Yeah, I'm thinking about what to sing though, it seems to have been nothing but nursery rhymes lately." He chuckles.

I get up and weave my way through the throng to reach the bar to let Carter know Den's going to sing. He smiles and walks out from behind the bar and comes with me to the small stage area East built last year. It only takes him a couple of minutes to get a stool and the mic set up.

"Ready, babe? You know what you're gonna sing?" I ask and he nods.

Then, walking past me, he sits on the chair and I know no one has noticed him yet; I know he likes it that way. He likes to be singing quietly to himself.

Den's voice starts and the rich, deep tones that always make the hairs on the back of my neck rise, stops the talking in seconds and the crowd turns as one to face the stage. There's no extra lighting but there's enough behind him to gently highlight him.

I watch as people stare at him then turn to whisper to their friends as smiles spread across their surprised faces.

Some start to sing along quietly or, maybe, they are only mouthing the words, because all I hear is Denver. I'm surprised by his choice but something must have triggered his choice and the chords of *Walls*, a Kings of Leon favorite of ours, starts as he plays. He looks around the bar. Then his head is back down as he finishes.

He moves straight into the next one and my heart stills. I look at East and we smile then, standing up, move closer to Denver as he sings John Legend's *All of Me*. Reaching the stage, he looks up, his mouth curves up on one side in his sexy half smile as he sees us. East has his arm around my waist and mine is over his shoulder and Denver sings to us like there's no one else in the crowded room.

I know he's in his own zone when he sings and I let him have one more before I'm ready to have him back with us. I watch as he scans around the room before bringing his eyes back to us, as he sings again and Vance Joy's *The Best I Can* starts up, and another lazy smile crosses his face.

When he finishes, he looks as if he's going to start another but East steps up and puts his hand on his, shaking his head. Then I see him bend his head and whisper something and I watch the light in Denver's eyes sparkle mischievously.

The crowd starts to clap and cheer and Denver smiles at them as if he's only now noticed them, a blush spreading over his face and he swiftly ducks his head.

I shake my head as he steps from the stool and walks to me. How can one of the country's youngest, smartest, and most talented trauma surgeons blush at some applause? I love how centered he is, he's purely Denver. His work no longer defines him: he prefers to be known as Phoebe's daddy or as mine and East's boyfriend.

East carries his guitar and takes it over to Carter to take care of. I open my arms and let Denver step up to me, his hands wrap around my waist and he takes my mouth with his. I love his long, lazy kisses, the slow burn as his tongue dances with mine. There's no rush but there's promise and I can't wait to claim it.

East walks back up as Denver breaks away from me, his eyes still glazed as he looks at his other lover.

"You ready to go home?" East asks and we nod our assent.

Turning together, I have hold of Denver's hand and East has his arm around his waist as we walk out of the door, heading for the truck, when someone calls out for Denver. I feel Denver freeze when he turns and sees the man who has stepped out of the bar behind us.

"Alec." Denver utters quietly. It's my turn to go rigid, I feel Denver's hand tighten around mine as I start to move forward, halting me.

"Um, hi, Denny." The man I have despised for so long steps closer to us. I take in his tall frame and dark eyes as he looks over the three of us.

I watch Denver's eyes narrow. Now it makes sense, why he never wanted us to call him that.

"It's Denver." East speaks up, his voice hard. Alec's eyes flicker over us and then narrow.

"What are you doing here, Alec?" Denver questions him.

"Um, yeah, I wanted to speak to you, to apologize for the way I treated you. I didn't expect to see you here tonight. I never thought I'd see you sing in front of people. You would never have done that before." He stutters, so obviously feeling out of place. "I was going to call you tomorrow."

"Why are you here? And I never sang before, because you always said it embarrassed you. What do you want?" Denver tips his head and eyes him. "Why now?"

"Yeah, I guess, because now I know how it feels. It seems that Michael likes the chase and the secrecy more than he likes the marriage and the permanency." He answers, and my fury builds as he looks at Denver, with what? Hope? Expectancy? I have no clue, I merely want him away from my man.

Denver chuckles dryly. "You mean, he cheated on you."

East and I laugh at that, making Denver's ex flush.

"Well, what did you expect, Alec? From me, now, I mean? What did you think you would find when you got here? It's been two years, Alec. Did you think I would want you back?"

"No, I mean, shit! I don't know what I expected; I just wanted to see you and to say I'm sorry." He looks at the three of us again. "I admit, I didn't expect you to be in this sort of situation. Are you with them, or have you just met them?" He sounds snide now.

I pull my hand free from Denver's and move in front of this piece of shit. I watch his eyes widen as I get in his face.

"Now listen here, you worthless piece of shit. I don't care if your husband fucked the whole town behind your back; the only person I care about is the man you broke. The man that is worth a thousand of you, the man who is the father of our child, the man that has been with us for the last two years. So, I think, you've said your piece and you now need to turn around and fuck off, back to where you came from. Before I get really pissed and break your fucking nose." I take another step towards him as he steps back.

He nods once and I back down and return to Denver and East.

"I think you need to leave, Alec. I'm sorry he hurt you too, but you are not welcome here. Goodbye." Denver looks at him, then turns away and we walk to our truck, leaving him standing on the pavement, looking totally pissed off.

We back out of the space and drive home when, suddenly, we all burst out laughing.

"Did that really happen? Shit, Kes. I love you all caveman." East sniggers.

"I can't believe he turned up here. Did he really think he stood a chance with me again? Fucking idiot." Denver laughs.

"Seriously though, are you okay, babe? That must have been a hell of a shock for you." I ask.

"Fuck that! I wish I'd told him I'd just picked you up; that would have been so much fun." Denver laughs.

"I guess I could play along with that, you wanna play that game tonight?" I look at Den and his eyes darken.

"Hell yeah!"

□ □ □

DENVER

As Kes and East sleep, I slip quietly out of bed and, pulling on some shorts, I walk out of the room. Instinctively, I go to check on

Phoebe but remember she's with my parents tonight and I smile, knowing how loved she is.

Walking out into the garden, I stand on the deck and look out into the darkness. The tapping of Missy's paws behind me make me turn my head; my girl is getting old but is still the faithful, devoted dog as she slows down.

Seeing Alec tonight was a shock, a face I never thought I'd see again. What surprised me was the lack of any emotion I felt when I saw him; he really meant nothing to me. I expected something, even if it was anger but he stood there, a stranger to me now.

But because of him I have found the greatest love. I have men who love me completely, a daughter that adores me as much as I do her. My life is full and rich, being called home was the best thing to ever happen to me.

Denver's Calling
The End

Acknowledgements

This is always the toughest part of writing: my fear of missing someone out plagues me.

So, thank you to my PA Rachel Hadley. The wonderful lady keeps everything running smoothly for me when I have to lock myself away to write, for cheering me on every day. I owe you a bottle of vodka □

To Whynter and Heather, for the tireless pimping and posting, keeping all the books out there.

Thanks to Harper's Honeys. You guys help and support me way more than you realize. To Jackie Thorogood, for the wonderful name of Kes' Bar - The Last Drop Inn. I love it! <3

To Petra, for her wonderful editing. I love you hard, I don't tell you this enough. You get me and you get my men. I'm so pleased I didn't make you cry this time.□

To Louisa Mae, for letting me moan and witter about these guys, for

your amazing support: I can't thank you enough.
To my lovely husband, Paul. He had to put up with living with three hot men this time. Thanks, for never moaning at me and my research methods.

To my Nutters Rae and Fee, the sisters of my heart: I love you girls so much more. Denver would never have been as wonderful as he is without you two amazing ladies.

To JC Clarke at the Graphics Shed for my amazing cover: thanks hun; it's a stunner.

About the Author

If you can take a moment to leave me a review on Amazon, I will love you forever

Please look out for me here, come along and say hello to me

www.jjharper-author.com

Other Books

The Reunion Trilogy

Reunion
Reunited
Elysium

The Troy Duology

Troy Into the Light
Troy Out of the Dark

Narrow Margins

The Finding Me Series (M/F)

Rising Up
My Turn
Missing Pieces
Set to Fall

Made in the USA
Columbia, SC
22 March 2018